"I WANT TO BE LIKE MY FATHER."

Wyatt spoke with firm conviction. "All he knows how to love is business. He doesn't give a damn about anything else. I'm tired of him using me. Family is all I've ever wanted."

"And you'll have it."

Beth leaned forward, her lips brushing over his like a whispered promise, then returning as a heated vow. He didn't so much as breathe, letting her mouth move on his, letting her tongue curl and stroke his hungrily. Then the reality of her desire hit and hit hard. "Wyatt, I want us to make love."

His eyes opened, staring up into hers, reading of a need that rivaled his own. And flat on his back with his leg in a cast, he smiled.

"As long as you don't expect any fancy athletics, we should do just fine."

She sat back on her heels and reached for the knot to her belt and parted her robe. "I'm all for old-fashioned simplicity."

DANA RANSOM'S RED-HOT HEARTFIRES!

ALEXANDRA'S ECSTASY (2773, $3.75)

Alexandra had known Tucker for all her seventeen years, but all at once she realized her childhood friend was the man capable of tempting her to leave innocence behind!

LIAR'S PROMISE (2881, $4.25)

Kathryn Mallory's sincere questions about her father's ship to the disreputable Captain Brady Rogan were met with mocking indifference. Then he noticed her trim waist, angelic face and Kathryn won the wrong kind of attention!

LOVE'S GLORIOUS GAMBLE (2497, $3.75)

Nothing could match the true thrill that coursed through Gloria Daniels when she first spotted the gambler, Sterling Caulder. Experiencing his embrace, feeling his lips against hers would be a risk, but she was willing to chance it all!

WILD, SAVAGE LOVE (3055, $4.25)

Evangeline, set free from Indians, discovered liberty had its price to pay when her uncle sold her into marriage to Royce Tanner. Dreaming of her return to the people she loved, she vowed never to submit to her husband's caress.

WILD WYOMING LOVE (3427, $4.25)

Lucille Blessing had no time for the new marshal Sam Zachary. His mocking and arrogant manner grated her nerves, yet she longed to ease the tension she knew he held inside. She knew that if he wanted her, she could never say no!

DANA RANSOM
Lifetime Investment

ZEBRA BOOKS
KENSINGTON PUBLISHING CORP.

For Rick,

with whom I discovered
the beauty of the UP
on our honeymoon
twelve years ago.

Chapter One

Her mood worsened by the mile.

It was, without doubt, the most miserable trip Bethany Marston had ever taken out of her native Chicago. Everything on this one seemed to take twice as long as expected and proved three times more stressful. Wasn't that one of Murphy's Laws, she wondered, flicking the wipers on high as spray from an oncoming truck splattered her windshield.

It started badly. Because of a lengthy client call, she'd nearly missed her flight—the only one she could wrangle into Marquette. She hadn't had time to change from her work clothes before the mad dash to the airport. Then the weather turned terrible, knocking the small commuter plane about the sky like a bully flexing superior muscle. She'd come close to reaching for the sickness bag when they took an unscheduled dip in altitude over Lake Michigan. She'd rented the car in Marquette thinking, how long could it take to traverse the highest spur of Michigan's Upper Peninsula where it jutted out into the cold waters of Superior?

A long time, she discovered. The road skimmed along the inner Bay revealing flashes of the lake below before curving off into the lonely arcade of pines. It had only stopped raining within the last half hour. The rain had left the ribbon of Highway 41 slick as ice. On the map, the route across the peninsula appeared to be populated by small towns. What the map didn't show was that most of them had gone bust when the copper market plummeted at the turn of the century. The towns gradually became ghost towns with wilderness in between. How long would it take someone to find her if her car broke down? That question tormented her city-bred soul. She hadn't passed anything that vaguely resembled a gas station for miles and miles and the rental car had developed an asthmatic knocking beneath the hood. She needed a restroom. Her back hurt. The throb of a sinus headache threatened. And on top of it all was the chiding thought: Why was she going to so much trouble just so her husband could ask for a divorce?

"You're going where?" her father-in-law had shouted across his big desk when she'd told him. Boyd Marston looked as though she was suggesting an indefinite trip to Mars instead of a short hop to Michigan's UP. "Beth, this is absolute insanity. You've got a job to do here. Do I need to remind you of all the things going on this weekend?"

"No, you don't, but Wyatt said it was important."

"Important enough to leave our biggest and best clients hanging? It's one thing for Wyatt to just take off, expecting me to cover for him. Gretchen is still chewing on me over that one. She'd been plan-

8

ning to spend a month or two in Denver and you know how your mother-in-law gets when her plans are interrupted."

Yes, Beth did. Gretchen Marston was used to having her own way. It came from being the only child in a very rich family. Wyatt's stepmother may have given over control of her family's hotel chain when she married Boyd, even allowing him to change its name to reflect the new management, but she refused to allow any interference in her lifestyle. Though the business hub of the hotels was in Chicago, she still claimed the corporate headquarters in Colorado as her home, shuttling between the two points whenever her fancy shifted from shopping to the ski slopes.

Boyd sighed, trying not to look impatient with the entire matter. "Did he say what was so important about it?"

"He said it was business."

The hotel magnate was suddenly all sharp attention. "What kind of business?"

Beth could only shrug, embarrassed to admit she hadn't a clue. She'd had to read between the lines. Not too easy since those lines of communication had dwindled down to next to nothing over the last two months. She'd never dreamed it would go so far, that he'd stay away so long. The terse letters — notes, really — could have been penned by a stranger. What was she supposed to think when her husband of less than a year took off for parts unknown with only the meagerest explanation, then chose to stay gone?

"Why is he insisting you bring the stock portfo-

9

lio? He knows it was worth a small fortune when we gave it to the two of you for a wedding gift. Something worth a million shouldn't be carried around like yesterday's *Sun-Times*. It should be kept in the safety deposit box as an investment for your future."

Beth felt herself stiffen. The portfolio was a sore spot with her. "I know about the value of future investments," she countered tersely. "Remember where I grew up. I was an inner-city Chicago girl. I had to fight my way out of the tenement mentality so I wouldn't end up like my family and friends. I wouldn't have gone to college if I hadn't been able to earn a scholarship and then I still had to work my way through by booking catered parties for that restaurant."

"And then you met Wyatt and all that changed."

Yes. And all that changed. He'd been a guest at one of the affairs. He'd asked her out for coffee the next day. She accepted without knowing he was the son of a Lake Shore Drive tycoon, bankrolled by Denver millions. She didn't find that out until their fourth or fifth date. By then, she was already in love with him and the discovery was an added blessing. Icing on the cake. And it changed everything. It meant plunging into a world she knew nothing about. It meant mind-boggling shopping trips and endless lessons in social protocol from Gretchen Marston. And though she was intimidated by all the glitter, by all the intense pressure, Beth vowed not to be an embarrassment to Wyatt's family because of her impoverished background. She listened and she learned. And she was quick to adapt.

But it hadn't been easy. It wasn't without sacrifice.

The wipers slapped ineffectually. Finally, Beth gave up and reached for a tissue in her purse. She blotted her eyes angrily and blew her nose. She wasn't the weepy type. Teary displays were useless and she grew impatient with her own lack of control. For what lay ahead, she needed calm not rampant, raw emotions, even though they were what roiled beneath the crisp detailing of her Evan Picone suit. She could pretend otherwise, but inside, she was scared—scared she was about to lose everything despite her father-in-law's assurances.

It was Boyd who had made her the director of Public Relations in the big Michigan Avenue hotel—a to-die-for job for someone like Bethany. Wyatt had his office in the glamorous old building. Officially, he was the vice-president of the chain and worked out of a room across the hall from her. She kept to a hectic schedule during the first difficult months as she struggled to overcome the rise from working-class to society virtually overnight. She threw herself into her job, not because she loved it but to prove herself and make the Marstons proud. Boyd was. He praised her initiative and gloated over the Merit Award he himself hung on her office wall. Wyatt was oddly neutral.

Hers wasn't a nine-to-five position. Most of her contacts were made in the social arena, courting executives at galas, hostessing client lunches at the hotel's fine restaurants, attending Cubs and Sox games and maintaining a high media exposure on the charitable front. But it wasn't all black tie and entertainment, either. She worked hard, often coordinating up to ten events at once. She arranged everything from ballroom parties and retirement banquets to full-blown conventions. She was the liaison between staff and customer and was always on call in the case of a glitch. In the first month of their marriage, she and Wyatt managed less than a dozen dinners together. He told her he didn't mind; he understood the demands of the job. And he smiled. However, his smile grew increasingly thinner as more dinners were missed and more weekends were sacrificed. He once said he saw her more on the evening news than he did in their kitchen. He made it sound as if he was amused. Why hadn't he told her he wasn't?

Beth stared down the lonely stretch of road, remembering. What else was there to do to fill the anxious hours? A potential investment opportunity. That's what he'd called it when she came home late to find him packing. He'd been brief, almost secretive. He was going to the tip of Michigan's Upper Peninsula. He wasn't sure how long he'd be away. He needed time to think things through. He'd kissed her coolly and he was gone. She was too surprised to get angry until later. And as the separation lengthened, as the days passed, Beth swung between feelings of panic and betrayal. If it hadn't been for Boyd, she would have broken down completely. But it was his blunt question that slammed her fears into overdrive.

"What does he want with the stocks?"

Beth was terrified that Wyatt meant to cash them in. And if he did, he was going to have one hell of a fight on his hands. Those stocks represented everything she'd dreamed of her whole life long, a security she'd never known. When her father had been injured on the job and they discovered his insurance and pension were practically nil, she learned what it meant to be unprepared for the worst. And she would never go through that again. Once, she'd thought Wyatt represented stability. Now, she wasn't so sure. If he wanted to dissolve their marriage along with the shares in Marston Hotels, he was going to have to spell out his reasons loud and clear. Because she was tired of guessing what was behind his silences.

"He didn't say what he plans to do with them. Maybe he just wants to read over some of the clauses, but I'll make sure they come back safe and sound."

Boyd nodded confidently. Then he added, "Bring Wyatt back with you, too. Or at least, talk to him. I'm going to need an answer from you about Denver. I can't hold off on it forever. The job's yours if you want it, Beth. I need you there. It's the opportunity of a lifetime. Doesn't Wyatt realize what he's keeping you from?"

"We hadn't really discussed it." Two months ago, she'd mentioned to Wyatt that Boyd had offered to make her his administrative assistant in Denver. She'd had great hopes. They'd move to Colorado and build on their future within the company business. It sounded so perfect. So why hadn't Wyatt jumped at the idea? Why had he looked at her so expressionlessly and said it was out of the question? No, that wasn't exactly a discussion.

Seeing her distress, Boyd shook his head in sympathy. "I know, Beth. I don't understand him either. Since his mother died, I've done my best for him. You'd think he could be just a little grateful. He's always had everything, whereas you and I know what it's like to have to work for what we want. Don't worry, Bethany. If things don't smooth out between you and Wyatt, I'll see you get everything you deserve. I'll see you have all the financial security you've ever desired."

But what Boyd didn't understand was it was Wyatt she desired, as well.

On the long, tiring drive, Beth had more than ample opportunity to consider her choices. Reconciliation with Wyatt was what she wanted foremost, but if that wasn't possible, Boyd's option would provide her with the freedom to start again. And on a plane far higher than a poor girl from a blue-collar neighborhood could have ever imagined. She couldn't lose.

Or so she told herself.

The lake was now on her left as she passed the arcing sweep of beach and cresting dunes on the western rim of the peninsula. The towns were farther apart and looked to be inhabited more by ghosts than by human form. The stillness of these skeletal outposts unnerved her, as if time had stopped with the sound of spectral footsteps lingering on the dusty boardwalks.

"Come on, car, don't fail me now," Beth muttered, goosing the accelerator as it sputtered to hurry them back onto abandoned blacktop. The empty boomtowns gave her the creeps.

She glanced at Wyatt's sketchy directions and realized with some relief that she was almost there— there, being the edge of nowhere. She smiled somewhat wryly to herself, thinking she was experiencing what the first brave settlers must have felt as they broke through inhospitable wilderness. Only if she'd been in their shoes, a good deal of the virgin countryside would have remained undiscovered. There was no pioneer stock in her blood. Give her the comfort of a crowded sidewalk and the security of store credit cards and room service, any day. What was up in this godforsaken place that anyone would want to buy?

Following Wyatt's arrows on the map, she made a left off the pavement and took to muddy two-track. Pine boughs scraped the side of her rental car. Ruts jarred her spine and tortured her bladder. But it was the expectation of seeing Wyatt that had her fingers white on the wheel and every muscle clenched tightly. Anticipation warred with anxiety, but caution advised her to wait and see. She wouldn't allow herself to feel panic until she heard what he had in mind.

For a moment, all her doubts were pushed aside as she turned a sharp bend and had her breath snatched away. There, nestled in a pine and birch tree embrace, was a huge two and a half story log lodge. Though rustic in appearance, it was by no means simple in construction. Second floor bays angled out, gleaming with long, multiple pane windows. From the side, she had a glimpse of rainbow colors as afternoon sun struck stained glass. A quick visual scan guesstimated at least 13,000 square feet of northwoods opulence. But closer scrutiny revealed the signs of neglect, like a grand dame sadly gone to seed. Could this be Wyatt's project? she mused as she eased the rented car to a stop in the circular gravel drive. Some undertaking.

Nothing like the haughty character of the typical Marston hotel.

No sooner had she cut the engine than a stocky man appeared on the front porch. He was dressed in wool plaid and heavy boots, as if he'd stepped out of a logging camp from days gone by. Dark in both hair and complexion and broad of features, Beth had no doubt of his Indian ancestry. His eyes were of a startling blue.

"Can I help you?"

"I'm looking for Wyatt Marston," she called through the open car window. She wasn't quite ready to get out. City living bred caution.

"He's here but not here."

"What do you mean?"

"He is living here, but he's not here at the moment."

A sigh betrayed her aggravation. "When will he be back?"

Massive shoulders casually shrugged.

It was then necessity overruled annoyance. "Do you have a restroom?"

"Sure. Inside. Come with me."

Taking the portfolio and her purse, Bethany climbed out and took a minute to enjoy a limbering stretch before following the stocky figure. Stepping inside, she was immediately impressed by the soaring majesty of exposed white pine walls rising two stories up to heavy ceiling beams. Her heels tapped upon oak floors where planks were secured by wooden pegs. Hand-hewn open staircases rose on either side of the central hall to a bridgelike balcony connecting opposite wings of the lodge.

"Wow," she murmured.

"Top of the stairs to your right. If you'll give me your keys, I'll park you out back."

Bethany looked to him in surprise. "My keys?"

The broad features puckered as if suddenly uncertain. "You are Beth, aren't you?"

"Yes."

"Keys, please. Wyatt's been expecting you."

If he was expecting her, why wasn't he here?

"I'm Jimmy Shingoos. Wyatt and I practically grew up together."

"Can you take me to him?"

"I could, but . . . it'd be better if you were to wait here."

"I've come a long way to see my husband, Mr. Shingoos. Can you take me to him or not?"

"If that's what you want." He caught the keys she tossed to him and grinned with some private amusement at her business attire. Beth didn't ponder over it. She was too busy hurrying up the steps.

Once the urgency of her situation was seen to, she returned to the main floor with nothing to distract her from her irritation. Wyatt knew she was arriving this afternoon. So where was he? If it was some scheme to avoid her, he might as well give it up. She and her errant husband were going nose to nose and without further delay. As soon as she could find her Indian guide.

"Mr. Shingoos?"

She moved toward the front door and abruptly came to a stop. There, suspended on one of the antler coat hooks, was Wyatt's leather jacket. She'd given it to him on the occasion of their one-month anniversary. She'd missed the romantic dinner he planned because of a late meeting with the

17

theater council, arriving in time to share the last of the champagne he had chilling. He'd smiled thinly as he accepted her gift, the way he would take a bribe or a guilty peace offering. She hadn't noticed the quiet of his mood at the time. She was just getting to know him. And just beginning to realize how little she did know. It was one of those twenty-twenty hindsight things.

Beth fingered the butter-soft leather, remembering how it felt with him inside it. A painful tightness swelled in her throat as she was lost to the memory of man-warmed leather and misty Chicago rain.

"You might want to take that unless you have one of your own. It can be cold on the lake."

Beth gave a start. She hadn't heard Jimmy come up behind her. Her hand dropped from the coat, then rose defiantly to take it from the hook. It was a link to a shared past, one she wasn't about to let Wyatt put behind him. There was a sense of strength and comfort in going to meet him with those memories wrapped around her. Folding the heavy jacket over her arm, she regarded her husband's friend with a grim expectation.

"Shall we go?"

He glanced around for luggage. "If you want to change, I can wait."

"Let's just go." It had been a long day and she had no more patience with delays. She was anxious for her meeting with Wyatt and he could take her as is. Jimmy just shrugged, noncommittally.

"Follow me and watch your step."

Steps, would be more accurate. About a million of them made of smoothed railroad ties embedded

18

in a steeply slanted bank as they descended from the lodge to the rugged beach frontage on Lake Superior. When she finally dared look up from the placement of her feet, she was swept away by the view. Only the roofline of the lodge was visible atop a bluff that seemed to soar a mile above them but was actually about two hundred feet of natural craggy rock retaining wall. The wave-tortured shoreline they stood upon was of pebbly stone and coarse sand, washed by the rhythmic cut of Superior surf. It wasn't the sort of place one would be tempted to spread a beach towel. The wind was sharp, slicing across the ripple of dark blue water and right through her business suit. Gratefully, she bundled herself in Wyatt's jacket, protected by its bulky folds and by the feeling of being close to him.

"Just where is Wyatt, Mr. Shingoos?"

"He's over on the island scouting out hiking trails."

Bethany squinted. All she saw was choppy blue surface stretching all the way to the horizon. Her stomach clenched. Oh, she hoped she didn't have to brave a small boat across those bumpy waves. Maybe she should just wait . . .

"Is there a bridge or something we can drive across?" she asked with a weak optimism. They were picking their way down the rocky shore.

"Nope. Only way over to Isle Royale is boat or plane."

They rounded a small spit of land and Bethany's heart plummeted. There, bobbing gently, with its tail wedged up against the beach, was a red-and-white seaplane.

"Wyatt flew over this morning in his own plane. If you don't mind, I'll just drop you off. I've got some supplies to taxi into Eagle Harbor and there looks to be some weather moving in — second half of the front that soaked us a couple of hours ago. Wyatt can bring you back over with him."

Bethany was only half-listening. Panic was thudding loudly in her ears. She hated small planes. When they were dating, Wyatt took her up for a tour of the Chicago shoreline in one he'd rented and she'd promptly disgraced herself all over his instrument panel. If man were meant to fly, it would be in a 747, not wrapped in an aluminum can on wheels . . . or floats.

"Hop aboard while I do a quick preflight."

She stood rooted on solid ground while he leaped out onto the twenty-four foot long pontoon and walked along it as if it were a dock, crouching with manual pump in hand to force water out of the hollow float compartments. She wasn't certain if she was reassured or more anxious as he checked the cables and underbelly of the plane then gave the twin-bladed prop a few loose turns. Then he looked to her.

"You coming?"

Bethany drew a fortifying breath and put one foot on the float, testing its stability. Muttering softly, she climbed out as if walking a tight rope and edged toward the cabin door he held open. She would have liked to knock off his sassy grin, if she'd dared let go of the wing struts for even a second. Setting her purse and the portfolio inside, she took the two steps up and settled into the copilot's seat.

"Buckle up," Jimmy advised as he slid beneath the steering yoke. It was an odd configuration, branching off from a central column in a Y, serving both front seats with dual controls. Bethany watched nervously as hers mimicked the movement of his. She was careful to place her feet far from the twin floor pedals as her shoulder harness gave a satisfactory click. He was observing her anxious behavior.

"Do much flying?"

"Not if I can help it."

Jimmy chuckled. "Don't you be worrying now. I'll get you where we're going. This ole de Havilland Beaver is the one-ton truck of the sky. You can load 'er up and if she doesn't sink, she'll fly."

Bethany responded with a watery smile. She noticed a plaque bolted to the dash. Don't Do Nuthin' Dumb! Sound advice.

"Wyatt and I picked up two of them fit for the scrap yard—about the only thing I could afford. We tore them down to bare bones, fitted them with new avionics and rebuilt Pratt and Whitneys. Nothing better for bush hops. Bet you didn't even know Wyatt had his seaplane rating."

"No, I didn't." Or that he'd bought his own plane. What else had happened during their two-month separation? She was gripping the edge of her seat, eying the rows of dials and levers with their ominous arcs and slashes, buttons and lights.

He tapped an impressive looking panel. "See. VHF Nav Com, ADF transponder and LORAN. You're in good hands." He spoke casually, as if the average novice had a clear comprehension of flying jargon and would take comfort in it. Beth had no idea what he was talking about and wasn't the least bit consoled.

Jimmy turned the starter key and master switch and began to work the manual fuel pump up to a five-pound pressure, then primed it by hand. There was a sputtering *chugga-chugga* and a puff of smoke rose from under the fuselage. Bethany held her breath as the coughing settled down to match the rhythm of the whirring propeller. Jimmy adjusted the flap switch on the center of the dash and the elevator trim overhead and dropped the water rudder lever between their seats. And they were moving. The floats cut through the water, creating more of a wake as speed increased.

"Okay," Jimmy crooned to himself. "I'll just slide the stick to the sweet spot and get us out where we want to be for takeoff. This little baby is great for STOL: short takeoff and landing." He glanced at his pinch-faced passenger and continued to talk so she'd have something else to concentrate on other than the throb of the engine's nine cylinders. "Time to pull up the water-rudder, feed in some throttle, nudge it up to 50 mph and we're up."

Bethany sucked air as the feeling of weightlessness grabbed at her stomach. It was a gentle ascension out over the choppy Superior waters with a line of spray trailing from the floats as the horizon fell away.

"I'm going to set the flaps to climb. You'll feel the plane sink a little when she settles into cruising altitude. I'll just trim her out and lean the mixture." There was a drop in engine noise as he made his adjustments. "There. Sit back and relax. She's a good, stable instrument machine. The island's about fifty miles. I used to make the trip every day when I was working for one of the charter services. Won't take long."

Relax. Right. Beth's teeth ground as they were jostled by a small pocket of turbulence. Any second, she expected them to plunge from the sky into the cold waters below. Not the kind of anticipation that groomed a healthy flying attitude. To nudge her thoughts from those of sure and sudden death, she glanced at the pilot who was humming softly under his breath. Wyatt's childhood friend. She'd never heard his name mentioned. She didn't know her husband flew seaplanes. And she didn't like the way Jimmy said Wyatt lived at the lodge. Her fingers tightened on the leather lapels of her husband's jacket. It was as if she was learning about a total stranger and the feeling was far from comforting.

"There's Isle Royale."

She risked leaning forward. Against the blue shimmer of the lake was a deep green brush stroke.

"It's our only freshwater island national park," Jimmy continued as he put the plane into a gentle bank so they could survey the area. "A backpacker's paradise: no roads, no motor vehicles and lots of moose. Some of the most rugged trails east of the Rockies. You can go days without seeing another human being. You either hate it or you want to come back year after year." His gaze canted toward her, asking which it would be for her. The curl of his smile said he figured she'd run for home. It was a gesture of resigned understanding, not one of contempt. And Beth found she liked

23

Jimmy Shingoos, with his flat Indian features and his friendly blue eyes.

As the engine droned, they made a low pass over the isle. It was small—some forty-five miles long and only nine wide, studded with thirty odd lakes, textured with folds of pine ridges and guarded by deep harbors and reefs. Wilderness, pure and simple. And Wyatt was down there. They flew by the northernmost tip where a string of lodges hugged the shore. After that, there was a lot of nothing.

"Wyatt's checking out a cove in Siskiwit Bay. It butts up against the trail between Island Mine and Feldtmann Ridge. There's his plane."

Bethany craned to see the high-wing, single-engine float plane tucked into an abandoned stretch of shore. Dense forest crowded right up to the water. She couldn't imagine anything more isolated. Except being left there alone to wait.

Jimmy cut back on the power, gliding down at a smooth sink rate. She felt the jar of the floats touching rough water and Jimmy responded with throttle back, stick back and water rudder down while her copilot's yoke twitched in restless neglect.

"Not a smooth patch anywhere," he grumbled as he chopped power and they rode the hard bumps. "Have to plow in." At Beth's alarmed gasp, he laughed. "Not literally. That just means I'll have to up the power so the rear of the floats will dig in and the front will lift out of the waves. A lot easier on the prop that way. Where'd all this wind come from? When you see Wyatt, you tell him to get his tail out of here fast before the bottom falls out of the clouds."

No problem. She meant to grab Wyatt and get

24

back to civilization — such as it was — as soon as possible.

Jimmy had cut the power again as they began to sidle close to Wyatt's red over blue and white Beaver. "Open your door, Beth." He laughed again at her stark expression. "I'm not going to ask you to jump. Just open the door. The wind will turn us around and I'll park pretty as you please."

She did as he asked and amazingly, the plane slid sideways and backed right up next to Wyatt's. Jimmy kept his engine winding.

"Hate to drop you and run, but I'm on a tight schedule. Just climb on into the plane to keep warm. Wyatt should be back any minute."

Beth gathered up her things. "Thanks for the lift."

"Any time. See you at dinner."

Would she? Beth gave him a small smile. Would she be staying for dinner or on her way back to Marquette alone? She climbed out of the cabin, ducking beneath the wing as she hopped from one float to the next. Wyatt's plane bobbed in a gentle greeting.

With a wave, Jimmy guided his seaplane back out into the rough. In an amazingly short distance, he'd cleared the surface and the de Havilland was airborne. For a time, Beth stood watching until the Beaver was a speck then disappeared completely. Sighing, she opened the cabin door to Wyatt's plane. The interior was a complex arrangement of flight gear and compact seating for eight. After just escaping those claustrophobic confines, she wasn't exactly eager to crawl back in. Instead, she tottered along the length of the float and jumped ashore. Huddling there, she looked around her. A break in the pines revealed a well-marked trail. It looked wide and promising. The longer she stared at it, the less she liked the idea of waiting. Wyatt was down this trail. How far could he be? She was in excellent shape. The hike would do wonders for her nerves. She was tired of waiting for Wyatt to make the first move. This time, she was going to meet him head-on.

After all, how far could he be?

Chapter Two

How far, indeed.

Bethany slowed and took a long moment to suck air and shed the heavy jacket. It may have been some fifty degrees on the shore, but here in the woods it was a humid seventy-plus. Sweat made her silk blouse adhere to her skin, wilting its crisp folds into damp blotches. Strands of her hair escaped the neat confines of her French braid and clung along her temple and throat. Her stockings were torn and her feet throbbed. She wanted to kill Wyatt Marston. But first, he was going to take her back to the lodge so she could enjoy a good, hot bath.

Beth set down her briefcase and draped the coat over it. Both seemed to weigh a ton. Ignoring the temptation to slip out of her sensible pumps—maybe sensible for executive carpeting—she breathed in the north country air in great noisy gulps. What she needed was straight oxygen. Her lungs were laboring. Only her temper had prodded her up those last few yards of trail.

Trail. Hah! She looked resentfully behind her.

What had appeared to be a well-groomed, easy path had quickly become a mountain goat's nightmare of uneven rocks, slippery moss and pine needles. Her shoes weren't designed for an alpine hike. Stilts would have offered better stability.

Damn Wyatt, anyway.

Why couldn't he have been waiting for her at the lodge?

Why couldn't she have waited for him at the plane?

Because she was mad. And she was scared. And when crowded by either of those emotions, she wasn't terribly logical. All her instincts pushed into aggressive overdrive, the best defense being a good offensive. Her father taught her that. He'd learned it from Ronald Reagan in a Knute Rockne movie. Her dad had been a great armchair quarterback, just full of advice while the TV was blaring and his six-pack dwindled. He'd never seen the need to put that advice into actual practice. But she did. And she had. She just didn't know when to stop.

Beth couldn't give up now, not halfway between the proverbial rock and a hard place. Pride wouldn't let her slink back down to the plane. But neither did it supply the necessary staying power for the elevations ahead. Clutching her sides, she glared at the green-carpeted ground that disappeared into the trees. Oh, to sit down on the nearest boulder and hail a taxi!

She didn't even want to consider the possibility that Wyatt had left the trail and that he was even now on his way down to the plane, passing her unnoticed as she struggled upward. She didn't want to consider it but she had. Which was why she'd put a note on the steering yoke telling him that under no circumstances was he to leave this wretched place without her.

Well, it was onward and upward. Bethany heaved a heroic sigh and picked up her belongings. She swiped the back of her hand across her face in annoyance, then glared at the sky. Adding insult to injury, it was raining; a cold filtering mist drizzled through the pine boughs overhead. Great. Just great. What could be worse?

The sound of twigs snapping in the thick underbrush to her right froze her in her tracks. A low, menacing growl sent her heart catapulting into her throat. Wolves! Jimmy mentioned moose, but she'd never thought about the possibility of other wildlife—dangerous wildlife. Like wolves or bears or other creatures that would devour a businesswoman with no respect for her five-hundred-dollar designer suit. She clutched her briefcase handle with both hands, meaning to use it as a weapon if she had to. Over her panic came a calmer warning. Don't run. Running only made a predator chase. Well, this woman didn't plan to be a Chicago deli snack for any northern Michigan animal. She braced her feet and swept the underbrush with a tenacious stare.

"Aren't you a bit out of your element?"

Bethany nearly withered with relief. And she forgot all about the immediate unseen threat from the bushes. As her muscle groups collapsed into quivery Jell-o, Wyatt Marston separated himself from the thicket at the bend in the trail ahead. No sight had ever looked better. He'd never looked better. Since she didn't have the strength to move or utter a coherent sentence, there was little she could do but stare. She'd always thought of him as one of the most marvelously fit men she'd ever known with his long, lean build and broad-shouldered stance. Even in a three-piece suit, he exuded a raw energy. Here, with the northwoods at his back, he looked right at home. His usually styled dark blond hair was rain glazed and finger-combed and as ruggedly male as the two-day stubble shadowing the sculpted angles of his cheekbones and jaw. Wearing snug Levi's tucked into sturdy hiking boots, a dark T-shirt and a fleece-lined waist-length jean jacket, he gave off all-man vibes no woman was meant to ignore. He looked like a cover model from one of those Rocky Mountain beer commercials and Beth could have used a nice cold one to moisten her mouth, which had suddenly become dry. But before she could rush to Wyatt to tearily claim how much she'd missed him, he gave her a quick summing-up gaze with his inscrutable blue eyes.

"What are you doing here, Beth?"

No warm hello, no welcoming smile, just a curt demand. All the joy died inside her. She would have flung her briefcase at him if there'd been any strength left in her arms.

"You invited me here, remember." The lines were drawn, immediately combative. Apparently the two-month absence had done nothing to make his heart fonder. He was bristling with the same tension she remembered in him as she'd watched him pack. But instead of meeting her in a head-on clash, Wyatt was a master of subtle subterfuge. He held to his guarded distance and cool reserve, making confrontation impossible by sidling away with cool reason.

"I didn't mean *here*. I meant at the lodge."

"Well, I didn't know that. Your directions left much to be desired."

But Wyatt Marston didn't. He was everything Beth desired, right down to the narrow set of his finely shaped lips. Right to the easy power in his casually curled hands. Thinking of his mouth, his touch, made her burn with remembrance and she became more frustrated than ever with the invisible barrier holding them apart. She didn't come all this way to argue with him. She wanted to know what had put the wall of caution between them.

"Did you bring the papers?"

How that blunt question hurt. Was he that eager to sever all ties? Apparently. Pain made her react with equal frigidity. "That's why you asked me here, isn't it?"

For a second, he hesitated. For a second, she saw a trace of her loving husband where a stranger stood. The stiffness left his features. The line of his jaw softened. Something in his gaze reached out to her, a look so wounded, so lost, she was unable to comprehend the reason for it. If he'd opened his arms, she would have filled

31

them in an instant. But he didn't. When she couldn't respond, he spoke her name, saying it low and wistful as a whisper.

"Beth—"

"Wyatt—"

A blur of movement on her right was a distraction. She caught a glimpse of gleaming yellow eyes and a bristle of white fangs. That was enough to set her screaming. She lunged toward Wyatt, equating him instantly with safety. In her careless panic, she banged her shins with her briefcase and stumbled to her hands and knees. Teary-eyed from the pain, she tried to scramble up to escape the snarling woodland threat that appeared from the shadows.

"Artie, heel!"

Then Wyatt was kneeling in front of her, cupping her elbows in his big hands, affording her the familiar solidity of his chest upon which to sob away her fears. All the day's aggravations and anxieties burst free with those great, gasping sobs. She buried her nose in the warm cotton of his shirt and wailed. Her knees and palms stung, her frayed nerves jangled and beneath it all was the indescribable comfort of being within the circle of his arms.

"Hey . . . hey, it's okay. It's all right, Beth," he was murmuring in gentle reassurance. She could feel the heat of his words blow warm upon her damp cheek and the definite sweetness of his mouth tracing along her brow. Wyatt . . . she wanted to hang onto him forever. She never wanted the closeness to end.

But he was levering away, pulling her back at the same time with a firm pressure. Still grabbing for hitching breaths, Beth couldn't look up at him. She knew she must seem a wreck and look even worse for wear. This wasn't how she envisioned their first meeting. She took one hand from his jacket and began fumbling in her bag for a tissue so she could make field repairs to her face.

"Are you all right?" he was asking with a reserved concern. "You're not hurt, are you? Let me help you up. Just hold onto me."

Oh, no problem there. Letting go was going to be the hard part. But as soon as they were on their feet and it was obvious she could stand on her own, he edged away, appearing uncomfortable with the closeness they'd shared. And eager for a distraction.

Wyatt snapped his fingers and glanced down. "Come here, boy. Beth, this is Artemus. Sorry he gave you such a scare."

She followed his gaze and recoiled from the sight of a huge, wolfish creature with shaggy black-and-silver hair and erect ears. Artemus sat at the edge of the trail, regarding her through those glowing amber eyes. The bridge of his snout crinkled and his lips slowly lifted from sharp teeth. He growled with enough ill will to keep Bethany from any thought of extending her hand. She had doubts that she'd bring it back with fingers attached.

"Shame on you, Artie. He's not very good with strangers."

Beth winced at that. She wasn't a stranger. She was his wife. And she didn't like dogs, especially big, snarly ones who looked like they feasted on small children and old ladies who couldn't outrun them. She was a city girl. The closest she'd had to a pet was the gerbil in her seventh-grade homeroom. And the thought of its beady black eyes and pin-prickly little toes was enough to give her chills. Pets made her think of being tied to the house and hair getting all over things. And they weren't allowed in their apartment complex. Neither were children. Yet this was Wyatt's dog.

Why would he go through the trouble of getting a pet when he knew he couldn't bring it home?

Unless he didn't plan on returning to their apartment.

Beth regarded the animal with even less affection. *You're history, pal.* The dog's jaw relaxed and his tongue lolled out as if he was laughing at her.

"I ought to keep him on a leash," Wyatt was saying as if to himself. He was staring at the dog, not at her. "He's not even supposed to be over here. They don't allow dogs on the island, but I can't get into the plane without him. He loves to fly and howls up a storm every time I leave him behind. And he'd eat my upholstery if I left him shut in it. Bad dog," he scolded. Artemus thumped his heavy tail, unimpressed by the chastisement. "You can pet him if you like. He won't bite."

Who was he kidding? She was no master at

34

doggy communication but she understood this one, loud and clear. "That's okay. I'll just take your word for it." She had absolutely no intention of making friends with the glowering beast. Apparently, the feeling was mutual. "He looks dangerous. Like he's part wolf or something."

"He's something. Probably husky or shepherd. The guy I bought him from said there was wolf mixed in his ancestry somewhere down the line. I'm not sure I believe it."

Beth stared at the sly-looking creature. She did.

"Anyway, I've always wanted to get another dog. Gretchen's allergic to them or, at least, that was her excuse."

It was the longest conversation they'd had in months and Beth wasn't even a part of it. Not a real good start toward the dialogue she intended. "I guess there's plenty of room up here for an animal like that. I can't imagine him terrorizing the Chicago streets."

"Neither can I."

Silence settled.

Wyatt gave her a long, exasperated look, as if he couldn't figure out what to do with her. It irritated the hell out of her.

"How did you get over here anyway? How did you even know where to start looking?"

"Jimmy brought me."

"Oh . . ."

"It seemed like an easy hike so I started up after you."

Wyatt almost smiled at the trace of regret in

her voice. He was a seasoned backpacker, having learned on the big boys out in Colorado while he lived there. She'd been intimidated by the huge, hostile mountains when they'd spent their honeymoon at his stepmother's palatial home in Denver. Beth equated climbing with escalators. She resented his smug amusement at the expense of her current misery. It rubbed her as raw as the blisters on her heels. It made her tone sharp.

"And he said we'd better be quick about leaving. There's a storm front moving in."

Wyatt nodded absently. He was taking her in from the tips of her scuffed beige pumps to the tangle of her mussed blond hair. She didn't know what to make of that look. It was part amusement, part annoyance. And part something she wanted to see more than anything . . . attraction. At least that hadn't expired between them. And it was mutual. The brief feel of his embrace was enough to kindle a lifetime of longing.

"Looks like I caught you between meetings," he drawled out impassively. "Seems like that's the only time I can catch you. Well, don't worry. This won't take long. I'm sure you're in a hurry to get back to your busy social agenda."

Maybe she deserved the bitterness in his voice but certainly not the heavy tone of finality. Not if she could help it. "I'm in no hurry, Wyatt. We have to talk."

She could see the barriers building in the narrowing of his eyes, in the way he assumed a wary posture. Signals of his unwillingness to enter into

36

a messy discussion. She wasn't going to give him a choice this time.

His answer was carefully neutral. "You can stay at the lodge until we get things settled. I'll have a room made up for you. If that's all right with you."

All right? Separate rooms? No, it wasn't all right. But a rocky trail in a drizzling rain wasn't the place to discuss more intimate arrangements. But even as she made that vow to herself, she was desperately afraid he'd already made his decisions concerning their future together. And she was afraid she wasn't going to be a part of his plans.

"We'd better get going," he said abruptly. The rain was falling faster. "Sure you can make it back down to the plane?"

"The alternative being to stay here?" She squared up her shoulders and pretended her shoes weren't torturing her by slow degrees. "I got this far, didn't I?"

"Yeah, you did. You always get what you go after. I'll give you that." But he didn't give it very complimentarily. Nor was he inclined to offer any more. He reached down to hoist her briefcase and his coat and he started down the trail without even checking to see if she followed. Artemus was immediately at his heels, leaving her to bring up the rear.

Beth heaved a determined sigh and started after them, wobbling in her shoes and grimacing when no one could see her.

Wyatt strode down the path in long angry steps. It took all his willpower, but he didn't slow and he didn't look behind him. He knew what he'd see. A businesswoman in a rain-splotched suit and torn stockings, hobbling in her ridiculous footgear. What possessed her to come to such a place dressed as if he was her four o'clock appointment? Had she expected all the civility of State Street or Michigan Avenue? Did she even know other worlds existed? That there were places untouched by concrete and inaccessible by cab? Probably not. Or she probably wouldn't have come.

Why had she? She could have sent the papers, but she'd insisted upon bringing them herself. So they could talk. As if that would change things. As if they'd ever been able to talk. But she'd said she'd bring them and he'd been so hungry to see her, he'd foolishly agreed. He'd thought he'd be ready, that he could handle things unemotionally. More the fool. He'd come over to the island to get his thoughts straight, to plan out exactly what he had to say, how he was going to approach her. It hadn't helped that the sudden bad weather delayed his trip back to the lodge so that he wasn't there to meet her. He'd carefully choreographed their meeting in his mind, but then she'd gone and thrown everything off with her typical impatience, by rushing in, by crowding him into a back-against-the-wall position. All the calm, rational things he'd rehearsed immediately fled from his mind when he saw her standing on the trail, so lost, so engagingly distressed. Everything inside him had dissolved in an instant. Had there ever been another human being who could reduce him to such vulnerability with just a single look? No, he knew there wasn't. And it made him angry all over again. Because during the few minutes with her, he wanted her so badly he was willing to forgive and forget everything.

Rain brought a plunge in temperature and with it, a thickening mist as cold air met warm ground, warning of worse things to come. They'd have to get in the sky fast if they were going to beat the advent of IFR weather. It would be suicidal to fly into nothingness and rely on instruments alone. It wasn't as though he had a major airport tower to home in on. This was seat-of-the-pants flying up here and there was no margin for error. All the fancy, up-to-date equipment in the world wouldn't do him a bit of good if a storm system settled in for the night. And the last place he wanted to be stranded was in a wilderness with Mrs. Three-Piece Suit. The only way to smooth what had to be said was to treat Bethany to a hot bath, a good meal and a lot of fine wine.

What had she thought she'd accomplish by coming to the island? Was she in that big a rush to get business over with and on her way? Maybe she'd already made reservations at some four-star hotel halfway down the peninsula. How much time had she planned to allot him? An hour? Two? She hadn't come dressed to enjoy the northern clime. Oh, no. She came girded behind her briefcase and her office attire: impersonal, professional, impatient. One look had shot all his hopes to hell. They *were* worlds apart in what

39

they wanted. Seeing her reinforced that unhappy truth. He could make all the speeches he wanted, but they wouldn't change anything at all. His father had been right about that.

And Boyd Marston would know.

What made it worse—no, unbearable—was the way she'd felt in his arms. For that instant, he could almost pretend things were the same as in the beginning. When she'd loved him for himself. Maybe all the right emotional ingredients were lacking. However, nothing was missing when it came to the spark they made together. Beth still turned his heart inside out. She still made him as rut-crazed as a northwoods bull moose. He wanted her so badly he was almost willing to overlook what was wrong with what they had in favor of what was so very right. Almost. But that would solve about as much as her talk. Neither would heal what was irreparably broken. It was like trying to mend a massive coronary with a Band-Aid.

But, oh, he'd been tempted. He'd been ready to strip her right down to the soft woman that lurked beneath the austere suiting. He would have taken her on a bed of moss, beneath a canopy of pines if there was the slightest chance he could wake in her some of the passion of their first weeks together. When it was just the two of them. Before Marston Hotels came between them.

Better he didn't give way. Better he loaded them into his plane and got them back to the lodge. Better he listen to what she had to say and let her drive away. Back to the city where she had what she wanted without him. That way, he'd have a shred of his dignity left. And her respect, if nothing else. A far cry from what he really wanted from her. Better not to dwell on the impossible hopes he'd had when he proposed. It was his own fault. He shouldn't have been so naive. Especially after all the examples he had to follow.

Rainwater glazed an already slick trail. Wyatt was a veteran hiker. The corrugated bottoms of his boots were made to provide the best traction. But neither of those facts protected against a preoccupied mind or a careless misstep. And a rocky path was unforgiving.

He felt his foot give on a patch of uneven stone. Immediately, Wyatt shifted his weight to compensate, but he was a second too late, a heartbeat too slow. His heel skidded on wet earth even as he twisted to catch himself. But down he went as Beth's briefcase undercut him, left foot going straight out ahead of him, right leg angling behind as he hit with jarring force. The sound was like a rake handle snapping in two. He was slow to associate it with his awkward descent. Until he tried to move. Until he tried to untangle the unnatural bend of his body.

"Wyatt? Are you all right?"

His voice was faint with surprise.

"I broke my leg."

Chapter Three

"You're kidding, right?"

But as she bent down, she could see he was already pale with pain and was breaking into a sweat.

"Oh, my God. You're not kidding, are you?"

"I wish I was. Of all the stupid—Argh!" He leaned forward and rolled to one side, levering to ease the awkwardness of his position. With both legs more or less in front of him, he could judge the damage for himself. Somewhere between ankle and knee on his right leg, all the fires of hell were burning.

As he felt along the closed break with unsteady hands, Beth watched anxiously. It had yet to sink in just how dire their situation was. Her concern was for the immediate, for the way Wyatt's features drew in lean, taut lines as he tried to contain the hurt. She wracked her brain, wondering if there was anything she could do to ease it. In her purse, she had a Midol and some sinus medication. Not much help.

"I can't believe it," he was muttering in a

strained voice. "I've walked these trails a hundred times. I've played rugby, polo, ski jumped down-hill and on water, I've parasailed and mountain climbed without breaking more than a sweat. And now I break my leg falling down on a clear path. I can't believe the bad luck. How could I be so careless?" He was panting softly into the pain, trying not to come to an answer. But he knew what it was. Beth had distracted him from his usual precautions. And now he was going to pay a price for that momentary lapse. Unlike his city-bred wife, he knew exactly what they were up against out in the rugged wilderness, miles from even the meagerest excuse for civilization. Time, foremost. The weather was closing in fast. They couldn't afford to delay.

"Beth, help me up. We've got to get to the plane. It's not very far."

She pursed her lips into a silent expression of doubt. Yes, it was. She was intimately acquainted with every torturous step. And a man with a bro-ken leg was not going to make it. But there was no arguing with the mulish set of his features. She dipped down so he could put his arm about her shoulders and straightened slowly, hauling up with all her might. Wyatt struggled to get his sound leg under him and for a moment, it looked as though it might work. Until he took his first wobbly hop on the uneven path. Balance gave way and both of them went down. Wyatt fell with a ragged cry and Beth sprawled across him. Artemus, who had run ahead, returned and be-gan to trot in a wide circle around them, whining

43

in uncertainty. Beth righted herself quickly. The sound of Wyatt's pain did more than alarm the dog. It started her thinking with a crisp, desperate logic and as much as she didn't like the direction of her thoughts, it would be foolish to ignore them.

"Wyatt, lie back."

"No. Come on. Give it another try. I can make it. Maybe if you cut me a branch to lean on . . ."

"No," she interrupted firmly. "No. Even if I dragged you down to the plane, how are you going to fly us out? We've got a storm right over our heads. What happens if you pass out halfway back? I don't know anything about flying, Wyatt. We'll just have to wait for help to come to us."

He was breathing harshly, considering what she said. And he was scowling. He made his words concise and brutally clear so she wouldn't mistake their situation. "There won't be any help, Beth. Not before morning, anyway."

She was silent, regarding him and slowly processing what that would mean.

"We're going to have to rough it here overnight."

"I can radio Jimmy," she began.

"He won't be able to get here and take us back before the storm system closes in."

"There must be someone I can call."

"No. Once the fog settles and it gets dark, Santa Claus couldn't find us with Rudolph leading the way."

"I can walk for help," she insisted a bit more frantically.

"Beth, if you haven't noticed, we're in the middle of nothing. There's no place to go," he impressed upon her quietly. He let that settle as he anxiously studied her expression. She looked scared but she was controlling it. "The nearest ranger station is in Windigo. That's close to ten miles away, twice that if you count all the up and down hills you'd have to climb. It would be dark before you got halfway and you're not a seasoned hiker. Even if you got there, do you think they'd just run on over here with an ambulance?" He shook his head. "There aren't any motor vehicles on the island. The chances of anyone stumbling over us is just about nil."

She swallowed hard and whispered, "So what are we going to do? We'll need some first-aid equipment to . . . see to your leg."

"We'll set up camp here. Our best bet is to button down for the night. Jimmy will come looking tomorrow when we don't show up at the lodge. He knows our location. I've got everything we'll need in the plane. It's going to be up to you, Beth. I'm not going to be much help." He grimaced at that, hating his own helplessness.

Beth took a deep breath. "What do I have to do?" Her face took on that same cast of stubborn determination it wore when she was confronted with a difficult client. Wyatt smiled faintly. She was going to do just fine.

"All right. You're going to have to go down to the plane. I've got a survival kit behind the rear bench seat. It's in an orange backpack. I've got a

45

couple of sleeping bags, grab them. There's some extra clothes in a gym tote; you'll want to get more comfortable. I don't think you have to worry about dressing up for dinner tonight."

She returned his smile somewhat wanly.

He was breathing harder, with more of an obvious effort. Sweat began to dampen the hair along his brow and temples. But he was fighting to stay lucid, at least until they were set for the night. "Let me think a second." He closed his eyes, concentrating. When they reopened, there was a feverish brilliance in his gaze. "Water. We'll need fresh water. You can't drink out of the lake unless it's strained and boiled. I've got some two-gallon containers of bottled water stored in the float compartments. Oh, and there's a battery-operated lantern in the back. Look around, whatever you think we might need."

"Have you got a cellular phone so I can call 911 and order a pizza while we wait?"

"Sorry."

"Oh, well. I guess we'll just have to make do." She stood, mentally calculating how many trips she'd have to make, figuring she'd have one, maybe two at most, in her. She'd forgotten about her sore feet.

"Beth?"

"What?"

"I'm sorry about this. It's not exactly what I had in mind."

He looked so genuinely contrite, as if he thought she'd suspect him of purposely breaking his own leg just to make her life miserable.

Beth's heart went to mush and she vowed if she had any complaints to make, she wouldn't make them verbally.

"I won't be long," she said with a brisk efficiency because she didn't dare soften. He was counting on her to get things done. "You lie down and don't move. I may not have been a Camp Fire Girl, but I'm pretty good at problem solving. Here." She rolled up his coat and used it as a bolster behind the back of his head. "Are you going to be all right?"

"Sure. Go on. I've got Artie to keep me company."

She glanced at the big dog who, up to this point, had kept his distance. "Swell. You're in great hands."

He was in her hands and observing her tenacious expression, Wyatt was as content as he could be, under the circumstances.

"I'll be right back. Don't go anywhere."

"Like for a hike? Don't worry. And Beth, you be careful on the trail."

"I will. I have no intention of being at White Fang's mercy."

"Right back" was a relative term. The rain had stopped, but a dense fog was swelling up from the lake surface, wreathing the trail ahead in obscurity. They never would have made it out in the plane. Beth didn't have to be a pilot to know that. Not when she could barely see three feet in front of her face. After skidding the first few hundred yards, Beth kicked out of her office footwear before she joined Wyatt flat on her back. The ground was cold and springy under stockinged feet. The relief of escaping her heels was indescribable. She picked her way cautiously downward, coming upon the plane almost without realizing it. She could see only as far as its propeller. Beyond, the lake was shrouded in mist. She couldn't see it, but she could hear the movement of its tidal current, just like she could feel the forest crowding at her back. It was an eerie sensation, like something out of the "Twilight Zone."

Beth edged along the float and climbed into the cabin. The first thing she fumbled for was the pack of spare clothing. She needed something that would allow for a little more mobility than a business suit. After a few minutes of close quarter wiggling, she was bundled into a baggy navy blue sweatsuit and two pairs of woolen socks. She stuffed a third pair into the toes of Wyatt's running shoes. His size tens felt like a pair of pontoons but were more comfortable than dress pumps.

Practically garbed to meet the northern elements, if not exactly a fashion statement, she began to assemble what they'd need to get through the night. She found everything right where Wyatt said it would be and, loaded down like a pack mule so she would only have to make one trip, she began the upward plod. Thankfully, there was no time to ruminate on their situation. She was too busy with the basics of minute-to-minute survival to worry about what would come later. Shelter first, then Wyatt's leg. She knew enough sketchy first aid to realize the break would have to be splinted. And she wasn't looking forward to it any more than he would be.

Wheezing and weary by the time she'd completed the climb, Beth dumped the supplies in the center of the trail and went to check on Wyatt. And there, she was faced with her first obstacle. Artemus. The big dog stood at his master's shoulder and had no intention of letting Beth anywhere near him. Artemus's first warning was a throaty growl. When Beth tried to ignore it, the hackles rippled up into a bristly display on the back of his neck. He growled again, deeper, with even greater menace. Wyatt was shifting restlessly on the ground, his eyes closed, his face ashen and wet.

"Move, you wretched animal," Beth snarled back, but the dog remained unimpressed. So she tried another avenue. Lowering her voice to a sugary cooing, she edged closer. "If you'll just get out of my way, you nasty creature, I can take care of him. I'm not going to hurt him, but you're going to be sorry if I have to take a branch to your thick head. Let's not make things unpleasant, shall we."

Artemus's head lowered, his thick neck sinking into his chest and shoulders as his fiercely protective rumbling intensified.

Beth circled wide, thinking to approach the prone figure from the other direction. The dog flanked her, stepping carefully across Wyatt, continuing to stand between them. She was too tired and agitated to fear one aggressive animal.

"All right, you. I've tried to be a good sport about this, but you and I are going to tangle. And I can guarantee my bite is worse than my bark."

"Beth?" Wyatt mumbled, rolling his head toward her. "Who are you talking to?"

Feeling suddenly foolish, she explained, "Old Yeller here seems to have some misguided ideas about protecting you from my good intentions. I was trying to talk some sense into him. Maybe he'd listen to you."

He looked at her as if she was delirious.

"Never mind. Have you got any suggestions as to how I'm going to get past him?"

Wyatt reached up to grasp the dog's collar. "Sit, Artie. Good boy. I've got him. He won't hurt you."

"Yeah, right." Beth gave him a cautious berth while the gleaming yellow eyes never left her. She knelt at her husband's feet. "I'm going to take a look. Just pretend I know what I'm doing. I'll try not to hurt you."

As gently as she could, she placed her hands on the calf of his leg, kneading slightly. About the time she encountered an obvious swelling, Wyatt gave a sharp cry and Artemus lunged with enough strength to pull him halfway up. She fell back on her rump, crab-walking backwards as vicious jaws snapped together inches from her nose.

"No. Artie, no. Sit. Aggh . . . damn. Artie, sit!"

The dog finally yielded and Wyatt sank to the

ground, gasping unevenly, clutching the collar with all his waning energy.

"This isn't going to work," Beth concluded as she brushed the dirt off her seat. She was shakier than she'd let on. She'd felt the dog's hot breath, he'd been that close to taking off part of her face. "I can't take care of you if he won't let me within five feet."

"There's a nylon rope in the survival kit. Toss me an end and I'll tie it to his collar. You can wrap it around one of the trees and pu!l him off."

Now, why hadn't she thought of that?

After Wyatt tested his knot, Beth took her end of the cord and looped it around a sturdy oak on the other side of the trail. As she began to walk, Artie was yanked from his guard position by the ever-shortening lead. When he was safely detained some twenty feet away, she tied off the rope to another tree and went to Wyatt's side. After a few tugs, the animal realized he'd been outsmarted and began a restless pacing with the nylon stretched taut.

Brushing back her husband's damp hair with a gentle caress, Beth asked, "How are you doing?"

"Nothing a steady morphine drip couldn't cure." His smile was feeble. He was trying not to groan. He hadn't a great deal of faith in either of their fortitudes at the moment. Bravado was all that was holding him together. He didn't know what kept Bethany from coming unglued. Pride, probably. She wouldn't want to appear less than completely competent in any given crisis. He was

51

glad for it now. He was no hero. "There's some Tylenol-3 in the kit. I could sure use a handful about now."

"Coming right up."

"Wish I had about a quart of Jim Beam to wash it down with."

"Settle for some nice cold bottled water?"

"Not quite the same."

Smiling, Beth rummaged for the pain medication, shook out two tablets, then added a third, bringing them to Wyatt with a tin cup full of water. He tried to lever up on his elbows and was grateful for the support of her arm behind his shoulders. Every movement encouraged a jarring agony down his leg. He opened for the tablets and gulped down the water. She eased him back down and gave the side of his face another lingering stroke. The last thing he saw before he closed his eyes was her caring expression. He turned his head to one side and waited for the analgesic to take effect. Hurry, hurry, hurry, he chanted mentally with every pulse of misery. Hurry and work.

Dismissed from his attention, Beth confronted the task of shelter, consciously avoiding what she dreaded the most — splinting the break. Settling on her knees, she spread the contents of the survival kit out before her for inventory. She never expected so much to be packed into a six-pound package. There were first-aid supplies for every kind of wound or bite and to tend the body's ails from insects and sunburn to sensitive intestines. Besides the rope, there were copper wire, safety pins, a utility knife, razor blades, a compass, waterproof matches, fuel bars, a cook pot and toilet paper. To hasten rescue, there were light sticks, a whistle, red aerial flares, a smoke signal, a candle and a signal mirror. She was delighted by the discovery of six tropical chocolate bars, four soup packets, three granola bars, some instant oatmeal, tea bags, fruit drink mix, sugar envelopes and chewing gum. There were water purification tablets, too, but Wyatt had said not to trust them. And, along with two space blankets, there was an orange two-person tent. Home, sweet home. Now all she had to do was set it up while the light held out.

After draping Wyatt with one of the gold foil blankets, Beth turned to the puzzle of erecting the tent. She read through the directions. It sounded easy, but the minute she began threading lines and matching ends and securing stakes, she felt reduced to the level of a fumbling idiot. No sooner had she secured one end, than the other would topple. She'd drive in the stake in the rear and the front would pull free. As an intelligent adult, she was frustrated by her inability to complete the simple task. As a desperate, unwilling survivalist, she was ready to cry. She settled for cursing very colorfully under her breath and calling down all manner of ill wills upon the individuals who smugly pronounced the device as easily assembled by one person. They were probably thinking of Paul Bunyan in a flat, dry campground, not a frightened city female in the rocky wilds.

Finally, she sat back on her heels to observe her handiwork. Not a prize winner by any stretch but not bad. There were a few sloppy sags here and there, but it was tethered firmly, even if it was higher on one end than the other. At least they'd be sheltered from the bad weather. Now to roll out the sleeping bags and make everything cozy.

While she was musing over the bags—one was an expensive down and the other a light, synthetic fiber—Wyatt eased up on his elbows to observe their slipshod shelter. She waited somewhat sheepishly for him to denounce her woodland skills, but he merely smiled.

"Not bad for not being a Camp Fire Girl." He nodded at the bags. "Put the down one on the bottom for insulation and the nylon on top. It's more waterproof."

That made sense. So did zipping them together into one intimate sack. Except the man she was bundling up with was hardly going to be in a romantic mood.

As she maneuvered the bags into the crooked tent, she was poised half in, half out on hands and knees. Wyatt enjoyed a leisurely study of cotton knit molded to sweetly rounded derriere. Hot thoughts were a brief distraction from the pain pounding up his leg. Bethany looked great in his sweats. Of course, she was a gorgeous woman with a figure made for designer clothes. Dressed for business, she was all chic and style. But something about the way she looked in his sagging workout clothes reminded him of the woman he'd met and fallen so desperately in love with. That woman had been soft and touchable. She'd needed him. But he'd been wrong about that. Needed and used were two very different terms. And even now, he was the one on the needful end, not Beth. She was always on top of everything. Even when wrestling up a tent and faced with a night in the wilds. That was her job, crisis management.

How he wished it wasn't just a job to her. He eased down on his back and let the pain ebb and flow. It couldn't hurt worse than the constriction in his chest. What he wouldn't give to have Beth here because she wanted to be. To be sharing the things he loved, the things he longed to do. If she had her choice, she'd be speeding back toward civilization right now, not plumping up their bedding for the night. He was being unfair, he knew. You can take the girl out of the city . . . Had he really expected her to feel any differently about this place? He was dreaming. Just like the shabbily garbed female whose rump was waving so enticingly in his direction was just an illusion. She was a briefcase not a backpack kind of woman. She'd taken to his family's lifestyle with gusto. And all too soon, she was backing out of the tent and he was forced to return to his indifference.

"Did you lay down a tarp first?"

Beth pushed strands of hair from her face. "What?"

"Did you put a tarp down under the tent to keep the water from leaking in?"

A tarp down? Where had it said that in the directions? She sat back on her heels to study her sloppy structure. How was she supposed to know such a thing? Placing a tarpaulin under a camp tent was not a subject discussed in business college or a ready topic of conversation at a Gold Coast cocktail party. There was no way she was going to pull down the tent she'd sweated and sworn over just to prove she was too incompetent to think of the obvious. So she smiled and lied.

"Yes, of course. All snug for the night."

How would he ever know the difference?

"You'd better help me get inside while I can still give you a hand." His tone had gone flat, but she could have sworn just before he looked away, there was a hint of anger in his tight expression.

Beth took a deep breath. No more avoiding the necessary. "Has the pain medication kicked in yet?"

"A little. I don't think it's going to give me a nice numbing buzz. That'd be too much to hope for."

"Wyatt?"

The tentative nature of her voice alerted him. The way she avoided his eyes when he turned toward her had him worried. "What?"

"Before I move you, shouldn't I splint your leg?"

He noticed her pallor and her hesitation and said softly, "You've done more than enough already."

Dark eyes rose in challenge. She had marvelously expressive eyes. "Don't baby me, Wyatt. This is serious stuff. I think I'm supposed to immobilize that break."

"Sure you're up to that?"

"No." She supplied a wavery smile. It firmed as she added, "But I'll do whatever it takes."

Wyatt's features spasmed with an internal agony. "You've more than proven that to me." She frowned slightly. However, before she could question the cynical twist of his words, he said with a somber gruffness, "Get a couple of sturdy branches and you can use that gauze out of the first-aid kit."

Given a task, she was able to respond without thought, without crippling emotion. Without wondering how on earth she was going to do what needed to be done. She scrounged around in the underbrush until she'd located two straight sticks of over two inches in diameter, then brought them back to Wyatt. He had his forearm braced across his eyes and was breathing shallowly. She guessed the pain medication wasn't doing diddly. That didn't make her chore any easier.

"Wyatt, I'm ready."

He lowered his arm and gave her a steady stare. "This isn't going to be pretty," he warned. "I'm probably going to yell my head off."

Funny, she couldn't remember ever hearing him raise his voice. "You go right ahead and yell. It'll scare off any wildlife that might be lurking near camp. I'm sure I'd do the same in your position." She lined up the limbs along his right calf and secured them to his ankle with a couple of quick turns of the gauze after lifting his foot gently atop her lap. Wyatt's breathing became a noticeable chugging.

"That's not so bad," he gritted out.

"Not bad at all," she reassured soothingly. Then she gripped his toe and heel and pulled.

He yelled. The sound echoed wildly through the dusk-draped trees and behind her; Artemus surged against his rope and began a savage barking. Beth didn't pay attention to either noise. She wedged Wyatt's foot between her thighs to keep the elongating tension on the bone and wrapped as fast as she could, binding the supports to denim in a snug cocoon. By the time she was finished, she was panting almost as irregularly as he was. Very slowly, she lowered his bound leg to the ground. She was near tears as she scooted up beside him.

"Wyatt?" Her hand touched his damp face. He seemed unaware of it. There was a blanking glaze to his lidded stare. He was hanging on to consciousness by a whisper of will. Beth swallowed hard and tried to control the quiver of her chin. If she lost it now, they'd both be in desperate straits. Everything inside her was shaking like unmolded gelatin. Composure was slipping fast. "I'm sorry, Wyatt. I didn't want to hurt you. I'm sorry." Her chest began a painful laboring for sufficient air and tears came.

She felt the brush of his fingertips over the hand she had resting on his seesawing middle. His fingers curled around hers and held tight.

And with that stabilizing grip, all returned to proper balance.

With her free hand, Beth dashed away any signs of tears. She attempted a smile. It was a poor excuse, all wobbly and trembling, but it gave hope.

"Hey, that's done. What could be worse? All downhill from here, right?"

His hand clutched hers and she nearly came apart again. She took several determined breaths and forced her mind to focus on the immediate. It was easier than drowning in helpless empathy.

"Do you think you're up to a little trip? Our room's ready for the night."

"Four-star accommodations," he murmured.

"Not the best in the Marston chain, but it was close and it happened to have a vacancy." She squeezed his hand then impulsively lifted it so she could place a warm kiss upon his knuckles. Then another. Then she was pressing his palm against her cheek, her eyes clamping shut to ward off more weeping. His fingers unfurled so their pads could sketch over her smooth temple and fragile jaw in a sensitive sweep. Beth didn't think she'd ever loved Wyatt as much as in this tender moment. But they couldn't afford to linger over sentiment. Not until he was tucked in safe and warm. She gave his palm a quick buss of her lips and released his hand, all business once more.

"Okay, here's the plan. I'm going to drag you and you do what you can to help out."

"That's the plan?"

"You have a better one? Like maybe hiring a forklift?"

"No. No, your plan's fine."

"Glad you agree. Now, if I can just lift you a little." She squatted and threaded her arms beneath his underarms, lacing her fingers over his chest. "Ready?"

He hoisted his bad leg so it cleared the ground by a couple of inches. "Set."

"Let's go."

As she backed out slowly, Wyatt pushed with his heel. It was awkward but effective until they got to the tent. There was no room inside for her to precede him. She couldn't risk knocking the whole thing down.

"You're just going to have to wiggle in on your own," she pronounced, easing him down at the open flap.

"No problem." He sucked in a quick breath and hauled himself across the threshold with the strength of his arms, plopping down on the opened sleeping bags with a grateful groan. Beth ducked in and fussed for a moment, arranging the top bag over him, but he was lost to her attention. Once situated, he had no further need to hang on. Consciousness was gone in an instant. Beth sat beside him, hunching so her shoulders wouldn't bump the angled overhead. She stroked his hot face and let the emotions swell.

"Oh, Wyatt, we're going to get through this. We are."

And that one sentiment summed up all.

Chapter Four

A fire. That was the first thing Beth thought of. Heat and light—a spark of civilization to cling to as the mist-shrouded pines closed in around her.

Something hot, like tea, maybe soup would be just the thing to calm her fractured nerves. And if Wyatt woke, she'd get some down him, too. It would give her something to do as darkness gathered in the forested interior. She wasn't quite ready for all that blackness, she who was used to streetlights and marquees and lighted billboards. She'd need wood and that meant leaving the security of her woebegone campsite. Better now than after the sun set and it really started to get dark and cold. And she imagined it got downright frigid during the course of a northern Michigan night.

Beth stayed on the trail, searching along its edge for small dry branches she could burn. She'd put on Wyatt's jacket because a seeping chill had already settled in. Her breath plumed faintly as she bent to scoop up several sticks.

When she straightened and looked down the path, at first all she saw was a big patch of fog. Then, as it dissipated, a dark shape formed behind it. A huge shape. The mist formed again and she realized it was the big animal's breath clouding the cold air.

"Oh, my God."

Beth froze, firewood clutched to her chest. Never had she seen such a monstrous and unattractive creature. The moose regarded her with like surprise and for a moment, they were at a standoff. It lowered its massive, ugly head, giving a threatening shake of stubby antlers. She knew absolutely nothing about moose. Were they timid creatures, like deer or aggressive monarchs of the wilderness? She was on its home ground and it looked like it was used to going wherever it wanted. Beth considered screaming. The hysterical sound welled up in her throat, but she clamped it off. Who would hear and come to her aid? Wyatt? The thought of him trying to drag himself to her rescue with a broken leg was enough to hold her silent.

The moose took a loose-limbed stride toward her and the stack of wood rattled with the trembling of her arms. What was she going to do? What if it decided to charge? How would she ward off a ton of slack skin, huge haunches and slashing hooves? With a handful of kindling? A petrifying helplessness overcame her. The animal snorted and took another step. Beth's knees went rubbery, barely holding her up. Panicked breath sobbed from her.

Then the thought came to her: What would happen to Wyatt if she was trampled on the trail? This big, hulking creature stood between her and the care of her camp and her injured husband. Her knees steadied. Her shoulders squared. And a frown firmed her features.

"Shoo," she whispered. The animal blinked. "Go on. Get away."

The sound of her voice seemed to confuse the beast. It scuffled backwards a few steps. Feeling more powerful, Beth raised her volume.

"Go on. You heard me. Go terrorize some other camper. I don't have time for this. Get!"

The moose obviously decided she was nothing it wanted to bother with. With one last snuffling snort, it shambled off into the darkness. Beth didn't move until the sound of it crashing through the underbrush had stopped. Then she scrambled back to camp in a dead run.

"That damned letter, the bumpy plane, the long drive, then no Wyatt. I ruin my best hose, tangle with a wolf-dog, skin my knees, set a broken leg and now a moose." She was muttering fiercely as she tented the sticks in a small circle and began stuffing in pine needles. Her hands were shaking. Only her anger kept her from succumbing to shock.

"I've had it." She tried a match. It flickered out before she got it halfway to the wood. "I'm outta here." She tried another and this time the needles caught with a surprising burst of flame. She blew on them softly and continued her agitated monologue. "Come morning, I'm on that plane, in my car and gone. Let him have his woods. If he wants to rip my future out from under me, he's going to have to come to Chicago to do it. Or Denver. I don't want any part of this."

As if she felt a provoking stare, Beth glanced up to see Artemus watching her. He was sitting at the end of his lead, his yellow eyes glowing. His tongue was lolling as if to mock her misery.

"What are you laughing at?" she growled. "Fine. You win. You can have him. If this is what he wants, he can keep it. Give me my fitted sheets, my cappuccino maker and my season tickets to the Cubbies. Give me muggers over moose any day. If he wants a divorce, he can have it. I don't care. I just want out of here." The words dammed up in a painful knot. For a nonweepy woman, she certainly had shed a record amount of tears in the last few hours. She brushed at the hot dampness tracking down her cheeks, but more tears cascaded down. She gulped through the thickening emotions, then gave a wondrous little cry.

"Oh, look. I did it. This is great."

Her fire was burning brightly, giving off a cheery warmth that pushed back the night shadows to a respectful distance. Beth put out her hands to feel the heat and the warming pride of her accomplishment did much to quell her self-pitying mood.

"Now for some dinner."

She smiled wryly as she thought of moose chops. Imagine jumping the gigantic beast with a stick of kindling wood and skinning it with a Swiss army knife. Soup would be just fine for tonight's menu, thank you very much.

As she poured water into the small cook pot, she noticed Artemus had clambered to his feet and was moving his thick tail in what could have passed for a wag.

"You thirsty?"

He whined softly in response.

"Okay, but you've got to promise not to bite the hand that feeds you. I could always settle for fillet of dog steaks on my open fire. You're dealing with a desperate woman here. You remember that."

Beth approached cautiously. She had nothing that could serve as a water dish, so she bent and scooped an indentation in the soft earth while watching the dog with a wary eye. He kept his distance. Quickly, she splashed water into the hole and backed away. The dog moved in and lapped it up before it sank into the ground. Then he parked on his haunches and stared at her.

"I suppose you're hungry, too. Sorry, no moose burgers. How about a nice nutritious chocolate bar. Best I can do." She got one of the bars from the survival kit, unwrapped it and tossed it over. Artemus gulped it whole. She pitched him another one. "Make it last." He devoured it in a bite. Apparently satisfied, he lay down and pushed his nose between his paws to watch her.

After stirring the soup mix in the pan, Beth wedged it in on top of the glowing wood and sat cross-legged to watch it steam. She sighed as a sense of deep quiet settled over her. Probably just exhaustion, she rationalized, because she was actually feeling mellow. The woods were now completely dark and the stillness was peaceful to one raised on traffic sounds and human movement in neighboring apartments. Relaxation eased over her, soothing the knots of tension and the threads of strain. She couldn't remember ever experiencing such total serenity within herself. There was nothing pushing to occupy her thoughts, nothing pending to demand her attention, no phone to answer, no work sheets to tally, no schedule to juggle. Just the gentle curls of steam rising from her supper, teasing her appetite with its tempting aroma.

Funny, how it took a forced moment of quiet for her to see how little of her own private time she had left at the end of each hectic day. For as long as she could remember, she'd been striving fiercely for something. At first, it was to escape the trap of poverty, then it was to hang onto her good fortune. There'd been so much to learn. It had been such a big step into Wyatt's world. She'd wanted to make that step, regardless of the cost to her, regardless of the shock to her social system. Marrying Wyatt pushed her into an intense limelight. There was always some function to attend, some charity to contribute to, some event to host as one of the well-to-do and community conscious Marstons. She'd taken private time for granted until there was none. Surprisingly, she discovered the life of the wealthy wasn't the expected life of ease. It was an outward life, one of causes and claims upon personal energy. It required high public visibility and involved a high degree of stress for someone who was ever conscious of being a society pretender. Beth hadn't inherited her role, she'd bought into it when she married a Marston. The jet-set profile was an obligation and it was one she felt uncomfortable with. The parties, the entertaining, the constant cultivation of the right people, it was more studied effort than enjoyment. Until now she'd never had the time to sit back and analyze how much she really hated the shallow socializing and glittery surface show. But she couldn't complain. It was part of what marrying into money meant. She shouldn't complain because it got her where she'd wanted to go.

The soup was simmering. When she couldn't wait any longer, she used the ribbed cuff of Wyatt's coat as a pot holder to pull the pan from the fire. Then she set it aside to cool while she went to check on her husband. He did not move beneath the bulky sleeping bag; he was either asleep or still unconscious. His forehead was damp and hot, which she considered a good sign. At least there was no clammy chill of shock to worry about. She could reheat some soup later, but for now, she'd dine alone.

As Beth sat sipping her soup, lost to her own wondering thoughts, a breeze came up. It rustled through the branches overhead and brought the loamy scent of approaching rain. She bundled closer into the leather coat, paying it little attention until her gaze happened to focus on the fire.

Her eyes followed, mesmerized, as the currents of air carried glowing sparks up like a swarm of fireflies that flickered and fluttered . . . right toward the tent!

Beth jumped up with a gasp of alarm. Tiny embers dotted the nylon awning. She grabbed a twig and frantically brushed the embers off, chastising herself for not having built her fire upwind. No great damage done, just a pattern of tiny pin-sized holes. She sighed tremulously as she thought how close she'd come to setting her shelter ablaze with her husband inside it. Anguished by that guilty thought, she doused the fire and kicked dirt over the smoldering remnants. Immediately, it was dark. She stood for a moment until her eyes adjusted to the gloom enough for her to make out the outline of the tent. She'd left the lantern inside. She ducked beneath the loose flap and fumbled until she found it, flicking on the bright yellow beam. It made an eerie circle on the tent roof, illuminating the holes like a reverse negative of the constellations. She scowled, displeased by the sight.

As she got ready to slip out of the jacket, Beth realized there was one more trip she needed to make before turning in for the night. Armed with lantern and toilet paper, she stumbled out into the woods only as far as she thought absolutely necessary. And again she found herself muttering curses upon her husband, their situation and the cold of the air against her backside. She stomped back to their wretched little camp and crawled beneath the orange roof—not quite Howard

Johnson's! She lashed down the flap and shed Wyatt's coat and borrowed shoes before wiggling into her side of the sleeping bag.

The sensation of warmth was immediate and familiar. Lying beside Wyatt Marston had become the rule rather than the exception for almost a year. Until this moment Beth hadn't realized how much she'd missed it. There, in the intimate darkness, she forgot the peril of their situation in favor of the pleasure. The low hush of his breathing was an enticement. The need for closeness was a compelling force. She wanted with a desperate longing just to be near him, to touch him, to hold him with all the manner of love welled up inside her heart.

She had so much love to give and restraining it had been a constant frustration in their marriage. Wyatt was uncomfortable with overt displays of affection. He shied away from her impulsive hugs, from her want to kiss him when and wherever the mood struck her. He'd made a joke of it, pretending to be embarrassed by her impatience. However, that didn't erase the momentary sting of rejection, no matter how slight. When had she stopped making those spontaneous overtures? When had fear of his recoil overcome the need to demonstrate how much she cared for him?

In their shared bed, she had no complaints. There, he'd always been a hot and enthusiastic lover. There, he let passions have full rein. But eventually, even the pleasure of their lovemaking was tempered by the reserve of their daily relationship. When had she given up trying to figure out a way to breach the growing sense of isolation? When had she quit reaching out to him? Had it been a conscious thing or had she simply allowed her frantic work schedule to lure her away from having to make the attempt?

Now, there was nothing to distract her, no excuses to make. She thought of all these things as the sound of gentle rain began to patter on the slope of nylon overhead. She mourned for all those barren months of being with him and yet feeling so far apart as she reached out to place her palm upon his slow rising chest. She moved her hand in a lingering caress. Lord, he felt good. She'd missed the simple luxury of touching him. Carefully, so as not to disturb his uneasy rest, Beth curled against him, reveling in the private knowledge she had of his every hard plane and tempting contour. She sighed with the pleasure of reestablished contact. As she nudged her cheek atop his shoulder, Wyatt shifted. She wasn't sure whether it was by instinct or design. His arm then lifted, opening an intimate hollow against his side. This encouraged her to pillow her head beneath his chin as he pulled her in for a tight fit along the curve of his ribs and angle of his hip.

He was still for a time, so she thought he'd fallen into a deeper slumber. Then his hand rose, brushing over the disarray of her thick blond hair, fingers meshing and tugging loose the last semblance of order in her French braid. He'd always told her how much he liked her hair down and free. It wasn't practical for work, but he'd insisted upon it when they were alone. At least, he had at first. Then, he'd stopped commenting on her neat, sophisticated up-does and chic braids, and the times she wore her hair down became few and far between.

Beth closed her eyes and sighed, seduced into forgetting everything by the strong kneading of his fingers. He had the most sensuous touch. He could reduce the day's stresses within seconds with a massage. He knew just the right spot where tensions massed and just the right pressure to dissolve them into eddies of liquidlike pleasure. The high point of her day had been kicking off her shoes after coming home late and sinking down onto the floor in front of him so he could work his magic upon her knotted muscles. And when he'd relaxed her to the consistency of putty, there'd be soft kisses, the first of many in an escalating intensity that led from living room to bedroom. When had those sensual sessions ended? When had she started coming in to find him busy with his own work or already in bed asleep? When had she stopped waking him to tell him she was home? Oh, to have those early days back when she'd happily taken his touch for granted.

His fingers tightened in her hair, drawing down in back to lift her face to his. His kiss was slow and searing, shaking her from her grip on time and place. She was no longer a woman who'd endured a dreadful day, who was stranded in the wilderness with an injured man who no longer truly loved her. She was Wyatt Marston's wife and lover, and it didn't matter if they were in a sagging tent in the middle of nowhere. This was where she wanted to be.

Wyatt eased from her eager lips to whisper, "I love you, Beth," and suddenly, everything was worth it—the flight, the drive, the hike, the fright, the struggle to compete where she had no experience. Hearing him say those words erased all else.

"Oh, Wyatt, I love you, too. I never stopped loving you."

She lifted up on her elbows, needing to see the tenderness in his expression. She was starved for it. Her palm soothed over his cheek and it was then she felt the scorching heat. He was burning with fever. His gaze was glassy with it.

"I wanted to wait up," he was saying, "but I must have fallen asleep. How did your meeting go?"

"What?"

"You work too hard, Bethany. I wish you wouldn't. I miss you."

She was very still as his fingertips sketched her jaw.

"Don't go with Casey this weekend," he continued.

Beth's mind scrambled. Mark Casey was head of Casey Computation. They held three four-day seminars in the hotel every year. These gatherings were spare-no-expense deals for over six hundred employees and were one of the hotel's biggest money makers. She'd seen Casey a half-dozen times, at different social events, some of them involving Friday or Saturday overnights. She was ashamed to say she couldn't pinpoint what occasion her husband was referring to. She'd spent so many weekends away.

"I don't want you to," he rambled in mounting distress. "Beth, please don't go. Please stay with me. I love you, Beth. Don't go with him." His breathing quickened in agitation. His hand dropped away, falling slackly atop the sleeping bag as his head rolled restlessly from side to side. He was clearly lost between fever-fed delirium and a Tylenol-3 cloud nine. What shook Beth were his words—words he'd never spoken aloud to her.

"Don't go. Don't do this to us. It'll get better. I'll make it better."

Now, she was lost and he was no longer speaking rationally. He was the one who left her. She didn't try to argue. The best she could do was quiet him.

"Shh. Wyatt, I'm not going anywhere."

He responded to her voice by jerking his head toward her and to her gentle touch with rapid pants of anxiety. Obviously, he didn't believe her.

"Don't go. Don't leave me. Stay with me, Beth."

"Shhh. I will. I will. I'll stay but you have to be quiet. You have to rest now. Will you do that for me?"

"I'll do anything. Just please . . . don't go." For a moment, his gaze seemed so lucid, so desperately searching hers for reassurance. She'd never seen him with all masks of reserve and proper upbringing stripped away. And what she saw startled and alarmed her. He looked fragile and uncertain, not at all the self-possessed man she knew. Or thought she knew. Was this what was behind the barriers, this despairing insecurity? Or was it a product of the pain and pills? She prayed it was the latter because she couldn't bear to think she had hurt him so. If these were the things he was feeling, why hadn't he ever told her? Just one more of the many mysteries to solve before she'd let him push her away. But for now, neither of them were going anywhere.

"I won't leave you, Wyatt. I'll be right here when you wake up. Close your eyes and try to rest."

His eyes shut obediently, but he continued to thrash until he was moaning softly with every ragged breath. Beth grew frightened for him. His fever was worsening. Had she the strength to restrain him should it become necessary? She didn't dare give him any more medication.

"My leg hurts," he complained weakly.

"I know it does. Try not to move and it'll be better."

"It hurts . . ."

"Shhh."

His eyes reopened, bright, unfocused. "Beth?"

"Right here."

"Where are we?"

She brushed his damp hair back from a fiery brow, nearly choking on her quiet words of comfort. "Camping. Don't you remember? You fell

74

and hurt your leg. But it's going to be all right. Jimmy will be here in the morning to get you to a hospital."

"Jimmy."

"That's right."

"Camping . . . I didn't think you liked to camp."

"I'm having a memorable time." Oh, how very true that was. She continued to stroke his brow and the side of his face, stilling the toss of his head with the slow repetitions. "You have to rest now. Close your eyes."

They flickered, seemingly reluctant to stay shut. "The tarp. Did you remember to put the tarp down first?"

"Yes. Hush now. Go to sleep. I'll be right here beside you all night. You rest."

His eyelids dropped, then dragged back open to sag again and remain unmoving. Beth kept up the rhythmic caresses until she was certain he had lost consciousness. Only then did she settle into the cove of his shoulder, frowning slightly.

What had he been talking about? Fiction from a fevered mind or jealousies restrained behind his stoic front? He'd never mentioned any qualms about her weekends away. But did that mean he didn't have any?

She felt a splash of dampness on her cheek and rubbed it away, impatient with further tears. She'd done enough weeping to last a lifetime. Again, the trickle of wetness and she looked up just in time to have a big droplet of water hit her in the eye. She blinked frantically and gave a soft cry of dismay. The tent roof was leaking.

Rain sieved in through dozens of tiny holes. Beth mumbled a dire obscenity and jerked the sleeping bag up over her and Wyatt's heads. It kept the moisture off, but then there was the incessant drip—drip—drip upon the nylon covering. Something sharp and unyielding dug into her hip through the downy thickness of the bottom bag. She'd forgotten to smooth the ground before unrolling the tent. As time passed in slow, agonizing seconds, she became more and more aware of the ripply texture beneath them. She wanted to fidget but was afraid of disturbing Wyatt. So she squeezed her eyes shut and hoped for unconsciousness to overtake her.

It seemed like hours, but it couldn't have been that long. She lay stiff and uncomfortable, trying to convince herself that she didn't have to go to the bathroom. The rain had stopped so she nudged down the sleeping bag now that the danger of leaks was past. It was cold—a deep, bonerattling cold. And wet, she realized in distress. The sleeping bag beneath them was resting atop puddles of water that had seeped up through the floor, because she hadn't put the tarp down first. Something was buzzing about the inside of the tent. In the stillness, it sounded like a B-52 bomber. She sighed in exhaustion. At least Wyatt was resting peacefully. She was glad someone was.

About then, she heard Artemus growl.

He gave a deep-throated rumble that meant business. Beth was instantly wide awake. Some-

76

thing . . . or someone was out there. Artemus sensed it. And the two of them inside the tent were helpless prey to whatever had the big dog snarling. Artie could provide no protection. He was tied up. Beth's imagination went wild. Huddled down in the sleeping bag, clutching at her unconscious husband, she tried to ignore the dog and pretend whatever predator it was would soon go away, leaving them unharmed. Her mind played scenes from every *Friday the Thirteenth* movie she'd ever seen. Visions of a hockey-masked killer stalking helpless campers reeled behind her tightly closed eyes.

Then Artemus began to bark.

Beth scrambled from the tent without thinking and ran to where the anxious dog was tied. Forgetting her reservations about him and her worries that he might bite her, she quickly released the rope from his collar. Hanging on with all her might, she dragged the animal toward the tent. She may have hated the beast, but he was the best protection they had. The dog might not have cared a hoot for her safety, but she was sure he'd fight to the death for Wyatt. Good enough. She shoved him inside and secured the flap.

The tent was small for two people. It was absolutely claustrophobic with one big, smelly dog thrown in. Artemus did what any wet dog would do. Immediately, he shook, spraying droplets of water everywhere. Then he lay down at the head of Wyatt's sleeping bag and became suspiciously silent. If she believed it possible, Beth would swear the animal staged the whole thing just to get in from the cold. But she did feel better knowing he was with them.

Cold and tense with agitation, Beth burrowed into the bag. It was quiet outside. However, she imagined threat even in the loud silence. She did her best to ignore the wet wool stench of musty dog, the restless murmurings of a delirious human and the drone of one blood-thirsty mosquito in her search for desperately desired sleep. Finally, she had to turn off the lantern because the light brought hundreds of winged things to beat against the nylon tent walls. The thought of them swarming inside was more distressing than her fear of unknown darkness. Beth hadn't known night could be so black. She shifted and muttered, counting the seconds as they dragged by, praying for the light of day to come soon.

It was the longest five hours of her entire life.

Chapter Five

An odd, snuffling sound awakened Beth. She opened her eyes into immediate panic, having forgotten her circumstances while she slept. She stared at the sloping roof uncomprehendingly. Then Artemus stepped on her in passing and she unhappily remembered all.

It was light, finally. She must have drifted into some level of sleep some time before that cold dawn ascended. She did not feel at all rested and she was stiff all over. She sat up only to be swatted with Artemus's bushy tail. He was standing at the tied down tent flap, whining to get out.

"Oh, for heaven's sake, dog. Cross your legs for a second, will you," she grumbled under her breath as she dragged out of the warm covers and loosened the flap. Artemus slipped out and was gone. "Go catch breakfast, why don't you? Or better yet, run away."

She took a minute to limber up as much as possible in the confined space, then twisted to check on Wyatt. His eyes were closed, but he was shifting fitfully. The light touch of her palm upon his brow brought his gaze up instantly. It was cool and aware of who she was and where they were. There was none of last night's confusion.

"Hi. How are you feeling?"

He didn't need to answer. His lean features were pinched and drawn. Pain put bruiselike circles beneath his eyes. But he managed a wry smile. "Like an elephant decided to sit on my leg."

"Ah, humor. That's a good sign."

"You want a sign? I could give you one that's a lot more explicit."

"Oh, and ill-tempered, too. I think you're going to survive."

"Oh, goody." In his present state, that was more a punishment than a pleasure.

"Any idea what time it is?"

He lifted his arm with an effort to check for her. "About seven. Jimmy should be here soon. Man, I could go for some hot coffee and some steak and eggs."

"How about tea and a granola bar?"

"Terrific," he mumbled. He let his arm drop. His knuckles hit the tent floor with a definite splash. Beth stiffened, knowing what was coming. He lifted his hand and shook the wetness off, then glanced at her. "I thought you said you—"

"I lied. All right? I lied. So don't hire me on here at Camp Mini-Ha-Ha next spring. At least you didn't drown, so quit crabbing at me." She rolled over and started to crawl on hands and knees out of the tent. Wyatt snagged her ankle.

"Where are you going?" There was the mildest touch of anxiousness in his tone. It made her remember how truly helpless he was and that no matter how awful her night had been, his had been worse. It was enough to temper her mood. But not enough to curb her tongue.

"To take a hot shower. Want to join me?"

"Sounds good." He gave a sigh of fatigue and it broke the last of her resistance. Her tone gentled.

"I'm going to fix up a northwoods breakfast. You take it easy, okay? Want some more Tylenol?"

"No. I'm holding my own."

Beth paused and looked back at him chidingly.

He glowered back. "Give me a dozen," he growled.

"Two, coming up."

She got him the Tylenol and a cup of water, easing his head up so he could swallow them. When he was resting again, she let her hand trail over his shoulder and chest, marveling at the hard symmetry in an unintentional second of distraction. He caught her hand and without saying anything, meshed his fingers between hers. She waited, heart in her throat, for him to say something meaningful, something tender. For him to thank her for her heroic effort.

"Can you manage the fire by yourself?"

So much for sentiment. She pulled her hand

away and scrambled from the tent, calling over her shoulder, "About as well as I managed the tent."

"Don't burn down the forest. The rangers tend to frown on that."

"Very funny," she shot back, wondering what he'd say if he knew how close to being toast he'd been last night. She made a mental note to get the tent replaced before he had the time to inspect it more thoroughly.

After hauling herself to her feet, Beth was halfway through a stretch when she paused and really took a look around her. The view was beautiful. More, it was breathtaking. The woods were all wet and glistening. Last night's rain glimmered in prisms of brightness as the first rays of morning sun pierced through the tall pines. The scent was wonderful, like Christmas—all fresh and clean and pungent. And the sky was blue. That was the best news of all. Beth inhaled until her lungs ached. And she found she was smiling as she looked for wood that wasn't completely sodden.

It took longer to start her fire. Everything was damp and the small curls of flame were sluggish. She knew just how they felt. Finally, they caught and she put water on to heat while she went to tend her own call to nature in the wet underbrush. Oh, for a toothbrush, some mousse and a tray of cosmetics. She didn't even want to think about how she must look. The way her brush snagged through her hair was evidence enough to create a frightening picture. *The Bride of Frankenstein Camps Out*. But her purse only contained so many miracles. Mouthwash and hot rollers weren't among them.

Her pot of water was bubbling nicely. Not being much of a hot tea drinker, she opted for oatmeal since they were limited in the tableware department. More stick-to-the-rib power. With two cups in hand and the granola bars, she slipped back into the tent.

"Breakfast is ready. Let's see, you ordered the oatmeal, plain, slightly stirred."

Wyatt levered up on his elbows, but that was as far as he could go before pain spasmed across his features.

"Here. Let me give you a hand."

Beth knelt behind him and edged up until the slant of her knees was supporting his lower back and his head rested quite naturally between the soft contour of her breasts.

"How's that?"

He wasn't sure what to make of his position. It was nice. And he would have given anything to have two healthy legs to go along with the healthy dose of growling hormones. But since he didn't, he mumbled, "Fine."

"Here you go." She handed him the meager fare. "No comments, please. The cook is extremely sensitive to criticism this morning."

"Look's fine. I could eat a horse."

"You almost had a moose."

"What?" He craned his head, trying to look up

at her. He got an eyeful of lush bosom and he couldn't seem to distract his gaze further.

"Never mind. Eat. You'll have to spoon it up with the granola bar. I guess real men don't use silverware because there wasn't any in the pack."

Despite his claim to the contrary, Wyatt was able to finish only half his scant allotment. He set the cup and partially eaten bar aside disinterestedly and his head gave a listless roll against its yielding pillow.

"I know it's not steak and eggs, but surely you can do better than that."

He didn't answer.

"Wyatt?" She put her own food aside. "Are you all right?"

Even as he shook his head, her hand was there upon his brow, feeling the return of heat and perspiration.

"I don't feel very good," he murmured unnecessarily.

"You're not going to be sick, are you?" Beth asked with a queasy faintness. "Tell me you're not going to be sick. I can handle just about anything else."

Again, he shook his head. Hard shivers began to work up along his limbs, the vibrations sending shattering waves of pain through his badly swollen leg. He clenched his teeth, but a groan of anguish forced its way out. Beth's arms became an immediate bond about his chest, holding him, hugging him as if her embrace could discourage his discomfort. It was a nice try, but nothing short of a few CCs of serious painkiller was going to take the biting edge off his misery. He would not be sick, he told himself sternly as a disquieting roil stirred up his belly. He'd just about been stripped of every other scrap of dignity. He refused to go that last humiliating mile.

That's when Artemus stuck his nose inside the tent flap.

Wyatt grinned weakly in welcome. "Hey, Artie. Where you been, buddy?"

But instead of coming in at the invitation of Wyatt's outstretched hand, the big dog backed out. They could hear him bounding off, then his barking. It wasn't a challenging noise, not like the night before. In a few minutes, the shush of footsteps followed.

"Hope you're decent."

With that call of warning, the tent flap parted and Jimmy Shingoos knelt to peer inside.

"I'd have knocked, but there wasn't anything to knock on." He eyed the two of them in obvious amusement. "Not interrupting anything, am I? Artie was rather insistent that I come right away. I was expecting a scene of distress."

Relief had Bethany close to babbling. "Oh, Jimmy. Thank God! Wyatt's broken his leg. We couldn't get down to the plane and had to set up camp here for the night. There was this moose and something prowling around in the dark and Wyatt's in such pain. I was afraid no one was coming. We've got to get him to a hospital."

The smile faded from Jimmy's flat features. He

flipped back the top sleeping bag to check the sturdy splint and his friend's general condition. "How are you holding up?" He touched blunt fingers to the sweat-slicked brow, then felt the base of Wyatt's throat to monitor his pulse rate.

"Could be better," Wyatt mumbled.

Jimmy's blue eyes took in the position of his head and the possessive curl of Beth's arms and he smiled. "Looks like you're in pretty good shape. Considering." He glanced down at the tent floor where the knee of his denims was rapidly soaking up water. "Did you forget to put down—"

"I did it," Beth cut in brusquely. "I forgot to put down the tarp. So shoot me. Geez! I'm never going to live this down, am I?" She abandoned her place behind Wyatt, letting him drop rather suddenly atop the half-saturated bottom bag. Pushing past Jimmy, she strode across their shabby campsite and began to stuff things back into the survival pack.

Jimmy looked after her with a cocked eyebrow, then back to Wyatt. He offered no explanation, so Jimmy didn't pursue it. "Let's get you out of here and into the fresh air."

"I don't think I can get up," Wyatt admitted gruffly.

"No problem. Just hang on."

Jimmy grabbed the bottom of the sleeping bag and dragged the whole thing outside with a minimum of trauma to the injured man. In full daylight, Wyatt appeared pallid from the ravaging pain and gaunt with the effort to control it. He lay with eyes closed, breathing in shallow little pants. There was no way for him to disguise how badly he was hurting, so he didn't try.

With Jimmy there to take charge, Beth was left uncomfortably on the outside. She'd done her best, but in the light of day, her best seemed fairly pathetic. Her tent was a soggy disaster. Her fire had nearly burnt the roof over their heads. She'd proven herself inept in the forest and had panicked at the slightest provocation. She'd cried enough tears to float a good sized ark, and now that it was over, she was still faced with the papers in her water-stained briefcase and the uncertainty of her future. She was a wreck, inside and out. And Wyatt was no help. He was zoned out on the Tylenols and had probably forgotten she was there. Even Artie ignored her; he wove happily around Jimmy's legs as he took down the tent and poured off the water. She might as well have been invisible for all the use she was to anyone in this godforsaken place. Feeling about as low as one could get without digging a hole, she plopped down on her briefcase and waited for Jimmy to arrange their rescue.

He made quick work of it. From his plane, he radioed the Coast Guard, who in turn contacted the island ranger station with their exact location. A rescue boat was dispatched and within the hour, Wyatt was on a stretcher bound for the hospital in Houghton. That left Jimmy with Beth's good-intentioned help to dismantle the

87

woeful camp and travel back to the lodge in Jimmy's plane to drop off an agitated Artemus. There, they paused long enough for her to grab her travel bag from the rented car, dash through a shower and hurry into a pair of slacks and a sweater. Then they were headed south on 41 with Jimmy at the wheel of his four-wheel drive.

Beth thanked heaven for Jimmy Shingoos. She couldn't have managed the trip on her own. Short on sleep and raw of nerve, she didn't think she could cope with a hangnail at this point. Until they arrived at the hospital and she was met with a mountain of insurance forms. Jimmy got her coffee while she balanced the clipboard on her knee and started filling in the blanks as best she could on what little brain function she had left.

It was almost two hours before Wyatt was officially admitted and settled into a private room. Beth stood at his bedside, a disaster of emotional loose ends and caffeine shakes by then. The sight of him so pale and motionless in his unnatural slumber nearly unstrung her. Of course, no one looked healthy in a faded hospital gown, hooked to an IV drip. Especially when a bulky cast was suspended by a complicated network of cables and pulleys. She was afraid to get too close, afraid of bumping something important if she eased down upon the edge of the mattress. So she stood, ready to wilt from weariness and worry and settled for clutching Wyatt's slack hand between hers. It was good enough.

"Mrs. Marston?"

Beth glanced around to see a young man in jeans and a pullover shirt. The only thing that separated him from a member of the janitorial staff was a clip-on name badge and the drape of a stethoscope about his neck.

"Hi. I'm Dr. Randolph. I hear you're the one I should thank for making my job so easy."

Beth blinked. "I'm sorry? I don't—"

"Before he went under, your husband said you splinted his leg. Good job, too. Made everything come right together for me. Thanks."

He put out his hand and she took it reflexively. It clicked in her daze of thoughts that this was the first thanks she'd received for a job well done. A load of anxiety rolled off her sagging shoulders.

"He's going to be all right then?" Her voice shook.

"Fine. Oh, don't let the IV scare you. Precaution. He was a little dehydrated from the fever and the circumstances. Can't hurt." He put his stethoscope to prescribed use, listening intently for a few seconds beneath the loose neckline of Wyatt's gown. After unclipping the earpieces, he tapped into a limp wrist while consulting his watch. He nodded and scribbled a couple of notations on the chart he'd carried in with him. Then he looked back to Beth with a marveling smile.

"Good thing you were there, Mrs. Marston, and kept a level head. If you'd tried to move him

89

or hadn't gotten him under shelter, things could have been a lot stickier. We end up with a lot of summer visitors who think they can scale Mt. Everest just because they can climb a flight of stairs in their climate-controlled office building. They've got no respect for the term "roughing it." Even a sprain can be serious business in that kind of isolated situation. You confined the site of injury, kept him quiet, kept him warm, gave him fluids and didn't panic. You did all the right things. He's in good shape. Should be out of here in a couple of days. Of course, he won't be up to hiking for a while."

She returned his smile somewhat shakily. She'd done everything right. Relief weakened her to the point of collapse. Seeing how unsteady she was, Dr. Randolph supplied a hand beneath her elbow.

"You'd better take care of yourself, Mrs. Marston. We'll see to your husband. He'll be out for a while."

"No. I'd like to wait, if I could."

He shrugged. "Sure. We've got a so-so cafeteria. Ask the nurse for directions if you get hungry. I'll be back on my rounds tonight, providing there are no complications. And I don't expect any."

"Thank you, Doctor."

"Thank you, Mrs. Marston." He pressed her arm and strolled out, leaving her alone. But that condition only lasted for a moment.

"Hi. How's he doing?"

She smiled up at Jimmy. "Good, the doctor

90

says. I'm going to stay for a while but don't feel you have to. I appreciate all you've done already."

He waved it off as insignificant. "I do have some calls to make. I've got to arrange for someone to run me to the island so I can bring Wyatt's plane back sometime today or tomorrow. The rangers will keep an eye on it until then. Want me to bring you a burger or something?"

"Anything's fine."

"And you'll probably want to call his folks to let them know what happened." He said that in an odd tone, but she was too tired to question it.

"Yes." Funny. She hadn't thought about the civilized clime of Chicago for quite some time. It seemed so far away from everything that was important to her now. Yes, she'd call them. In a while. First, she just wanted to sit with Wyatt and hold his hand, content with the knowledge that she'd done all the right things.

Even if she did forget to put the tarp down first.

I love you, too, Wyatt. I never stopped loving you.

He fought consciousness, for it meant surrendering that caressing whisper. Words that meant everything in the world to him. He let awareness lapse, trying to call back that sweet dream, but it was gone. Reality beckoned with its cold, bright lights, with the nag of throbbing pain somewhere so far removed, it didn't seem like it could be part of his body. He was comfortable and un-comfortable all at once. Warm, reclined upon a good mattress yet oddly restrained. Curiosity teased him into opening his eyes. He blinked slowly, struggling to focus.

His leg was sticking up in the air, all swaddled in white. He stared at it for a long moment, un-able to comprehend. Then he remembered. He'd broken his leg. Snippets of recall wafted through his drug-induced lethargy. He was in a hospital. Then he heard that voice again and all the pieces fell into place.

Beth.

It was an effort to turn toward her. She was seated in a chair at his bedside, angled away so he could only see her profile. She was on the phone. Close but so impossibly far away for someone whose arms felt weighted with cement-lined sleeves.

Beth.

He tried to speak her name but his mouth was dry, his throat uncooperative. The attempt wore him out. He closed his eyes and waited for strength to gather. And he listened, loving the sound of her voice. Until he heard the words she was saying.

"I can't possibly be back before Monday. I know. I know all that. I'm sorry for the incon-venience, but there's nothing I can do."

Inconvenience. Pain buzzed through his tem-ples as he held onto that terrible word and its meaning. He was an inconvenience to her. One she'd escape at her earliest opportunity. Her conversation continued and his mood sank deeper into an ill-defined despair.

"Everything's right there—the tickets, the times. Just have Sam pick him up and tell him to have a good time. I can call Mark when I get back. He'll understand."

Wyatt squeezed his eyes shut. She was wheeling and dealing from his hospital bedside, for God's sake. Rearranging her rendezvous with Mark Casey while he was strung up like a bridge under construction. Why had she even bothered to wait? Just to keep up appearances? Well, to hell with that. He didn't want any shallow show of kindness from her. He flung his head to the other side, torment swelling so mightily within his chest he was surprised he could withstand it even with the numbing blunt of painkillers to serve as a buffer.

"Wyatt?"

She must have seen or heard the movement. He lay still, pretending to be under. How was he supposed to face her knowing she was running from his bedside to be with another man? He didn't know if he wanted to kill her or cling to her and beg that she stay. Even if she didn't care.

"I've got to go, Mary. Just take messages and I'll be back as soon as I can. I will. 'Bye."

There was the click of receiver upon its cradle and the stir of movement. He felt her fingers slide softly over the backs of his. They curled into a gentle clasp. He would have pulled away if he'd had the strength. Instead, with a despicable weakness, he hung on. Then, she knew he was awake, so there was no use faking. He turned toward her, braced, yet unprepared for the way her sweet smile tore through him. She looked awful, like she hadn't slept or seen her hairdresser in years. Yet she was the one to ask first.

"How do you feel?"

How the hell did she think he felt? Like she'd just ripped his chest open. What irony that she'd fuss over a broken leg and not care that she had shattered his heart.

When he didn't answer, her features puckered with concern. She bent closer. He could smell her perfume over the sterile hospital scents. Liz Claiborne. Her favorite. He'd gotten it for her birthday because she liked it better than the pricier scents Gretchen gave as gifts. He'd liked the fact that she went for preference over price tag. Her palm was warm against his cheek, wiping away a wetness he hadn't been aware of. Her compassionate pretense raked his emotions raw.

"Are you uncomfortable? Do you want me to call a nurse?"

"I want . . ." He couldn't continue. His vocal cords seemed welded together.

"What? What can I get you?"

He took a ragged breath. "I want you to go." That was very clear and she recoiled, snapping back with spine rigid.

"Wyatt—"

"Just go. I don't need you here. I don't want to

pull you away from your job. Just leave the papers at the lodge. You shouldn't have come up here in the first place. It was a mistake. I should have known better. I should have known."

"But—"

"Dammit, Beth, get out of here!" He looked away from her stricken expression, his own twisting into an agony of despair. He didn't need her pseudodevotion when her mind was obviously on her work in Chicago. He'd had enough of that while growing up not to recognize the pattern. The rest of his words were inflectionless, dead sounding. "You're making things worse. Can't you see that? You're just making things worse."

No, she couldn't see. And as she sat in the waiting room, she couldn't see anything at all through the haze of tears. For a long time, she was too drained of everything vital to move. After the hell and worry she'd waded through, to have this as the kicker. It was too much. All her determination failed her. She wanted to cry and yet she refused to give way in such a public place.

I don't need you here.

No, he didn't need her now. He had highly paid, impersonal staff members to care for him now. He wasn't forced to depend on her any longer. So he shoved her away, never minding that she just might want to stay.

Leave the papers at the lodge.

She was so tired, logical thought failed her. In her wretchedness, only one thing surfaced. If he didn't care, why should she? If he didn't want her at his bedside, why should she stay? She'd leave the portfolio. He couldn't do anything without her signature, anyway. And if he wanted that, he'd have to come to her.

"Calls are all made. Sorry I was gone so long. I got you a burger and some fries. Hope that'll do."

When she didn't respond, Jimmy dropped down in the padded chair beside her.

"Beth? Is everything okay? Nothing's happened, has it? Wyatt?"

She shook her head, fighting down the swell of remorse that lifted from her heart to her constricted throat. She heard Jimmy exhale in relief.

"Here's lunch. Can I get you anything else?"

Beth dragged in a pitiful breath. She sniffed and scrubbed her face with her palms. Then she straightened. Her tone was as flat as Wyatt's had been.

"I need a ride back to my car. I've got plane reservations to make."

Chapter Six

It was the first time Beth had ever taken comfort in the grimy Chicago skyline or in the crazy pace of its city streets. Normal confusions after the nightmare weekend she'd endured. She needed the familiar to hang on to.

She pushed open the door leading to the fourth floor business offices of the Marston Terrace Hotel. The atmosphere immediately changed from the quiet elegance of the old hotel to the noisy pace of corporate industry. Here, the sedate comfort of the French Provincial couch provided for those in wait clashed drastically with the ultramodern receptionist station, where the mammoth multiline phone system, computer banks and closed-circuit television monitors were all state of the art. Beth paused out of habit to pick up one of the sheets on the marble-topped end table and scanned the list of this week's hotel events, finding them typically hectic. A medical convention in the meeting rooms on two, a bar mitzvah and a fiftieth wedding anniversary party in the Continental Ballroom, a group of Future

Businessmen of America on three, complete with seminars, catered meals and presentation ceremony in the International Ballroom. Then a partial turnaround on Sunday when Casey Computations arrived. Some tight scheduling but they'd manage.

"Beth, here are your messages. That top one is ASAP."

"Thanks, Mary."

Beth reached over the high desk to take a two-inch stack from the dark-haired receptionist. The slip on top was from Mark Casey.

"How's your husband doing?"

Beth's smile was strained. "Fine." And she was quick to move down the hall toward the creative hub of the Marston Hotel chain. She shifted the papers into the hand that held her briefcase and juggled a cup of coffee in the other as she continued to her office. Purposefully, she didn't glance toward the closed door with its name plate, Wyatt Marston, Vice-President. With a feeling of finding sanctuary, she slipped into her own big room.

Stepping around the cushy wing chairs and her big mahogany desk, she dropped into her swivel seat and for a moment did nothing but breathe deeply. Keeping a lid on was proving much more difficult than she'd expected.

Finally, she riffled through the messages. Nothing earthshaking, nothing that seemed half as important as the troubles she'd left the day before. She added the messages to the stack in her

98

IN basket, having to stretch over a pile of folders and video tapes to do so. There were days when she wished she could clean her desktop by pushing the whole ream of work into the wastebasket. This was one of them. Oh, for just a few quiet hours of rote busyness.

"In the middle of something?"

She glanced up to see Gretchen Marston posed in her doorway. Not many women pushing fifty could get away with wearing a jungle print saronglike dress under a silvery Lynx coat, but Wyatt's stepmother was one of them. With her sleek black hair and wrinkle-free skin, both products of modern science, she could still pass for the model she might have been had she needed to work for a living. But with her dad's Denver millions, now, she was merely a professional shopper. She rationalized that her four-closet wardrobe was necessary for the social lifestyle she led. When she wore something once, and on rare occasions, twice, she then donated the item to charity. As if some homeless woman would have use for a twelve-hundred-dollar sequinned mini. But that was Gretchen Marston. She wasn't really concerned with practicality. Just the image of benevolence.

"Darling, can I drag you away this morning. They're having a sale at Bloomies and there's this zebra-stripe that is just you. I had to use considerable clout to get the saleswoman to hold it for you." She smiled as if that had really been necessary once she'd flashed her gold card bearing the

Marston name.

"I really can't today, Gretchen. But thank you. Another time."

The older woman whipped out her appointment book and put on her narrow reading glasses. "I could pencil you in for lunch on Thursday. That is unless there's a cancellation at my hairdresser's. I've been trying to up my appointment before these gray hairs get out of control."

Beth smiled. Nothing about Gretchen Marston was ever out of control. "I'll call you."

"Make it soon. It's been an age since we've had coffee together." They kept up the occasional social outings as more of an obligation than for the pleasure of each other's company. Gretchen Marston had no need for friends or intimate chats. She had her father's money. She dropped her social bible back into her big snakeskin bag and folded away her glasses. "I've got to drop in on Boyd for a second so I'd better run."

She started to turn away and Beth stared after her, stunned.

"Gretchen?"

"Yes, dear."

"Wyatt's doing fine."

The woman blinked at her with a remote curiosity. "Of course, he is, darling. Otherwise, you would have told me." Her logic was inescapable. And frighteningly cold.

"Don't you want his room number and the hospital address? In case you want to send flowers or call?" She added that, wondering why it would be necessary to make such suggestions to a mother.

Gretchen waved a manicured hand. "Oh, give that to Boyd. He has his secretary take care of those things."

Those things. As if their son was a trifling business formality.

Beth smiled thinly, the politeness in her tone showing wear. "I'll take care of it." It was something that needed to be done by someone who did care.

"You're a doll. 'Bye now. Give Wyatt my love."

Since when? Beth waited until the click of her mother-in-law's heels were muffled by plush carpeting, then picked up her phone. "Mary, connect me with the mezzanine florist, please." She waited, shaking her head in lingering disbelief. "Yes. Good morning. I'd like a get-well arrangement wired to Houghton, Michigan. Flowers? No, make that a plant. Something ferny, woodsyish. The card—Put 'With Love'—no, put 'Thinking of You, Mom and Dad.' " That should sound impersonal enough for him to believe they might have sent it themselves. She gave the address and told them to put it on Boyd's account. Let him puzzle over it when he got the bill. For a moment, she considered sending something with her own name attached, then decided against it. She'd given him a night and a day of total devotion and that hadn't been enough for him. Flowers saying, "Wish I was there," weren't going to do the trick.

Trying to shift her attentions back into a work mode, Beth switched on her computer, then spent several minutes staring at the flashing cursor. Her business mind was a total blank. She knew what needed to be done. Her daily routine was as ingrained as a Pavlovian response. Usually, her start-up time was nil. But this morning, she was running on a dead battery. The cells had run dry when she flew out of Marquette.

Why had he sent her away?

She closed her eyes, knowing it was useless to spin her emotional wheels when there was no way to gain traction. The answers were in a Houghton hospital and she wasn't going to find them inscribed on an empty green screen sitting behind her desk in Chicago.

She shook off the pensive mood by returning the calls that had piled up in her absence. The last one, to Mark Casey, served to lighten her mood. He was thirtyish and divorced and a confirmed flirt. Though she wasn't interested in encouraging his playful suggestions, they did make her feel attractive and alive again. And they made her wonder how long it had been since Wyatt had shown her half that much attention. When she concluded the call, the brooding settled in again.

Why had he sent her away?

"Hard at work?"

She looked up guiltily, hoping Boyd Marston hadn't been standing there for long watching her

102

in her daydreams. She set down her cup of coffee. It was cold. "Just taking a break," she confessed, as if making an excuse was necessary.

"Well, when you're back on line, you'd better recheck these figures you gave me this morning. I think they're off by about a week's profit margin."

"What?"

She took the folder from his outstretched hand and snapped on her calculator. After the second column, she began to see a dreadful pattern of error. Flustered by her unusual carelessness, she was alarmed to find herself close to weeping.

"Oh, Boyd, I'm sorry. I'll redo this right away."

The hotel owner sat himself on the rolled arm of one of the wing chairs and regarded her with an unswerving scrutiny. "I don't care about that, Bethany. I didn't bring it in to chew you out. I wanted to ask what was wrong. This isn't like you to make those kind of mistakes. Where's your concentration? Somewhere in northern Michigan, I'm guessing."

She smiled in chagrin. "You'd be guessing right."

"So why did you come back?"

"Not by my choice."

Boyd pursed his lips thoughtfully. He was a handsome man, still very youthful looking in many ways, like an elegantly aged version of his son. He never fell into the rut of a conservative executive who was content to let the years compound in face and form. Beth supposed having a

103

wife fifteen years his junior did that. Not that he was into blatant second adolescence. He didn't color his fading hair or comb thinning strands across the shiny circle on his crown to fool anyone into thinking he wasn't going bald. He didn't wear gold chains, drive a two-seater sports car or wear sweat jackets unzipped to the navel. His was a subtle denial of age. He played racquetball and jogged. He was tanned year-round from his time on the Colorado ski slopes when he and Gretchen bounced between the Midwest control center in Chicago and corporate headquarters in Denver. He dressed well, in the current style, without looking absurd. And he treated everyone, from the eighteen-year-old cleaning ladies to their geriatric female guests as attractive contemporaries. And he always behaved with Beth as if he was half father-in-law and half prospective suitor. And he'd always been as much friend as employer.

"What's going on with Wyatt, Beth? If it's none of my business, say so. If it affects my business, you'd better tell me everything."

"I don't know, Boyd. He's got some project going up there, some big old mansion he's thinking of restoring into a resort, I think. We didn't have a lot of time to talk before he had his accident."

"The lodge? The one he used to go up to with his mother?"

Beth nodded, puzzling over his sudden frown. When he spoke again, his tone was crisper.

"When is he coming home?"

"I don't know that he is."

Boyd absorbed that news behind a composed facade. She had no way of knowing if he was upset or angry or not at all surprised. "I guess I can't expect him to climb out of his hospital bed to come to work." Then why did his voice betray the impatient insinuation that he thought his son should try? "What about the stocks?"

"He didn't say anything about what he plans to do. But he did ask me to leave the portfolio."

"Maybe he's going to use it as collateral on a loan." Boyd Marston was astute. He saw the tightness around Beth's mouth as a sign of her displeasure and added softly, "Restoration can suck up a fortune real fast. Does it look like a fool's errand, Beth?"

She shrugged in an attempt to look unconcerned, but the shadow of worry lingered. "I don't know. I didn't get a good chance to look it over. It's a beautiful setting, though. Not your typical Marston style." Their resorts in Denver, San Diego, Lake Tahoe, the Catskills and Orlando were well-known for their contemporary opulence. The rest of the hotels scattered from coast to coast were all good, solid investments that brought in a steady profit. Not like a rundown woodland lodge on the outer limits of upper Michigan.

"So he's planning to strike off on his own, is he? After all I've done for him."

The hard edge of his words surprised Beth and she reacted to them with a feeling of indignation.

Boyd Marston of all people should understand a man's want to succeed on his own. He'd done it. Why should he begrudge his son the same opportunity? Did he expect Wyatt to be content in his plush office, building on what was handed to him?

Wasn't that what she expected of her husband?

Confused, she kept her thoughts to herself, but it was too late to keep Boyd from seeing her uncertainty.

"Risky business if you don't have the muscle to back it. If he acts outside of the chain's interest, there's not much I can do if he makes the wrong choices. He'll go down alone." Then he said very meaningfully, "And you'll go down with him. Is that what you want, Beth?"

She was rigid in her office chair. No, her instincts cried in panic. It wasn't. Wyatt had no business tampering with the safety of her future. Not without consulting her. If he had some great urge to go off on his own in shaky waters as a resort entrepreneur, why hadn't he ever told her? Why had he let her believe he was satisfied with the status quo? Or had he known she'd balk? Fear goaded her into self-preserving caution. "He can't do anything with the stocks without my approval, can he?"

Boyd smiled reassuringly and shook his head. "Half are yours, Bethany. That's the way we had them drawn up. He can sell his half, but he can't touch yours without your okay."

She let her breath out in an unintentioned

gust. Boyd's smile thinned with speculation.

"Even if Wyatt sells his shares, you'll still have plenty to invest upon. Of course, he'd need yours, too, if he was to make a real go of a place like that lodge. So unstable." He shook his head and Beth wasn't sure if he referred to the investment or his son. Regardless, the connotation frightened her.

"What's he up to?" Boyd mused to himself.

"He didn't confide in me. In fact, he couldn't wait to get rid of me." It was impossible to hide the pain in her voice. And she didn't try. Boyd Marston was one of her few confidants. And who would know the quirks of a son better than the father? "I just don't understand it, Boyd. If he wants to end this marriage, I wish he'd just come out and say so. If he doesn't, he'd better be doing something soon if he expects to save it."

"That bad?"

She nodded grimly.

"We talked about this before, Beth. I meant every word of it. You're going to come out of this just fine, either way. But you've got to make the decision. What do you want? Your independence or a relationship you can't depend on? I don't mean to sound disloyal to my son, but I don't like the way he's treating you. I raised him better. You deserve better after all the hard work you've done to fit into his life."

He sounded just like her own fearful self-talk. And she was distressed because she couldn't argue with what either of them said. All she could do was make excuses for a man who wasn't there. And she was tired of doing that. She wanted Wyatt to give his own reasons. And he wouldn't. She supposed that was an answer in itself.

"I don't know what to do," she admitted wearily.

"What do you want to do?" was his quiet challenge. He wasn't going to make it easy on her.

"Sometimes I just want to give up and say it's not worth the trouble. I've got a good job now. I can support myself. With what you've offered, I can get by almost in the lap of luxury. And sometimes I want to fight back and demand to know why he thinks he can get away with what he's doing."

Boyd smiled at that. "So what's it going to be?"

She smiled back wearily. "I haven't decided yet."

Then he became serious once more. "When you do decide, make sure you're doing what's in your own best interest. Wyatt can take care of himself, but you've got no one who's going to look out for you except you. You can come out of this ahead if you're smart, and I know you are. You're the best employee I've ever had, Bethany. I can see good things for you. With your talent, you can only go up within the Marston chain. Unless you let Wyatt drag you down.

"I hope you've been doing some serious thinking about becoming my administrative assistant at corporate headquarters. Someone like you

108

would fit the bill perfectly. It would mean a move to Denver, but it's something else for you to think about. You're important to us at the hotel. No matter what happens, I'll still think of you as family and Marstons look after their own. If Wyatt wants to make his marriage work, he'll come after you."

"And if he doesn't? What if he's set on this northwoods venture? He could lose everything, Boyd. I don't want to see that happen!"

"Beth, you can't stop Wyatt once his mind is made up. Maybe you can change it for him. Maybe he doesn't realize his decision could cost him his marriage. Whatever happens, Beth, you can count on my support. All I ask is that you keep me up-to-date on what's going on. That way I can be there for you."

The emotional chokiness his words created stayed with her for the rest of the afternoon. Yes, working for him did feel like family. It was Wyatt who always seemed to be on the outside. And it appeared that he preferred it that way. He didn't want to be a part of the unit and that exclusion applied to her, as well. Boyd Marston represented the security she needed. Wyatt was a big uncertainty.

She was afraid of being on the outside. She'd been there all her life, looking in, dreaming of the day she'd have what others took for granted. Well, now, suddenly, she was in that comfortable inner circle and its safe foundations were being threatened. Her instinct was to hang on at all

109

costs, even if her marriage was one of them. Here before her, Boyd was dangling her every dream come true—a job tailor-made to her ambitions. In Denver. A world away from the frustrations of Chicago. An escape of her own from the downhill slide of her marriage. But the loneliness she came home to in their sleekly modern apartment after being in the northwoods with the man she loved was a powerful argument against the job. She still loved her husband.

She sighed and turned off her computer terminal. There was no use pretending she was going to get anything else done. Her thought process was too far gone. The trip north had settled nothing. She'd allowed herself to be driven away as much in the dark as when she'd arrived. That hadn't been her intention. She didn't usually give up so easily.

Stay with me, Beth. I'll do anything. Just please . . . don't go.

She closed her eyes and rubbed them methodically. If he wanted her with him, why had he chased her out? Why had he claimed not to need her?

Don't go. Don't do this to us.

She wasn't the one doing it. He was. With his silence. With his refusal to communicate. If he felt those things he'd rambled about when he was lost to fever, why had he never told her?

And he never would . . . if he was up there and she was down here.

110

Beth picked up her phone.

"Mary, I need to make some flight reservations. No, for me."

At this rate, she'd soon be passing her luggage en route.

It took Wyatt forever to get comfortable. He'd thought things would be better once he was ensconced in his own room, but he hadn't counted on a nearly forty-mile drive with a cast wedged into the front seat of a Ford Bronco. Or on the difficulty of scaling a flight of stairs. His leg ached. It throbbed all the way up to his eyebrows. Jimmy's wife, Mani, fussed over him, propping his cast on pillows, making him swallow his pain medication over his protests that he'd be fine without it, shutting his drapes so the sun on the lake wouldn't bother him. As if the sight of either could after staring at nothing but the same sterile curtains and bland art prints for what seemed like months. Then she'd placed that damned plant at his bedside.

Thinking of you, Mom and Dad.

Yeah. Sure. Mom and Dad. He wondered who they'd gotten to send it or if one of the hotel employees had taken it upon themselves to do the good deed. Wouldn't Gretchen just die if he addressed her as "Mom." She'd always insisted he call her by her first name. After all, she was only fifteen years older than him and "Mom" made her feel positively ancient. Like there was any danger that he'd call her that, anyway. His mother was dead. Gretchen was his father's wife. Nothing more, and that suited them both just fine. If she'd sent him anything through a florist, it would have been some grand and gaudy display of wealth rather than affection. A plant wasn't her style. He didn't think she was aware that green things actually grew in the soil underfoot, and if she was, she certainly didn't want to be bothered with the responsibility of tending them. Any more than she'd wanted to be bothered with him. Nurturing was not her forte. If he'd been a green plant, he would have been brown on the stem weeks after they moved into her Denver mansion.

He was hurting and unhappy. It must have been the inactivity that turned his thoughts down such melancholy avenues. He preferred action to brooding, but in this case, he was relieved of choice. What else was there to do when one couldn't move and the brain cells were reduced to tapioca by the influx of numbing drugs? He wasn't quite far enough in the bag to ask for a television to be brought up so he wouldn't miss the next episode of *Days of Our Lives*. And he certainly wouldn't admit that he was wondering how Victor planned to get out of his latest scheme without the good guys catching on to him. Real men didn't get addicted to soap operas. He shifted restlessly, chafing at the knowledge that today was the day when the TV paternity tests were due. They'd probably be switched. The day-shift nurse who'd sneak in to watch with him told him that's how they always complicated things for a good four months or so. Still . . .

He was considering asking Jimmy to bring the set up from the kitchen when his medication kicked in. Then, he forgot about Victor and Marlena and the torrid doings in Salem. As he dozed off, he wondered if they'd ever done a soap in a hotel. Oh, yeah, that one with James Brolin. Funny how art imitated life.

Hours later, he drifted toward wakefulness with a dry mouth and a mind like cotton wadding. The first thing he tried to do was roll over onto his stomach, which was his natural sleeping position. His cast slipped off its stanchion of cushions, nearly fracturing his other ankle when it fell on top. Pain jolted, white-hot and blinding. As he struggled to recover, he felt someone lift his mending leg, positioning it gently. Mani, he thought, gratefully. Then fingertips caressed the side of his face. Definitely not Mani!

He dragged his eyelids open. They felt lead-lined. Nothing was in focus, so he let them slam shut again. He didn't need to see her. He knew instinctively who was at his side. He breathed in deep of Liz Claiborne. And he sighed out his contentment. Wetting the arid surface of his lips, he tried to speak. The sound was little more than a rasp.

"Glad you're here."

"Are you?"

He managed to nod. Why would she question that? Of course, he was. He loved her. She knew that. Every time he opened his eyes in the hospital, he'd hoped he'd find her there. When she wasn't, he found no reason to stay awake. Sometimes, he remembered why she wasn't and the sense of sadness overwhelmed him, but mostly he was hurt and confused by her absence. Why would she be with him? She was having an affair with Roman Brady. No. That wasn't right. His mind was mush. Roman was on the soap opera. Beth was *his* wife. Beth was having an affair with Mark Casey. But if that was true, she wouldn't be sitting with him. Would she? He wasn't sure what was real. Except Beth was here. Reality was in her gentle touch, in her whisper of, "I love you, Wyatt."

He nudged his cheek into her palm and surrendered to the healing darkness. It didn't matter who was having an affair with whom. Beth was here and when he woke, he wouldn't be alone.

Chapter Seven

Glad you're here.

Was he?

Beth stood watching him sleep, not so sure.

He looked good, smooth-shaven with a healthy color. The cast was, of course, a bulky obstruction to his otherwise clean lines. He was wearing a faded T-shirt and athletic shorts. She'd always thought he had great legs. Well, leg and a half from what she could see.

"This is it, Wyatt Marston," she said aloud. "Whether you like it or not, I'm here to stay until I find out what's going on with you. With us. You're going to talk to me, mister. Even if I have to break your other leg."

She turned at an odd clicking sound. Artemus regarded her from the doorway in a stalemate of ill will. With his ears laid back, he approached her Oleg Cassini pullman in stiff-legged strides to begin a thorough sniffing. As he circled it, Beth warned, "Don't you dare turn your leg up on that. It's brand new."

Having decided there was nothing of interest to

be discovered, Artie padded across the room and lightly hopped up onto the bed. With a couple of restless turns, he settled into a great furry ball at Wyatt's shoulder, making himself very much at home. Beth frowned.

"Guess again, pal."

The animal glowered at her and gave a territorial rumble.

"We'll see about that."

Artemus wedged his nose beneath his paws, apparently unworried by her threat, and went to sleep.

Dismissed by both of them, Beth recalled the invitation from Jimmy's Ojibway wife for coffee on the sun porch. Now, to find it. The house was huge, its upstairs host to at least ten bedrooms. Wyatt's—theirs—was centralized right off the left branch of the stairs, so there was no getting lost. Once back down in the front hall, she wandered deeper into the heart of the mansion into what probably would have been called the gathering room when the place was built.

"Wow," she whispered, awed once more as her eyes were drawn upward to the heavy beams of the cathedral ceiling. A two and a half story stone fireplace dominated the far side of the room, set majestically into a wall of roughly peeled pine logs. It was a massive space with marvelous potential. Unfortunately, it was crowded with tacky fifties-style furniture and a truly awful rug. If it were hers, she'd back an industrial dumpster up to the French doors and shove all of it out for a proper burial. But it wasn't. She continued through the cavernous room, exiting through another set of double doors. This must be the sun porch, she decided. The forty-foot expanse fronted the lake and had an unobstructed vista of glass. The view was spectacular, even through the dirty windows. She was so lost in it, for a moment she didn't realize she wasn't alone.

"Mrs. Marston?"

Beth turned toward Mani Shingoos with a smile. "I found you. This place is bigger than some museums I've been through."

"A dusty museum," Mani allowed, bringing her a cup of coffee. They stood together, admiring the sparkle of late afternoon sun on still water. The Indian woman only came up to Beth's shoulder in height. She wasn't pretty or petite of build, but hers was a striking appearance of strength and ancient ancestry. Her black eyes and small smile hinted of mysteries and secret contentment, and the hand she placed on Beth's arm made her instantly feel welcomed.

"Do just you and your husband live here?"

"Oh, no. I can't imagine our two boys running loose inside this maze. We're staying in the old carriage house. Jimmy made it over and it's quite comfortable. Up until Wyatt came, this old place hadn't been lived in since Jimmy's grandparents died. Mausoleum is the more accurate term. It's taking all our resources just in upkeep. That's why Wyatt's such a godsend. We never thought he'd really come back. You know how promises are when they're made by children. But he kept his. When it's done, it's going to be magnificent."

Beth took her words in without betraying her

own ignorance of Wyatt's plans. Pride wouldn't let her admit she knew so little of her own husband. So instead of floundering in an unknown past, she spoke of the present.

"How old are your boys?"

"Seven and nine. They're at school now. Trust me, you'll know when they get home. The ghosts in this house must love them. They're Wyatt and Jimmy all over again." Mani was smiling back on fond memory.

Beth fidgeted. Curiosity was eating her alive. Wyatt Marston running loose, a carefree boy. She couldn't picture it. She'd never known him to let go of his proper reserve. Since she'd met him, he'd always been the well-bred son of a hotel tycoon.

"Is he all settled in upstairs?"

Beth nodded. "Sleeping. With the dog."

"You're going to have your hands full, Mrs. Marston. If the man is anything like the boy, he's not going to like being penned up inside. I remember when he was eight and had the chicken pox, his mother had a terrible time keeping him in bed. If I recall right, he snuck out to play and we all ended up in bed for weeks, itching."

Learning intimate details of her husband's life from a stranger was a bittersweet pleasure. Wyatt never spoke of his real mother or of the time he must have cherished up in these northern Michigan woods. Beth wondered why. Was his childhood so inconsistent with the man he'd become that he was ashamed to reveal it? She couldn't believe that. She saw too much genuine affection in this native couple who knew Wyatt so much better than she

118

could claim. With these bits and pieces of the past, an understanding was beginning to form. This uncomplicated paradise was what he coveted behind his silence and sophistication. Who would equate the heir to the Marston millions with a boy running wild in the northwoods pines? Oddly enough, the image warmed her. She was glad to learn that he had some happy memories to look back upon.

"If you'd like, Mrs. Marston, I can give you a tour before my roughnecks get home."

"I would. And it's Beth."

Mani Shingoos gave her an accepting nod and led the way through a patchwork arrangement of cozy parlors and soaring spaces. Over thirteen thousand square feet of turn of the Century grandeur Keweenaw style. Jimmy's maternal ancestors had originated in Boston and had made a second fortune in logging, Mani explained. In those days when Calumet was being considered as the state's capital and East Coast wealth flowed like inland rivers, forty rooms was not so much an excess as it was a standard among the mining magnates and lumber barons. Few such reminders of Michigan's past were still standing, which was why she and Jimmy were so anxious to preserve the lodge. Not just for the sake of history but for family, as well.

As she went from room to room, Beth nervously tallied the cost of remodeling. All the furnishings were of that rummage sale variety. Plumbing was woefully inadequate. Heating was inefficient and the stench of mildew was overpowering. Lighting was nonexistent. But the view was priceless. The structure itself was built to endure centuries with unwarping grace. In the midst of a cluttered setting jewels of architecture shone; leather wall covering in the den, hand-painted wall murals in both dining rooms, that gorgeous pegged floor, surprising nooks of stained glass, fireplaces of gilded tile and marble, a six-foot tall Royal Oak parlor stove, a built-in wall-size oak, marble and tile icebox in the kitchen and all that precious hardwood. If atmosphere added up, Jimmy was sitting on a gold mine. If he could afford to get it working. And that, she supposed unhappily, was where Wyatt fit in. He was going to supply the bankroll.

"We'd like to get it on the National Historical Registry," Mani said as they walked through a huge empty room that must have been a ballroom at one time. Now, it was a home for cobwebs and birdnests. "We've been hanging on by our fingernails for the past few years. Jimmy had a trust from his grandmother, but that's almost gone. With the boys, and me working part-time and Jimmy trying to get his air service off the ground, so to speak, there just aren't enough hours or enough dollars to do what we have to do. We're just so grateful to you and Wyatt, we don't know what to say."

Beth felt uncomfortable accepting thanks for generosity she hadn't earned. She could see the merit of the lodge and the enthusiasm of its owners. But just where Wyatt fit in and to the tune of how much working capital, she was totally in the dark. And she didn't like being on the outside or being made to feel guilty because of her own reservation.

"So, where are you going to start?" That seemed a logical question.

"Wyatt's applying for a loan so we can get underway. It's a rather grand projection, but we'd like to have the place functional by next May. I must admit that beyond the funding stage, we're at a standstill. None of us has the background for such an undertaking. I suppose we'll have to hire consultants."

"Oh, don't do that," Beth heard herself saying. "They'll bleed you until you can't afford so much as a carpet remnant. I can help you out there."

Mani was looking at her hopefully. "Wyatt mentioned you'd taken some interior design classes and were a whiz at organization. But—"

"But what?" She wondered what else Wyatt had told them about his city-bred wife.

"He said you'd be too busy."

"Well, he was wrong." She said that firmly, as if her schedule was flexible enough to accommodate a whim. As if she was in total support of the plans she knew next to nothing about. As if she had the time available for such a draining task. How dare Wyatt just assume she wouldn't. But then, he had good reason for his assumption. Less forcefully, she concluded, "I'm sure something can be worked out."

Mani regarded her with a veiled smile. "You're not what I expected. I'm glad."

Just then, before Beth could ask what she'd meant by that, a cyclone of sound rushed through the staid rooms. A sound only two young boys freed of school could make. They raced into the

121

ballroom and skidded to a halt at the sight of a stranger. Both were stocky and dark, the older with Jimmy's blue eyes. They regarded her with wide stares.

"Beth, these are my boys, James and Wesley."

Wesley, the seven-year-old, tucked in behind his big brother to smile shyly. James, as gregarious as his dad, came forward with his hand outstretched.

"Hi. You're Wyatt's wife. He said you were pretty."

Beth took the small hand in grown-up fashion. "Pleased to meet you, James. And Wesley." She merely nodded to the younger boy, who was cringing back at the thought of extending his own hand.

"Well, I'd better go." Mani looped an arm about each narrow set of shoulders. "If I don't get these two a snack, they'll have the refrigerator cleaned out before supper. You're welcome to join us, by the way."

"Oh, I . . ." She wasn't sure what she'd planned for dinner so she broke off. For an organizational whiz, she hadn't thought that far ahead. She hadn't planned how she was going to actually care for herself and her husband. She didn't even know if there was any food in the big kitchen vault. Or where to buy some if there wasn't.

"I insist. Wyatt's been working dawn to dusk helping Jimmy so we've taken him under our wing like one of the family. We've made it kind of an unspoken arrangement. He stays here and eats with us. There's room for one more. I'll send one of the boys over when it's time, then you can bring a tray back for Wyatt. It'll be a while before he's ready to tackle those stairs, no matter what he tries to tell you."

Quiet settled into the big, musty rooms the minute the Shingoos family departed. Left alone, Beth went back upstairs to check on Wyatt and found both him and Artie snoring companionably. The queen-sized bed was angled in an unadorned window bay and soft sunlight warmed them. The rest of the room was simply furnished: a dresser, mismatched wooden chair and rocker, inadequate little boudoir lamps, an ugly reproduction print on the wall and a lovely hand-tied down quilt folded by the spooled footboard. Still, better than where she'd grown up. With a few touches, it could be a beautiful room, but as with the rest of the lodge, neglect was apparent.

Beth glanced at her suitcase and at Wyatt's chest of drawers, wondering whether she should mingle her things in among his or tactfully find herself another room. He'd mentioned separate quarters when they were on the island. She hadn't liked it then, either. When she looked back at the bed and saw Wyatt's hand resting upon his slowly rising middle, the first thing she noticed was the gold band he wore. That settled it. She was commandeering her half of the drawer space.

In the middle drawer, she found all his T-shirts and sweaters—not a custom-made, monogrammed cuffed shirt among them. She pushed them over to make room for her pullovers. Then her dainties went in next to his sensible cottons and her designer jeans and slacks beside his sweats and faded denims. She pursed her lips. Even though she'd picked the most rugged pieces from her wardrobe, next to his sturdy wear, hers looked made for a princess bound for the country club. Oh, well. At least she had stout shoes. Those she'd bought special for their fleece lining and waffled sole. She'd left the stockings at home in favor of a new pack of wool socks. No more blisters for this city girl. Clothing stashed and armed with her cosmetics, she headed for the bathroom. And stopped in surprise.

The first thing she saw was a whirlpool tub. Oh, heaven! All the fixtures were porcelain, wood and brass, new with the look of old. The dark green towels were thick enough to drown in. There was a standing shower. However, its nozzle and faucets were conspicuously missing. Eying the tub with anticipation, Beth deposited her necessaries on the oak vanity top, then noted the double sink with pleasure. Every woman craved her own bathroom space. As with Artemus, it was a territorial thing and she was quick to establish hers, flanking one side with her lotions and brushes and curling iron. Wyatt's toiletries were all neatly arranged on the other, not spread indiscriminately. As if he'd been waiting for her to stake her claim. That thought made her pause, but she couldn't afford the luxury of belief. If Wyatt had wanted her here with him, he would have asked her to come.

But he had, in a roundabout way.

Not good enough, she concluded. She wanted to hear it in plain English. And until she did, she would behave as if she was defending her right to stay as a more or less uninvited guest. At least until he told her to go. Then, there would be no coming back a second time.

"Mrs. Marston?"

Beth came out of the bathroom to smile at James Shingoos.

"My mom told me to come get you for dinner."

"Thanks. I'll be right there."

He glanced between her and Wyatt's still figure and mumbled, "I'll wait downstairs."

"Okay."

Beth paused at the bedside, feeling uncomfortable with leaving Wyatt alone. At the moment, he didn't look as though an atomic bomb would wake him. Artie's nose nudged over to rest atop the slow moving chest. His yellow eyes were open, and as Beth reached out to place her hand to Wyatt's cheek, the dog's lips curled back in a silent snarl.

"Knock it off," Beth hissed and the animal's nose smoothed. She gently stroked her husband's face. It was warm but not overly so. She spoke to the dog in a whisper. "You take care of him. If he needs me, you come get me."

Artemus rumbled gruffly as if to say, "We don't need you."

Feeling foolishly hurt by the dog's rejection, Beth backed away from the bed and with one last long glance, turned to hurry down to where James was waiting.

The Shingoos family had converted the big carriage house into a homey dwelling. As Beth sat at the table with them, she admired the northern Michigan decor. The furnishings were of rugged pine, fashioned from roughly peeled and bent wood. Mani called it Adirondack style, which made use of natural materials. The rustic simplicity suited the surroundings. Everywhere, Mani displayed native handicrafts from her own Indian background and bits and pieces of the peninsula's history. The blend was appealing. Just as the Shingoos family was appealing.

For two such rowdy boys, James and Wesley were faultlessly behaved at the table. Beth was impressed. The children she saw dining at the hotel restaurant with their parents were invariably demons to be avoided at all costs. She was as comfortable with children as she was with pets. But these boys charmed her with their manners and shy glances. Then, she was completely distracted by the food.

Mani had prepared a large game bird, and Beth found its golden juiciness and fruit stuffing beyond the realm of delicious. She couldn't remember the last time she'd had a home-cooked meal, and this one took her back to long ago weekends, sharing ethnic dishes at her mother's table. But here, there was no cramping course of tension to complicate the simple enjoyment of feasting.

"This is wonderful," she exclaimed, examining a forkful of the dressing.

"It's an old recipe handed down in my family from the logging camps. The secret's in the sourdough bread."

"Wouldn't this just excite the tastebuds of the spoiled Chicagoans I know." And as she chewed, Beth considered what she'd said. Yes, it would.

She asked casually if Mani had many such traditional meal plans.

"Oh, a whole cookbook, if you can call it that. It's mostly loose pages scribbled in my great grandfather's hand. For dessert, I've made one of Jimmy's favorites — pregnant-woman pie. The lumberjacks named it that because of the way the apples swell up."

That got a giggle from the boys and Beth's mental wheels started spinning.

"Are you having full food service at the lodge?" At Mani's nod, Beth jumped in with enthusiasm, forgetting her reluctance. "I hope you're planning to cook like this for the guests. That would guarantee a return clientele."

Mani and Jimmy exchanged looks. She raised her eyebrows and he grinned as if they agreed on some unspoken issue.

Over coffee and pregnant pie, Jimmy leaned back in his chair, his blue eyes lowering in a shrewd summation of his friend's wife. "How much has Wyatt told you about the renovation of the lodge?"

Beth started to bluff, then caught herself and admitted, "Nothing."

He exhaled in a rush and shook his head. "Nothing? Oh, boy. Maybe I'd better not step into anything then."

Beth smiled convincingly. "If Wyatt hadn't wanted me to know, he wouldn't have asked me here, would he? I'm sure he wouldn't mind if you filled me in." Someone had to. She'd rest a lot easier if she knew what she was up against.

Jimmy took a sip of coffee and searched for

where to begin. "The lodge has been in my family for generations, but the money to keep her is nearly gone. You've seen her at her worst. Unless something is done soon . . ." He shrugged eloquently and Beth shared his pang of regret that such a thing should happen.

"When Wyatt and I were boys, like my two there, we would listen to my grandmother speak of the old days and how fine it all was. Funny, back then, Wyatt's family worked for mine. His mother grew up in Laurium, a town about twenty miles south of Calumet with a whopping population of a couple of thousand. Anyway, his mother and father met when she won a scholarship to the University of Chicago. She'd bring Wyatt up every summer to spend several weeks with his grandmother, who worked at the lodge. Wyatt's father never came. Too busy at work to take the time off."

That hadn't changed, Beth thought ruefully. "So the two of you became friends."

"Best friends. We'd sit with our cherry Cokes on the sun porch and talk big dreams of how some day we'd be partners in owning the lodge. And we'd be rich beyond our imagination." Jimmy smiled without envy. "At least one of us made it." Then he looked about him and at his family and his expression softened. "Both of us made it." Mani smiled back and Beth's heart took a bittersweet twist.

"But the lodge kept going downhill," he continued.

"Wyatt's mother died and his father remarried, moving them to Denver. He went to some fancy business school there and I put in a couple of years at a junior college and we lost track of each other. But hearts don't forget as easily as minds. One day, he flew in and tied up at the beach and it was like the years apart were nothing. He was a big shot in his stepmother's hotel business, wearing suits and reading the *Wall Street Journal,* but he never forgot the boy who played in these woods and made promises to an old friend."

Jimmy smiled to himself, marveling at how strongly the ties had held over time and distance but Beth wasn't surprised. She couldn't imagine giving up the kind of closeness the two men must have shared. If she'd had something like that in her younger years, how different some things might have been.

"Well, it seems Wyatt had been thinking of ways to salvage the lodge and keep a bit of his past intact. We'd gone from cherry Coke to Lite beer, but those talks in the sun porch got both of us remembering and wanting the same thing. He suggested restoring the old place, making it into a resort, using the seaplanes to charter guests to the isle and to other attractions on the peninsula. We were full of ideas but couldn't do a thing until we had the money. Wyatt offered to put up his shares in Marston Hotels as collateral for a business loan. I didn't like the idea of him fronting all the bills, but he said I'd be doing the hard stuff—the managing and maintenance. He insisted on the full partnership, so I insisted he take over part ownership of the lodge. He has everything set up with the bank just waiting for the final approval . . . and for you to agree to the use of the stocks as collateral. Things got put on hold while he was in the hospital. A lot of things."

His gaze flickered to her and seeing her sudden stiffness, away. Though Beth wanted and needed to pursue the topic, it was getting late. But there would be other opportunities. From the Shingoos, she could learn what Wyatt wasn't telling her. Then, maybe she'd know how she fit into the scheme of things. And to the tune of how big an investment.

"I'd better get back to the lodge. I don't like leaving Wyatt alone." After she thanked Mani for her hospitality, the Ojibway woman went to the kitchen to fix a plate for Beth to take to Wyatt. It was then Beth remembered a promise she'd made in Chicago. "Is there a phone at the lodge?" she asked Jimmy, recalling that she'd not seen one.

"No. We've never gotten around to putting one in, but you're welcome to use ours."

"I've got to call Wyatt's father. I told him I would once I was settled in. I'll put it through on my phone card number."

Jimmy waved a hand as if that wasn't important and showed Beth to an extension in their cozy living room. While she spoke to the operator, he returned to the dining table to stack dishes and muse over Bethany Marston, whom he hadn't expected to like quite so much.

With the covered tray balanced on her hip, Beth let herself into the lodge. The flip of a switch illu-

130

minated the hall and stairs with a weak light from the tarnished brass chandelier overhead. This sufficed to guide her up the steps. Halfway there, she heard an odd sound. She paused to listen. Her brow furrowed. Whining? Artemus?

Thinking he probably had to go out, she hurried the rest of the way. The door to Wyatt's room was open and she wondered why the big dog hadn't met her at the front steps if he was in a rush to answer nature's call. The anxious whimpering escalated at her approach, and Beth was suddenly gripped with apprehension. The animal's cries were almost plaintive. Then she switched on the light and understood the dog's agitation.

Artemus was pacing in circles, whining mournfully as he nosed the motionless form stretched out on the floor.

Wyatt!

Chapter Eight

"Oh no!"

Beth nearly dropped the tray in her haste. It teetered on the edge of the rocking chair as she ran to kneel at her husband's side. Artemus backed away, for once putting his hostility aside, sensing she could help.

"Wyatt?"

He was sprawled full length. She guessed he'd tried to get out of bed on his own and had fallen. As carefully as she could, she rolled him faceup and waited anxiously for some sign of awareness to return to him. His eyelids fluttered, then opened. He looked up at her in surprise and blinked as if he expected her image to disappear.

"Beth?"

"I'm here." She clutched his hand. "Oh, Wyatt, I'm so sorry. I shouldn't have left you. I should have been here. Are you all right?"

"I think so." He sounded dazed, uncertain. He was staring at her strangely, still not believing she was real.

"Let me help you back into bed."

"No. No."

"Don't be silly. If you could manage on your own, you wouldn't be covering the floorboards like a bearskin rug. What possessed you to try such a thing? You're not supposed to be out of bed until you're strong enough to use your crutches. Here. Grab on."

Beth dragged the straight chair over close, and with one of his arms about her shoulders and the other on the seat of the chair, they were able to wrestle him upright with a minimum of effort. He hung against her, his body weight a telling sag of weakness, pulling on her neck like a heavy yoke.

"Now, let's get you back in bed."

"No," he argued wheezily. "I had a purpose in mind when I got out of it in the first place, and unfortunately it hasn't disappeared. I was heading in that direction."

He nodded toward the bathroom.

"Oh."

"If you could get me as far as the door, I'm sure I can handle the rest."

She hoped so. "Lean on me."

Together, they made it to the bathroom and once he had a firm grip on the edge of the vanity, he gave her a dismissing scowl. Beth backed out, uneasy with the idea of leaving him on his own. His balance was precarious at best and his color, none too good. But for the sake of his dignity, she obliged.

"Don't drown and don't let modesty keep you from hollering if you need help."

He gave her a small smile, one reminiscent of his heart-stopping grin. "Beth, I've been doing these kind of things for myself for quite a number of years. I don't think I'll need help." And he shut the door.

She waited, hearing bumps and bangs, hearing him curse and yelp several times, but she forced herself not to run to a premature rescue. Artemus padded over to sit beside her, his own anxious whine echoing her concern. Absently, she dropped her hand to the top of his head, rumpling the thick coat before she realized what she was doing. They exchanged a startled look as if both woman and dog were surprised by the temporary truce. But neither of them moved away from the other.

There was the sound of water running and more fiercely muttered curses. Finally, there came a rather sheepish request, "Beth, would come get me. And be careful, I'm right behind the—"

She opened the door and was greeted by a thump and a shout of pain. Wyatt had been standing up next to it and the jamb caught his bare toes. He gave a few backward hops and almost landed in the tub before she could grab onto his arms to steady him.

"Sorry."

"—behind the door," he concluded a bit too late to do his throbbing toes any good. He clutched at Beth's shoulders, letting her angle

134

him out of the crowded space. He was breathing hard, his features pale and taut with discomfort. There was no question that he was hurting badly.

"Come on," Beth coaxed. "We'll take it slowly."

Wyatt hobbled next to her, leaning heavily, depending upon her for support and direction while he panted and tried hard not to pass out before the objective was reached. She swung him about on the pivot of his good foot and let him down upon the edge of the mattress as easily as her strength allowed. He sat for a moment, sucking air, shaking with the strain.

"I feel terrible," he moaned in obvious understatement. He looked terrible.

"What about your dinner?"

But he was falling back at an awkwardly controlled angle, aiming for the pillow and a painless slumber. "Give it to Artie," he muttered. He battled with the bulky cast, trying to drag it up onto the bed. Finally he conceded defeat and flopped back breathlessly while Beth hauled his injured leg up onto the covers. He groaned, feeling too miserable to disguise it and found it was worth the humbling to enjoy the tender sympathy his wife heaped upon him. She fussed, tugging the sheet and blanket out from under him, then situating him as comfortably as possible before tucking him in. A relentless nag of agony pounded in his head. However, the light brush of her fingertips along his hot brow made it endurable. As he closed his eyes, he wondered what he would have done without her.

And just before he drifted off, he found himself wondering what she was doing here at the lodge.

Beth lingered at the bedside, wishing she could do something to speed along Wyatt's healing. The fact of his helplessness alarmed her. She'd never had anyone dependent upon her and it was a disquieting sensation. She'd never had to worry over anyone other than herself. The maternal instincts swamping her were new and so was the need to nurture. Both things were tempered by the facts of her uncertain situation. She felt guilt over not being there when he'd needed her and yet still ached as she remembered him sending her away from his hospital room.

"You need me, Wyatt," she told him softly. "We'll both just have to get used to the idea."

His eyes didn't open, so she had no way of knowing if he heard her.

Artie had finished the remnants of Wyatt's dinner and began to trot back and forth at the door to the bedroom. When Beth looked up, he gave a descriptive woof and bounded down the stairs. She followed to where he was prancing at the front door. The second she opened it, he bounded out and was gone. While she waited for him to finish his business outdoors, Beth wandered to the library, hoping to find something to ease the interminable northwoods hours. It was only seven. It felt like midnight. She was exhausted in body and mind and felt a book might

136

quiet the latter so the former could reach a comfortable point of collapse.

The library held an inestimable fortune. Beth knew books. One of the things she'd always enjoyed was making the rounds of collector bookstores even before she could afford to buy. She had little time to actually read anything older than the last week's profit tables, but she liked the idea of being surrounded with a sense of history. From the squalor of her childhood, books had provided a much needed escape, and then the past seemed to have so much more to offer than her own future. This library was that feeling, encapsulated. She scanned the shelves, astounded by the wealth of volumes dating from the mid-1800s. Aside from the mustiness, they were in mint condition. Everything from tomes on mining to the escape literature of the day. She wondered if anyone was aware of the collection. First editions, rare titles, family journals. A historian's dream come true. None of the books was published aftere 1940. Someone should know about a collection this well preserved, but she wasn't sure who. She'd ask Jimmy in the morning. For now, she selected an anthology and went to put water on to boil for some coffee.

The kitchen was a blend of antiquity and the chromy fifties. But at least, everything worked. It was stocked with the basics, and she remembered that while Wyatt lived at the lodge he ate with the Shingoos family. That explained the lean condition of the larder. While her kettle simmered, she went to let Artemus in. The dog made a dash up the stairs. She followed with her book and mug of coffee, turning off the lights to the rooms below. The sense of silence, of aloneness was as thick as the shadows closing in on the hall and lower stairs with a flick of the switch. It was a restless sort of silence for one city-born and city-bred.

Curled up in the rocker, Beth read until her weariness proved an obstacle to every word. At nine, she gave up. She prepared for bed, slipping on a short nightie and turning off the lights. When she tried to lift the covers, she was presented with an immovable object. Artemus was back on the bed.

"Get down," she ordered in a low, firm voice.

The dog growled.

"Get down, you big ox. Don't mess with me, if you know what's good for you."

He growled again, stubbornly defending his position next to Wyatt.

Beth reached for his collar, then jerked back as he snapped at her hand. "Oh, so you want to play rough, do you." She straightened and pointed toward the darkened hallway. "Artie, what's that? Go get 'em!"

The dog lunged off the bed in response to her excited tone. He'd reached the doorway before he realized he'd been tricked. Beth slid under the covers, chuckling to herself. She could swear she heard the animal grumbling as he trotted back and flopped down on the floor on Wyatt's side of the bed.

Wyatt was shifting fitfully in his sleep, probably uncomfortable even in his exhausted slumber. Tentatively, Beth slipped her arm about his middle and nudged in close. He sighed deeply and quieted as if aware of her presence. How long had it been since she'd slept beside him? The tent disaster didn't count. Too long, she decided as threads of desire intertwined with those of belonging. How good he felt. Lean and still so very strong. Cautiously, she burrowed her fingertips beneath the edge of his T-shirt, wanting, suddenly needing to feel the heat of his skin.

It was crazy. She knew it. She was getting herself all wound up with no possible way to release the tension. But she'd risk the frustration for the pleasure of stirring sensual memory. Her palm charted the pattern of his ribs and stroked across the furred plane of his abdomen. Her breathing quickened and her mouth went dry. Slowly, she rubbed her knee over the hard curve of his sound leg. Longing pooled inside her, that and a desperate need to reestablish intimacy. Her fingers followed the ridged waistband to his athletic shorts. Then, she made herself stop. Oh, if only he wasn't lying there with a broken leg . . .

But he was.

With a pent-up sigh, she rolled onto her back. Urgency gnawed at her. The craving for his touch had risen to an intolerable level. She cursed his leg cast and his unconscious state. She cursed the wilds of northern Michigan and her husband's reasons for coming here. And she cursed the fact that she should be driven to such a desperation within the bounds of matrimony. She wanted the man she'd married. She wanted him in bed beside her every night. She wanted to make love to him. She wanted to close her eyes to a sense of security, knowing that all was right and well. And she had none of those things. And it made her mad as hell.

They had to settle things. She couldn't go on like this. They hadn't been close for a long time, but now Wyatt was pulling away, showing all the signs of starting up a different life. One that didn't include her. All these plans—the lodge, the planes, the loan—and he'd said nothing to her. The pain of it was almost like betrayal. The sense of panic returned and she fought it off. No, it was too soon to be truly afraid. Concerned was what she should be. Concerned over the sad state of their relationship. But not yet terrified that it was over before she had the chance to effect repairs. Surely it could be mended. Surely the break could be healed, as his leg would heal. It would take time and care and a bit of caution. But it could mend.

Or she'd be on her way to Denver. Alone.

Wyatt opened his eyes to a devastating pain. It wasn't the nagging ache of his leg, but rather the emptiness of his bed.

140

He'd thought Beth was beside him.

It was the residual effect of the drugs, of course. They'd been feeding him the fantasy foremost in his thoughts. That of his wife cuddled up against him with her unbound hair streaming like raw silk across his shoulder. With her palm resting tenderly over the beat of his heart. Just an illusion. It was a killing reality to wake to.

He closed his eyes, trying to overcome the despair that lanced his soul. The dream had been so real he could almost smell Liz Claiborne on his sheets. Why couldn't he just put the past behind him? Why did he have to suffer the good memories mixed in with the bad? What good did it do to remember how much he had loved her? Past tense. That's what he had to remind himself of. Beth was in Chicago, getting on with her life, just as he needed to get on with his.

He was hungry. His leg hurt. His thoughts were painfully clear. He imagined he could smell eggs. Funny the tricks a shut-in's mind could play. He could tell that it was early by the angle of the sun over the lake. Mani would be getting her boys off to school. She wouldn't be bringing him breakfast any time soon. Oh, for room service.

"Are you awake? I thought you might be up to eating something this morning?"

Wyatt practically dislocated his head from his shoulders, he whipped it so fast toward the door. He stared, stunned, his heart staggered. Beth approached the bed, tray in hand, delicious scents

141

wafting up from whatever she carried. Artemus was at her heels, apparently hoping for a sample.

Beth was here, bringing him breakfast.

He was either dreaming or hallucinating.

"Steak and eggs," she announced as she set the tray down on the dresser. Her smile seemed small and wistful. "To make up for the lumpy oatmeal and granola bars. If I prop you up, do you think you can handle the tray?"

"Sure."

She looked at him strangely, wondering over the dazed quality of his voice. The medication made him fuzzy, she decided. He was following her movements with an alert, if somewhat confused gaze.

"Lift yourself up a little."

When Wyatt pushed up on his elbows, Beth wedged several pillows behind his back until the bolster had him almost upright. When she started to move away, he reached out, snagging her wrist within the tight circle of his fingers. He could feel the smooth warmth of her skin, the rapid beat of her pulse. She paused, questioning him with her expression. He released her, then sagged back against the pillows wordlessly.

She was here. He'd had to touch her to be sure. What was going on? He tried to pry the truth from his befuddled brain. So many images making so little sense. He couldn't be certain what was real and what had happened only in his fevered head. The camping trip he remembered. Her holding his hand in the hospital. *I love you,*

Wyatt. He wasn't convinced he'd heard that. He wished he could be. He vividly recalled sending her away from his bedside. He could see the whiteness of her face, the anguish in her features and remembered his own helpless anger that she should look so devastated. He felt that anger now. What had she expected?

So when had she returned?

His glance into the bathroom beyond showed evidence that she'd made herself at home in his room. He vaguely recalled silk and heat beside him in the night. Just how long had she been here to be so comfortably a part of things? In his bathroom, in his kitchen. In his bed. That last was what had him rattled.

"Here you go." She slid the tray onto his knees. Steak and eggs. His hollow stomach roared to life.

"Thanks."

"I'm going to run back down for your coffee." She started toward the door when his call brought her up short.

"What day is this?"

"It's Thursday."

"The date."

"The fourteenth. Why?"

"Because I feel kind of like Rip Van Winkle." She smiled at him indulgently. "That was the medication. Some pretty strong stuff. Is your leg bothering you? Do you need some more?"

"No." No way. No more of that. He had just got his senses back. He wasn't about to scramble

143

them again. He was afraid of what he'd find next time he awoke. "Just some over-the-counter. There's some in the bathroom cabinet."

"I know. I'll get it as soon as I bring up the coffee."

I know. How did she know? Thursday. It had almost been a week since the accident. Where had all the hours gone? He closed his eyes, feeling disoriented and unsettled.

When and why had Beth come back?

Then the insistence of his appetite took over and he applied himself to the meal at hand. And a good one, it was. Far better than the oatmeal. He was smiling wryly to himself as he cut into his steak.

Beth returned with a mug of coffee in either hand. He watched her without losing a beat between cutting and chewing. She looked good. She wore snug black stirrup pants and an oversized royal blue and black patterned sweater. And her hair was down. Another kind of appetite took hold, one he did his best to ignore.

"Careful, it's hot," she warned as she extended the cup.

He contained a rueful smile. How could she possibly believe she'd never burned him before? "Set it on the floor. I've got my hands full for the moment."

"How is everything?"

She bent and the sight of Lycra hugging gorgeous thighs almost made him swallow his tongue along with his mouthful of steak.

144

"Fine," he muttered, quickly averting his stare before he carelessly fed himself his own fingers by mistake. Beth assumed a seat in the rocker and the impartial distance allowed him to relax. Just a little. She was silent for a moment, watching him eat while she waited for her own coffee to cool. He could tell she was just dying to say something. Beth had a great poker face but her body language gave her away. She was tense and restless.

As he reached down for his cup, she let him have it.

"Why didn't you tell me about all this?"

Wyatt brought the cup smoothly to his lips, letting the question hang while he thought of how to answer it. His reply was remote. "Why would I? It has nothing to do with Marston Hotels."

That took her aback. But she responded equally civilly. "But it has to do with you. Shouldn't that concern me?"

"I don't see why it should."

When she paled, he continued more caustically.

"I could have the whole thing developed before I could schedule a few minutes of your time to tell you about it."

"Now that's an exaggeration and you know it." She was snappish.

Guilt? he wondered.

"Is it? Is it really? And I suppose you would have canceled your oh-so-important meetings to come up here with me to look the place over."

"We'll never know, will we. You never gave me the opportunity to say yes or no."

His jaw tightened and his tone flattened. "Oh, I think I could figure the answer to that one out well enough on my own." And he went back to his eggs. They hadn't lost their flavor, but he was suddenly no longer hungry. He moved the tray onto the empty half of the bed and concentrated on the coffee. And from the corner of his eye, he watched his wife.

"I'm not going to argue this with you, Wyatt. It's over and done."

"Right. Why argue when you know I'd win."

"I might have surprised you."

He grinned. It wasn't a pleasant gesture. "Yes, you have done your share of surprising me. A man can take only so many surprises."

"So can his wife."

A tense impasse settled.

Beth was frustrated. He was good, so good at evasion. He should have been a politician. He knew just how to turn things back upon the speaker. He made an accusation directed at him into his own defense. And he gave nothing away. He never betrayed an ounce of his own feelings. It would seem confrontation was not the way to go. At least not for the moment. His mood was too self-protective.

"It's a beautiful place." She said that warmly and felt the suspicious cut of his gaze.

"Really? I didn't think it would be to your taste."

146

Beth refused to be goaded down another destructive avenue. "Oh, I love grand old things. It practically oozes character. With a little elbow grease—make that a lot of elbow grease—some organization and a good deal of collateral, someone could have a potential gold mine."

"I intend to."

She gave him every opportunity to include her in his plan. To say "we" instead of "I" but he didn't. He clung to the first-person singular almost defiantly. And she backed down in momentary defeat. Where had all the hostility come from? He was treating her worse than a stranger and acting as if she were his enemy. She wondered why, but before she could venture in that direction, there was a soft tap on the bedroom door. She looked up to see Jimmy hovering in the hall. She smiled in welcome. He stared at her expressionlessly.

"Wyatt, I need to talk to you for a minute."

That couldn't be more tactfully or more clearly put. He didn't need to add the word "alone." She got the message. Beth gathered the tray and empty cups, trying not to look mildly offended. She'd begun to think that Wyatt's friend liked her. She got no sense of that this morning. "I'll take these down to the kitchen. Jimmy, can I offer you some coffee?"

"No thanks." He angled in, stepping aside so she could pass. He gave her plenty of room. His features were impassive. But something in his blue eyes gave her an uneasy pause. Something

147

was up and she wanted to know what, sensing that either directly or indirectly it involved her. And it definitely involved Wyatt. There were too many secrets already. She would have given anything to linger, but Jimmy stood there, waiting for her to go. Resigned, she headed for the stairs.

"Hi, Jimmy. What's up?" Wyatt was studying his face, keyed in to the blankness as if it was an expression all its own. Internally, he was bracing for the worst.

"Morning, Wyatt. How are you feeling?"

"Why do I get the impression that it's going to depend on what you have to tell me?"

Jimmy didn't smile. He came and sat on the edge of the mattress, drumming his fingers nervously along the inside of his thighs. He didn't quite know how to put what he had to say. He didn't like the idea of kicking a man when he was down. But there was no way around it, no way to stall when precious time was passing them by. He'd have to put it plain and hope his friend and potential partner could weather it.

"I just got off the phone with the bank."

Wyatt went ice cold inside. "And?"

Oh, hell. He might as well just say it. "They've refused the loan."

Chapter Nine

"What?"

Wyatt stared at him, too stunned to think of anything else to say.

"The loan officer called it a bad risk."

"Bad risk," he echoed. Then the daze lifted, leaving outrage. "Bad risk? What did he mean, bad risk? He couldn't possibly find anything wrong with the Marston shares as collateral. And as for this place, it's not in as bad shape as other places up here that have made good as B and Bs. What's their problem? I don't get it!" Agitation was making his leg ache. He gritted his teeth until that pulse echoed between his temples.

Jimmy wouldn't meet his eyes.

"What? Jimmy, what aren't you telling me? Come on, man. It's Wyatt here."

"It is you, Wyatt. It's not the collateral or the lodge." He lifted his unhappy stare. "It's you."

"Me?"

"They consider you a bad risk."

Wyatt slumped back against the cushions,

mind reeling. What? How could that be? There was some mistake. He was an heir to millions. He was the VP of the Marston Hotel chain. What on earth . . .

"What did they tell you, Jimmy? Word for word."

His childhood friend shifted uncomfortably, reciting the harsh conclusion. "They said they re-evaluated your application and further investigation showed you weren't a viable risk for their investment. They said something about a series of unwise collaborations when you were younger."

Wyatt went numb. "How did they find out about that?" His gaze challenged Jimmy's as if he could find an answer there. Jimmy had no more idea of what was going on than when he'd been on the phone with the faceless bank officer. Wyatt looked away in frustration. "How the *hell* did they find out about that?"

"An undisclosed source," Jimmy muttered quietly, hating it, hating the helpless fury in his friend's face and the sense of failure hovering over their dreams.

"Undisclosed source. No one knew anything about that except . . . except my father." His voice dropped off on a note of disbelief. His father had pulled the plug on his ambitions. That knowledge was devastating. But as stunned, as hurt as he was, Wyatt didn't ask why, even of himself. He knew why. For the same reason his father had bailed him out of his first few financial fiascoes. Because Boyd Marston wanted him to be part of the Marston chain. Because his father didn't believe he had the capacity to succeed independently. Wyatt had proved it well enough with his first sadly bungled attempts. But that had been years ago. Years ago. The question he asked wasn't why but how. "How did he find out about the loan?"

Jimmy fidgeted even more noticeably, not wanting to say, not knowing how to get around it. Again, he just came straight out with it. "Your wife called him last night."

Wyatt flinched and immediately sought a way to recover from this, the worst of the two blows. "But she didn't know any of the particulars."

"Yes, she did. Mani told her. She thought you'd told Beth everything. She acted as though you had. I told her about the loan. Even what bank. So I guess it's my fault," he concluded glumly.

"Not your fault." Wyatt said that with a hard edge of anger. He knew whose fault it was and it was eating him alive. Jimmy didn't have to ask what he was thinking.

"Maybe she let it slip by mistake. Wyatt, I don't believe she'd do anything to hurt you."

"You wouldn't think a man's own father would, either. Don't waste your breath arguing a case for my wife, Jimmy. She's a Marston. One of the few, the proud, the unswervingly loyal. Anyway, it doesn't much matter now, does it? What's done is done."

151

The two of them sat in a dire study of silence, feeling the weight of their hopes collapse yet not wanting to admit that all was lost.

"Is everything all right?"

Wyatt looked to where Beth was standing in the doorway, her expression hesitant and concerned. His reply was very smooth. "Depends on who's asking."

Jimmy got up, clearing his throat awkwardly. "I'm out of here. Wyatt, we'll talk later. I've got some puddle hopping to do this morning. Excuse me, Mrs. Marston."

Beth smiled stiffly as he passed. Mrs. Marston. Not Beth anymore. Wondering what uneasy ground their talk had covered, she advanced into the room. Wyatt was propped up with covers tented over his one updrawn knee, but his look was anything but that of a helpless invalid. He looked dangerous. His eyes glittered. His jaw was set like granite. He tracked her movements with the wariness of a wild thing backed into an uncomfortable corner. She didn't know what to do. She didn't know what was wrong. But she knew better than to try to reason with him now. He looked ready to crunch broken glass.

"How about you?" she asked gaily as if unaware of all the riptides of emotion she stepped in upon. "Can I get you some more coffee?"

"I think you've done more than enough already."

The chill index of that statement had her shivering inside. She continued to smile determinedly.

"I can take some of those pillows if you want to lie back down."

"I don't want to lie down. I don't want to be in this damn bed." He shifted angrily and grimaced in pain.

"How about those Tylenols? Your leg must be hurting you."

His leg was the least of his concerns, he thought wretchedly. And a couple of Tylenols wouldn't begin to get on top of what was killing him. He wanted numbness, sweet oblivion. Maybe that way some of the horrible agony of truth would be gone by the time it wore off. He couldn't deal with the facts just yet, and he couldn't handle being in the same room with the woman who'd betrayed him so unforgivably.

"I don't want anything from you, Beth."

She went rigid at the crack of his voice. He was panting, his breath hissing between clenched teeth. His hair was damp at his temples and the pinch of distress at the corners of his eyes was unmistakable. He threw aside the extra pillows and dropped back with a groan. He was looking purposefully away from her. Beth had seen the studied snub before. At the hospital. And the last thing she wanted to do was push him into sending her away again.

"I'll be downstairs if you change your mind about needing anything."

He placed his forearm across his eyes in lieu of an answer. The gesture was a fairly clear reply.

153

Beth frowned and left him to his brooding silence.

Jimmy strode into the big lodge out of habit, then paused. He wasn't used to knocking, but there was a lady in residence, whether he approved of her or not, and he supposed he owed her the courtesy of announcing himself.

"Hello?"

"Back here. In the library."

Curiously, he went through the great room and rear dining room, then drew up in the doorway, bemused by the sight that greeted him. All the book shelves were empty and gleamed of polish. The depth of satiny wood surprised him but not so much as the figure who straightened up from behind a mountain of volumes.

Sunlight streamed in through the mullioned windows, highlighting motes of dust that hadn't been stirred for decades. It shone on the perspiration dotting Bethany Marston's brow. She looked a far cry from a Chicago executive. Her heavy hair was bound back washerwoman-style in a bright blue bandana and she wore one of Wyatt's T-shirts that must have been white at one time. Her black pants were marbled with dirt and smudges of it tracked her cheeks. But she was smiling.

"Have you any idea of what a great collection of literature your family has?"

"I'm not much for this kind of reading," he admitted, giving the gilt-edged books a once-over. "If it's not fishing, fan belts or flying, it doesn't hold my interest past the table of contents. I think Wyatt was the last one who ever took one of them off the shelf. And if I recall, it was dusty back then. Surely you didn't have to go through all this trouble just to find something to read."

She laughed at his expression. "No. I have too great a respect for books to let them go so neglected. And I was curious. Did you know there are some first editions that are worth several thousand?"

"Dollars?"

"Each."

"No, I didn't." He looked the pile over with a new appreciation.

"Of course, the best ones have no real value except to a historian. Mani said something about you wanting to have this place put on the historical registry. You may have your ticket in right here."

"In my grandmother's diaries?"

"Oh these go back farther than that. A lot of them predate the house, itself."

"Hmmm." He sounded polite but uninterested in further details, so she put the book she was holding aside.

"I thought while I was cooped up in here pretty much at Wyatt's beck and call, I'd see what's hidden under all the mildew and cobwebs."

"And what did you find?"

"So far? More mildew and cobwebs."

He laughed at that and the warmth was back between them. She hadn't understood where it had disappeared to that morning.

Perhaps, it didn't matter. Jimmy was more forgiving than her husband.

"How's Wyatt doing?" he asked, offering his hand to help her over the obstacle of books.

"Sleeping last time I looked in on him. And not in the kind of mood you want to wake him up from."

He nodded in understanding and made a face. "Then we won't wake him."

She liked Jimmy Shingoos and was glad Wyatt had had him for a friend while growing up. He was a simple man, an easy man to be around. A man of the woods and the sky. And she was dying for a little comfortable conversation. "How about some sun tea? I've got some brewing on the porch."

He would have preferred a cold beer, but he smiled at the mussed and very pretty Mrs. Marston. "Sounds good."

While she poured warm amber tea over the ice in their two glasses, Beth looked around the sun porch, repressing a grimace. "Jimmy, do you have any great sentimental attachment to this furniture?"

He looked around, sharing her distaste. "No. None in the least. An eyesore, isn't it?"

"Wonderful. I want to get started out here

156

next. This could be such a gorgeous spot. I figured I'd empty out the junk, give it a good cleaning and then order something in wicker with—"

"Ummmm, Beth," he began cautiously. "I'd go easy on the spending if I were you. There's no rush."

"But Mani said you were hoping to have the place ready for the public next spring."

"Well, that *was* the plan."

"So what's the plan now?" She was watching his face, frowning slightly.

"The loan got turned down." There was no subtle way to put it. This was shaping up to be his day for bearing bad news.

"What? Oh, no. But you were counting on that money to—Does Wyatt know?" Of course he did. That would explain his mood of that morning. But not his antagonism toward her. She should have felt relieved. Now, there'd be no reason for him not to follow her back to Chicago and on to Denver. But she wasn't. She hated to see him fail in something he obviously had his heart set upon.

"He's feeling pretty low about it. Seems it was some snag in his credit rating."

"Wyatt's?"

She sounded too astounded for Jimmy not to believe her. And too genuinely distressed for him to think she'd taken part in engineering their troubles. At least knowingly. She stood at the windows, looking out over the lake.

"Then we'll just have to think of some other way to arrange for financing."

She said the "we" unthinkingly, but Jimmy caught it and he began to smile with new hope.

She brought him a dinner tray.

Wyatt watched her move about the room through slitted eyes. His mood was far from friendly. He'd lain in his bed of misery all afternoon, aching in body, tormented in soul. And he'd found no means to resolve either agony. The hurt just kept getting bigger, one feeding upon the other until it was all he could do to lie still.

He didn't want to lie still. He was bored. He was restless. He was helpless in a time that demanded action. He needed a phone and a miracle. He wanted desperately to choke someone. Preferably his father. But Beth was closer. And at the moment, seemed a suitable substitution for all his grievances.

Pain and betrayal gave a sharp, glittery edge to his thoughts. Confined as he was, the same ones played over and over until they became distorted by repetition. No loan, no restoration. His father had effectively nipped that in the bud. Now what? Back to Chicago with an air of proper humility? Or to Denver where he could watch his wife dance attendance upon his father's whims? Back into the Marston fold where he could perform as an extension of its owner? Back to tailored suits and restricting job and a marriage that

158

was as empty as his future now seemed? Everything inside him rebelled against it. Against the idea of defeat. Against the sham of pretending he didn't care if the wife he loved was careless in her infidelity. Damn them both, Boyd and Bethany Marston.

Why couldn't his father trust him? Why couldn't his wife love him?

There was nothing to go back to. Nothing. He decided right then, as he watched Beth slide his tray atop the dresser, that he'd rather slave for pennies flying off the cold surface of Lake Superior as second man in Jimmy's flying service than rake in the expected thousands living a lie in the cold emotional climate in Chicago. It had been in the back of his mind ever since he'd set foot on the land of his childhood dreams. The sense of belonging overwhelmed him. He hadn't expected it to still be so strong, for its embrace to satisfy what had long been missing in his life. It was the loamy scent of the damp woods, the springy feel of pine needles underfoot, his easy inclusion within the Shingoos family as if the years had never passed. This old place with its pride and its memories. He'd come with a half-formed idea and it burst full bloom the second he'd stepped in the great hall below.

He'd meant to just take a financial and advisory position in the restoration of the lodge. He'd never consciously planned to sever his ties with Chicago, to resign his predictable job or move out of his stylized apartment in favor of these musty rooms. It wasn't a conscious decision. It was one that continued to grow inside when each day ended in silent lengthening shadows. Each time he looked out over the restless lake and felt energy build within him. Each time he took to the air and soared like one of the neighboring eagles. Freedom. It was freedom from the strictures of his family and his regimented lifestyle. And it was the means to heal from the debilitating wound in his heart and soul. He'd stayed, each day moving unnoticed into the next, until weeks amassed and then months. He didn't notice the passage of time until his yearning for his wife was too intense to ignore. As much as he rationalized it would be the best thing to do, he couldn't seem to wrest her out of his thoughts or out of his very explicit dreams.

Beth had changed into a formfitted Henley pullover. The snug powder blue cotton knit did glorious things to her firm, high breasts as she stretched to pull the curtains open. Her new crisp jeans hugged where they were meant to hug and looked devastating. His beautiful wife. His faithless wife. Anger and anguish crowded into his throat. Loving her was a weakness he couldn't control. Wanting her was a madness that writhed inside him. It had been months since he'd held her and made love to her, but he never stopped imagining either pleasure.

He wondered grimly how long it had been for her.

The wondering had kept him from calling for

her when he was half crazy with need. Because he was afraid he couldn't touch her without speculating on whose path he was following along her lovely skin. With his father and Gretchen, it was a matter of pride and upbringing to overlook marital indiscretion. With him, it was heartbreak.

It was his own fault. He'd fallen in love with a sweet, caring woman and had introduced her into the Marston clan. How had he thought she'd survive that indoctrination intact? Wealth corrupted. He'd seen it happen to his father. Ambition overruled emotion. He'd seen that on a more personal level. It hadn't taken any time at all for the Marston hierarchy to swallow his beautiful wife whole. And she did them proud, pulling in the traces just like his father.

Had she used him as a career stepping-stone? Had she ever loved him at all? If she had, would it have been so easy for her to push her social ambitions and career plans ahead of their marriage? He didn't think so and he didn't like what he was thinking. Boyd had married for prestige and money. So had Bethany. His stepmother was well known for her affairs. So was his wife. Sort of a shameful family tradition.

He'd been crazy to contact her. He'd been foolish to think he could charm her with the natural beauty of the northwoods and sell her with his own enthusiasm upon his ideas regarding the lodge. And he'd been naive to think he could woo her away from her coveted office and exciting social schedule. To be with him. To live here.

He was very afraid "here" had nothing to offer his gregarious wife. And that he didn't, either. Everything had gone to hell over on Isle Royale. All his plans to sweetly seduce her in this very bed were ruined. All his hopes of starting their marriage anew, destroyed. She'd be crazy to want what she'd seen so far: a dangerous, inconvenient wilderness and a husband with a handful of futile ambitions and a broken leg.

But that didn't stop him from wanting her.

How he wanted her, wanted to see if there was any reason left for hope. If there was a spark worth relighting, if there had ever been a genuine flame at all. It burned hot on his side but it was a carefully contained heat. At least he'd thought so until she turned toward him and all the fiery glory of a Lake Superior sunset framed her lovely face and form.

"Hi. I wasn't sure if you were awake. I brought dinner. You must be starved."

Beth leaned down to plump his pillows and froze at the look of ravenous hunger she saw in his eyes. When she didn't straighten immediately, he reached up to cup the back of her head in his palm and pulled her to him. Desire exploded as her mouth opened over his, inviting the probe of his tongue and the drenching sweetness of exploration that followed. To his surprise, she was kissing him back with a matching urgency. Her hands were on his face, in his hair, rubbing, clenching with a restless fervor. He couldn't remember the last time it had been so good.

She'd come down on the edge of the bed and was leaning across his torso. In a second, his hands had wrenched her clingy shirt from the band of her jeans and were thrust up to surround the lace-covered fullness of her breasts. She moaned softly into his mouth. She didn't seem to mind his rough handling. In fact, her response encouraged it. And he needed damn little encouragement as passion swamped all else.

Wyatt shifted, using his upper body for leverage to topple her onto his sheets. But when he twisted to follow, a sharp shock of agony bolted up his leg. He tried to ignore it. He wanted to ignore it. He wanted to pursue the soft delights of the woman below him, but as he started to breathe hard into the pain, Beth's compliance ended. She pushed against his shoulders, rolling him onto his back.

"No, Wyatt. We can't."

Rampaging need surpassed common sense and he rejected her protest. When he tried to tug her back into his arms, her resistance became more marked. She pushed against him, trying to wriggle free. Struggling brought more stabs of pain until he was unable to contain his groan of discomfort.

"Wyatt, stop."

"Why?" he panted, angry and too aroused to question the reason for it. "Don't you want me to make love to you?"

Before she could answer, he shoved her away, coming to his own fierce conclusions. When she tried to stroke his cheek, he tossed his head to the side in avoidance. His leg pounded from the exertion. His blood roared. And his body shook with the strain of denial.

"Don't bother, Beth."

"Wyatt." She said his name softly. The sound shivered along his tautly strung nerves. "It's just that I don't want to hurt you."

His laugh was short and bitter. "Too late."

"I'm sorry. I shouldn't have let things get so carried away." She was panting softly, trying to rein in her own rampant emotions. "It's my fault."

She was totally missing his point.

Then she said all soft and honey sweet, "I've missed you, Wyatt."

He went stiff. His voice was chill. "Really? When did you find the time?"

She sat back then, all the tenderness in her expression erased in an instant. He might as well have slapped her. The impact of his words had the same sharp result. Hastily, she struggled to draw up her own defenses. How fast the mood had changed. It seemed impossible that a moment ago, they'd been feverishly kissing. They regarded one another for a silent, combative moment, then she stood.

"I brought your dinner."

"I'm not hungry anymore."

"I'll leave it just in case."

"Don't bother. And if you're so worried about hurting me, maybe you should take one of the other rooms so I can rest better by myself."

"That's probably a good idea."

And while he watched stoically, she pulled some of her clothes from the dresser drawers, slamming them noisily in a show of temper before marching to the door. She paused there and flung back at him, "Call if you need me for anything."

"I don't."

She stiffened. "Yes, I seem to remember you telling me that. I should have listened."

And she was gone.

Chapter Ten

None of the spare bedrooms were fit for human habitation. Sure Wyatt was aware of that when he'd suggested she find other accommodations, Beth stewed. She was sorely tempted to find her lodgings halfway back to Chicago. Let him drag himself where he needed to go. Let him go hungry and thirsty. Let him holler at empty rooms. He deserved it. He didn't *need* her.

But the kiss stopped her. As angry as she was, as hurt as she was feeling, the passion of that kiss would not release her. Wyatt cared.

He may have had a strange way of showing it, but he cared. And she wouldn't leave him knowing that.

So she did her best to make do with a musty room, with its rusty and antiquated bathroom, with sheets that hadn't been aired for a millennium. She tried to forget a time when this was little better than she was used to. Life as a Marston had spoiled her with finer things. In less than a year, she'd grown accustomed to comfort, to having the best ever at hand and she'd liked that benefit even if she wasn't so particularly pleased with some of the others.

When did you have time?

His sarcasm wounded because it wasn't far from the truth. She'd become more caught in the rewards and requirements of being Mrs. Wyatt Marston than she was in living out the role itself. Deep in pensive thought, she stretched out on the bed. And she drove herself half crazy trying to figure out what made Wyatt Marston tick.

He was upset about losing the loan. She could understand that. She shared his frustration. So why didn't he confide his feelings instead of lashing out at her? Didn't he realize that together, they just might be able to come up with something? No, not the self-contained Wyatt Marston. And why the continued jibes at her job loyalty? What had she done that was so wrong? She'd married into a family with high expectations and high visibility. Gretchen had been quick to let her know what would be required of a Marston wife. She'd knocked herself out learning to fit in, to not be an inner-city embarrassment. Boyd had been just as quick to tell her how she could be an asset to the family. She'd so wanted to be a part of Wyatt's life, to work together as a team, the way she did with his father. How could her husband resent her for that? How dare he resent her for that! He'd never told her what he expected from her. If he had a problem with her long hours, why hadn't he said so? If he felt neglected, why didn't he do something about it?

Well, he had. He'd left for parts unknown instead of confronting her. He sidestepped the issues, then blamed her for the fallout that followed.

He hadn't mentioned divorce, but the shadow of it hung over their every meeting. He was so bitter, so discontent. He had to be thinking about it, too. Maybe she should push Boyd's offer of Denver, establishing that she'd be fine without Wyatt's support in case his sense of responsibility was all that was holding him within their marriage. Would she be easing his conscience or throwing gas on the fire? But if he wasn't thinking about it, she didn't want to be the one to bring it up. She didn't want to be the one to plant that particular seed of disillusionment as the only solution.

Beth tossed on the old mattress, shifting to find a spot between its broken springs. She didn't want to lose her husband, but she knew things couldn't continue as they stood.

So where did that leave them?

Unable to sleep, for starters.

"Beth."

She stirred on the lumpy mattress and the smell of mildew made her grimace. Morning had broken. Light streamed weakly through the cloudy window glass. She ached all over. A sleeping bag upon cold ground had been more comfortable, but at least this roof didn't leak.

"Beth!"

She realized then what had woken her. Wyatt's cry of distress. She bolted from the bed and raced into the adjoining room. There, she paused in the doorway, confused by the room's emptiness.

"Wyatt?"

"In here," came the begrudging reply. From the bathroom.

She went to look in and couldn't contain her smile. Wyatt was reclined in the big tub, his cast resting on its edge and his features a glowering study of annoyance.

"Yes?"

"Don't just stand there smirking," he growled. "Give me a hand."

"You can't manage the soap?"

"Very amusing. I'm clean, I just can't get out. Are you going to help or do I have to call a wrecker?"

"I'll help." She struggled to compose her face. That became impossible when she drew close enough to view his naked form. Oh, he was a gorgeous man. An irritable man, at the moment so she didn't dare linger over the scenery as she would have liked to. She put down her hand and scolded, "What are you doing in there, anyway?"

"What do you usually do in a tub? I'm washing off about two inches of sweat. I got tired of my sheets sticking to me and I needed a change of clothes. When Artemus wouldn't come downwind of me, I knew I had to do something before

169

he decided to bury me. I knew I should have finished plumbing the shower."

Beth was grinning. She couldn't help it. She
grabbed hold of his slippery forearm and he
gripped the tub edge with the other hand. It was
like wrestling a beached whale. Once momentum
took over, the weight of the cast dropped him
onto the carpet on hands and one knee with a
shout of complaint.

"Okay?"

"Oh, hell yes. What do you think?"

She thought the gleam along his sleek back
and hard buttocks too tempting to ignore. Her
hand skimmed down that slick terrain under the
guise of offering assistance. In doing so, she created her own private misery. The feel of him kin-
dled all sorts of needs.

"Think you can get me up without a crane?"

Now there was a thought.

Beth shook her mind out of the sensual gutter
and forced herself to concentrate on the immediate problem. "You grab on and we'll lift together
on three." His hands curled over the caps of her
shoulders as he levered up on his bad knee. His
breath was coming faster, with more difficulty.

"One . . . two . . . three."

They struggled for a few awkward seconds but
managed to get him standing. He leaned into her,
wet and shivery from the effort. Beth held him
easily, loving the damp heat of his skin against
her, wishing she could feel it more personally
from top to bottom. Her palms curved around

170

his ribcage, feeling it expand in jerky spasms. Another time, she would have continued that caress but now, she was too aware of his distress to allow her desire for him to escalate. Better she care for his pain than encourage her own passions.

"How you doing?"

"Better." He was breathing hard. "Well, I'm clean anyway and that's something. Hand me a towel."

Reluctant to surrender even one damp inch of him to a covering of terry cloth, she begrudgingly did as he asked. He wrapped the towel around his neck, not about his hips. They'd been married almost a year. A gesture of modesty wasn't natural between them.

But neither was the tension.

Wyatt didn't step back, at least not right away. He continued to hang onto to the stabilizing strength his wife offered while indulging his senses in the more fragile aspects of her. Like the faint tease of perfume. The softness of her unbound hair as he rubbed his scratchy morning face into it. The gentle rock of her breathing that moved her breasts against his chest in a delicate rhythm. For a moment, those frail things held the power to conquer his pain and he reveled in them, grateful and greedy for more.

Beth would have gladly stood there all day just to hold him, just to experience the hard beat of his heart up against her and to know the security of his embrace. But he was dripping and chilling

171

where exposed to the cool air. And their massing awareness of one another wasn't going to accomplish anything. At least not within the crowded boundaries of the bathroom.

"You'd better dry off."

"Thanks for the helping hand. Will you accept my road service card for the tow?" His words brushed warm along her brow and that was payment enough.

"I'll bill you," she said in a husky rumble. Then she stepped back before things got carried away. The atmosphere was definitely getting steamy in the enclosed space. "Can I give you a lift someplace? Back to bed?"

"No way. I've spent enough days horizontal. I've got my crutches. I'm going to brush my teeth and shave, then I'm going to sit in a chair and vegetate from a vertical position."

Beth almost protested that he shouldn't push himself, but he sounded too determined to be dissuaded by cautious concerns. So she bowed to his choices. "While you're finishing up in here, I'll get you something to put on. The clothes you were wearing and your sheets could stand up by themselves. Is there a machine here or do I have to beat them over a rock?"

He smiled. That flash of white teeth against lean, stubbled cheeks was heart-melting. "Mani's got a top loader you can use. We're not totally in the Dark Ages up here."

"That's nice to know."

"Do you know how to wash clothes?"

"There are a lot of things I know how to do that might surprise you."

She slapped her palm against his bare flank without thinking. The intimacy of that gesture surprised both of them. Then Beth gave a strained smile and backed out of the bathroom. Wyatt balanced on one leg, leaning his hip against the vanity while applying the towel to the damp contours of upper body. And he watched his wife move about the bedroom. She was wearing little more than lace. Beth had a collection of the sexiest underthings he'd ever seen and she looked great in them. This morning, the beige skim of her short nightgown over the familiar swells and hollows of her body was almost more than he could take. Especially when that scrap of fabric clung with dampness borrowed from their close contact. She bent over to strip the sheets and he tore his gaze from the graceful column of her long legs and the provocation of barely clad bottom to swaddle the evidence of his arousal with the towel. And he began to scour his teeth with a vengeance.

Cleanliness feeling one hundred percent better on him, Wyatt began to hobble back into the bedroom under his own awkward steam to the chair she'd angled by the window bay. So he could look out and watch life passing him by, he assumed wryly. When he collapsed into the chair, slightly winded and flushed, and let his crutches drop on the floor beside him, Beth brought him a pair of sweat bottoms and a T-shirt.

"I tore the elastic out of the right leg," she was saying. She was looking everywhere but at the towel so briefly shielding him. "You should be able to pull them on over the cast." She dropped the garments on his lap, grabbed a pair of her jeans and a sweater and headed for the door in a hurry. As if she wanted to escape the sight of him dressing. "I'll bring up some breakfast," she called without looking back. He could hear her quick, light step on the stairs. And Wyatt smiled pensively to think of her so flustered as he began to put his clothes on.

The day dragged on interminably to a man confined to cast and chair. Within an hour, Wyatt grew bored watching the light play on the surface of the lake. He wanted to feel the moist, cool air on his face, to stride across the pine-laden ground, to something—anything. Beth appeared long enough to deliver his tray and remove it. She supplied him with some magazines he'd already thumbed through in the hospital and was so spare on conversation, he was left moody and lonesome. The confrontation of the night before had obviously made him persona non grata except at feeding time. Apparently, her conscience wouldn't allow her to starve him to death. Even if she was willing to let him waste away in boredom. Even Artemus was a poor companion, preferring to race about outdoors rather than lie faithfully at his master's immobile feet.

What drove Wyatt truly crazy was the sound of industry from the rooms below. He could hear

Beth moving, could recognize the tunes she was humming. He heard the sounds of water and pails and the shush of stiff brush bristles, and that filled up some of the time as he made his imagination work to supply the visuals. What was she doing down there? Spring cleaning? His Beth who sent their clothes to the cleaners and did no more in the kitchen than switch on the coffee maker?

Mani brought his lunch, but she was in too big a rush to tend the bread baking in her oven to spend much time talking. So he sat alone and he moped over his isolation. And he fretted over the future of the lodge and his marriage, wanting desperately to save both. But not knowing how.

"You look like a man in deep thought," came a sudden wry observation.

Wyatt turned toward Jimmy as his friend sauntered into the bedroom and grinned, grateful for the interruption. "You mean in deep coma."

Jimmy laughed and came to settle on the edge of the bed. "How are you feeling?"

"Tired of people asking how I feel. I'm bored and I'm climbing the walls."

"Well, then, at least you're getting your exercise."

"Ha, ha. How did the flight to Ontonagon go? I saw you take off this morning." His tone reflected his envy.

"Fine. Made us some ready cash which we can use just to keep your pretty little wife in cleaning solution."

175

Wyatt frowned in confusion.

"You didn't tell me she was such a whirlwind. She's got half the downstairs shining like the finish on a new Oldsmobile. And she's been weeding out the more offensive pieces of furniture."

"Beth? What's she doing that for?"

Jimmy shrugged. "Maybe she doesn't like living in the collected dirt of ages."

"She's not living here," Wyatt corrected tersely.

"Oh? Could have fooled me. She isn't acting like someone just passing through."

"What do you mean?" He absolutely refused to recognize the lurch of hope shaking through his chest.

"She's just full of suggestions for the lodge—remodeling, rewiring, setting hottubs on a private patio overlooking the lake. She's even talked to Mani about using her family's recipes in a cookbook, you know the old way on one side, the nineties version on the other. She said one of the hotel chefs would help convert the old logging recipes to fit modern appliance and time constraints. Said it would be a great money maker with the tourists. Clever, huh?"

"Yes. Beth's very clever." He said that sourly. "But all the great ideas in the world won't add up to squat if we don't have the money to get this place off the ground."

"We could apply for another loan at another bank."

Wyatt sighed heavily. "What good would it do if my father has sabotaged my credit rating? If only I had some other kind of liquid assets. All I've got that's worth anything, that I can get my hands on, that is, is my half of the hotel shares and they wouldn't be enough."

"Unless Beth put in her half, too."

Wyatt stared at him.

"Wouldn't hurt to ask, you know. The answer might surprise you." Jimmy slapped his hand down on his friend's sound knee and stood. "Well, some of us have to work for a living. You think about it. A woman who would clean house is not a woman to be dismissed lightly."

And Wyatt had little else to do for the rest of the day but think.

The air was cool and the coffee hot. Add to that, the vivid splendor of the sunset and Beth was certain things didn't get any better this side of a television commercial.

She sipped the dark brew and enjoyed examining the fruits of her labor. The sun porch was close to perfect. Its streakless windows gave a clear view of the lake. The smooth stone floor and rough pine walls attested to the rugged heritage of the land. She liked the stark simplicity, swept clean of cobwebs and clutter. The only things she'd add were unintrusive sofas lining the interior wall so guests could comfortably sit and soak up the peaceful surroundings. Much the way she was. Never had she seen a palette of colors like those melting into still waters. Never had she experienced such marvelous tranquility. Such pleasant exhaustion. Anyone who complained about fatigue after scheduling appointments and attending meetings had obviously never spent the afternoon on hands and knees scrubbing a floor.

How had she lost those feelings of attachment to simple physical routine? She'd been raised to believe honest toil was a sign of responsibility. Her mother had taught her that to do for a man was a woman's greatest accomplishment. Of course, she'd dismissed that in a hurry in the waning of her adolescent years. She was too liberated to believe such antifeminist ideas. Too independent. But she couldn't dismiss how good it had felt caring for Wyatt these last few days. It hadn't been a particularly pleasant job but it had been satisfying. Had she been pulled so far up into the machinery of the Marston hotel chain that she had forgotten how to relate on less than a corporate level? Wyatt had once remarked that she was a caring and compassionate person. Would he still say that today? Or had the stresses of maintaining her success weaned simple, strong emotions from her? She didn't like to think so.

Mani had taken Wyatt his dinner so Beth could finish the windows while the light held. A reasonable excuse, she thought. One that wouldn't sound as though she was trying to avoid the inevitable. One that wouldn't betray her cowardice when it came to going upstairs where Wyatt was waiting.

Beth took another sip of her coffee and tried

to draw the serenity of the woodland scene in as a balm to her troubled soul. Her hesitation aggravated her. There was no point in slaving to please empty rooms. There was no great accomplishment in blisters and a sore back, not if they meant nothing in the long run. This wasn't her home to care for. She needed to come out of hiding behind her scrub brushes and mop pails and get down to business. Unless she came to terms with the distance levering between her and Wyatt, she'd have no place in his current plans. And the fear that she could never fit into them was the fear that had her lingering alone watching the setting sun.

Never had she dreaded or anticipated a meeting more. Wyatt Marston had her heart and mind in a turmoil. On a practical level, she knew just what she had to say and what she had to hear from him in return. However, whenever the opportunity was ripe, her emotions mucked up her clarity of vision. Sensory stimuli kept intruding upon her rational thought processes. The way her husband looked all bed-rumpled in the morning and how it had felt to wake beside him. How enticing the sheen of bath water appeared upon a form she was hardly unfamiliar with. How good it felt to be close, to be held, to share heat and heartbeats. And how quick the passion of a moment could be destroyed by a moody chill or an unexplained reserve. She was a basket case of indecision. The words demanding a confrontation wouldn't come, not when she feared the outcome would devastate her. As long as she continued the tenuous status quo, she could remain with him. If only she could bear the pain of distance.

But she couldn't. She couldn't pretend she wanted to spend another night on a lumpy mattress in a room separate from the man she longed for. She didn't want to scourge herself with laborious tasks rather than face the consequences of her shaky marriage. She didn't want to be content with her own company when she could share the satisfaction of the perfect sunset with the man she loved.

If he tried to push her away, it was time to hold her ground.

"Hey, how about some coffee?"

Wyatt greeted the suggestion with a small smile and a husky, "Sounds good." He was propped up on the bed, bolstered by pillows with his bum leg stretched out in front of him. He'd been watching the sun set, too. But he took greater pleasure in watching his wife move across the room. He was as eager for companionship as he was hungry for the sight of her. So he was careful not to rock the boat of truce.

"Here you go. It's hot."

He took the cup and cradled it between his hands. Nice hands, Beth noticed. Strong hands. The hands of a man who could work the woods for a living. Funny she'd never viewed them quite that way before. Or him. The awareness gave her a decidedly vulnerable quiver. She liked the sensation.

Wyatt stared into his cup and mentioned, "Jimmy's been singing your praises. He seems to think you could save even a sinking albatross like this."

She didn't smile and for a moment, he feared he'd taken the wrong kind of risk in bringing it up. Then she sat down on the foot of his bed, not intimately close but comfortingly near, and she regarded him sincerely.

"I'd like to."

"Why?"

"Because I want to see you succeed in this, Wyatt." When he didn't answer—when he couldn't answer, she continued softly. "I'm sorry about the loan. I wish there was something I could do."

Ask her, his logic prodded but he held back, uncertain and too cautious to plunge into trust so easily. What reason did she have to invest such a sum in a mutual goal when their future together was unstable? Why should she pledge her security on the chance that he could make this place work? It was his dream, his risk, not hers. And what if she should say yes, and he should fail?

Instead of answering, Wyatt shrugged philosophically. "I'll come up with something."

She smiled and her confidence was a sweet shock to his system. "I know you will."

Perhaps it wasn't the wisest time to ask, but

suddenly, he had to know. "How long are you staying, Beth?"

As long as you need me, she wanted to answer. As long as you want me. But she didn't quite dare. She was afraid he'd say he didn't and she'd have no reason to linger on. Instead, she told him, "I took two weeks off."

"Two weeks." Did he sound as shaken as he felt inside. Two weeks and she'd be gone. Having a time limit put the pressure on and made the inevitability of parting a terrible reality. He wanted to plead, don't go, but he heard the sarcastic drip of his own voice saying, "I'm surprised my father would allow it."

"I didn't give him a choice," she responded grittily.

Good for you, he thought. Stand up to the old tartar. But for her, there was a doubtful smile. "Vacation time? I'd have thought you'd want to save that to go to Europe or on some luxury cruise."

"This seemed more important. At the time." Her temper was chafing. Her words snapped. He didn't have to be a genius to figure her meaning. If he wasn't careful, he was going make her regret that decision. He softened his tone and his features, sparing a thin smile.

"What? Soaping floors and putting up with grumpy invalids?"

"Humbling penance for the rest of my charmed life, I'm sure." Then, she smiled. It was just a small break in the surface of her stoicism, but it

182

was just the crack needed to break the tension apart. Wyatt grinned and suddenly their gazes were mingling, filled with warm, inviting things before either of them thought to look away.

"I'm glad you're here."

He'd said that before but she hadn't dared believe it. But now . . . Beth held her breath. Her heart was hammering like crazy

"I'm mean," he concluded awkwardly, "I'd have hated to put all this onto Mani. I know I've been a real pain."

She smiled but didn't deny it. Didn't, because he'd just snatched back all the tender things that had started to wake inside her. Why couldn't he have just left the compliment alone instead of turning it into a backhanded remark. He wanted her here to ease the load on his friends. Not because he wanted anything else. She started to get up but Wyatt possessed himself of her hand.

What a stupid thing to say, Wyatt scolded himself but he couldn't take the words back. Couldn't even though he wanted to. He saw the way they hurt her and that was the last thing he'd wanted to do. But in a way, he wasn't sorry. Because if the thought of his indifference could wound, it meant she still had feelings for him. He let his thumb ride over her recently roughened palm.

"You'd better put some lotion on these."

"Not exactly the hands of someone who does nothing more strenuous than push buttons for a living." She laughed. The sound fell flat.

"You've more than earned your keep today. Why don't you go sink into the whirlpool for a while. I can amuse myself. I'm getting damned good at it."

Beth hesitated. The idea of a hot, pulsing bath was delicious. But she was still smarting from his attitude. "Thanks but I've got a tub in my room."

He laughed then. It was a full-bodied snort of good humor. "I've seen your tub. The water level will leave rust marks on you." The stroking of his fingers in the cup of her hand grew more sensuous, more insistent. "Use the whirlpool." He broke off before he admitted, *I got it for you.* He'd done the whole bath for her, wanting her to sink in comfort, to enjoy her nights before coming to bed. To his bed. All warmed and relaxed and ready to be loved. That's what he'd been thinking when he designed it. "Go ahead. I want you to."

Beth smiled somewhat weakly. "All right."

She took a few things from the drawers and disappeared into the bath, shutting the door but not quite closing it tight. He could hear the water run. He could hear the throb of vibration as the motor started it churning. And he didn't think there could be any agony on earth worse than sitting helpless, imagining his wife easing naked into the frothy tub.

Chapter Eleven

What could possibly keep a woman in the tub for an hour?

Wyatt wondered as he shifted uncomfortably on his bed. His skin had begun to itch beneath the cast. Nothing he could reach could effectively scratch it. It was almost as bad as the chafe of his celibacy. But not quite. Nothing could ache that badly.

Then Beth came out of the room, switching off the lights behind her. She was wearing an apricot-color fluffy robe with a quilted satin collar. Against it, her hair glimmered like gold and her skin, like rich ivory. She was bare footed and he speculated wildly on what she wore underneath. Some scrap of lace? Some skimp of silk? His mouth went dry just thinking about it. Now, if he could only manage a look-see to satisfy the foment of curiosity. He'd had few things to look forward to over the last week. This was one of the most exciting.

"Feel better?"

"Ummm. Thanks." She rolled her shoulders with a catlike grace and his muscle groups froze with tension. "I'd better go let Artemus in for the night before someone thinks he's a bear and shoots him for their stew pot."

"I didn't think you cared."

She responded to his teasing with a smile of her own. "If anyone's going to make a rug out of him, it's going to be me." Then she was gone before Wyatt thought to ask if she was coming back.

He waited, restless and anticipating, straining for the sound of her on the stairs. He heard the click of toe nails and Artie trotted in with his doggy grin and musty outdoor aroma.

"Hey, fella." He gave the beast a quick pat but discouraged him from jumping up on the bed. Wyatt wasn't too keen on sharing the space with his dog. Not tonight.

Then he made out the soft pad of her bare feet on the landing. He was about to call out to her, hoping to come up with some viable excuse, but in the end, he didn't need to. She returned to his room.

"I'm going to turn in. Do you need anything else before I do?" She paused there in the doorway, features expectant.

"No, thanks. I'm fine."

She nodded and he thought in sudden panic that she was leaving.

"Beth —"

"Yes?"

186

"Stay a while."

She didn't ask for a reason. She said, "All right," and came across the room. She stopped at the window and looked out with a wistful contentment etched upon the lovely contours of her face. "It's so quiet up here. I didn't think I'd get used to it at first, but now it feels like Mother Nature is tucking me in at night." She smiled at him somewhat sheepishly as if expecting him to laugh at that sentiment from a city girl.

He didn't. He was holding his breath.

She said it casually, as if her whole future didn't hang on his reply. "No wonder I couldn't talk you into going to Denver. How about Chicago?"

He hadn't planned to tell her yet. He wasn't aware he'd fully committed himself until he heard himself say, "I'm not going back, Beth. Even if I can't get this place going, I'll find something else. I don't want to go back to what's there."

Beth didn't look surprised. Her expression was carefully schooled to betray little if any emotion. "I don't really blame you," was all she said.

She was taking it too well and he didn't know how to take that. If it mattered to her, wouldn't she get all panicked or ask questions or . . . something? But she didn't. She looked out into the night with an air of acceptance that scared him. She didn't ask for reassurance. He didn't want to think she was relieved that he was stepping out of the picture and she was grateful to be spared the trouble of a nasty scene. Didn't she want to know where that left the two of them? He did. He was the one panicking. He was the one who needed reassurance. He had to do something to hold onto her.

Then she turned away from the darkening glass with a sigh. "I'd better let you get some rest."

"I'd rest better if you were here beside me." That slipped out, too. And to cover his clumsy attempt at seduction, he patted the comforter gently. "Unless you like that unsprung excuse for a mattress next door."

She chuckled nervously. "No. I can't say I do." Her gaze scanned the space beside him.

"Then climb on in here with me."

By flipping up one side of the covers, he was able to scoot onto the bottom sheet and pull the blankets up over him. Then, he tossed back those on the other side and looked up in invitation.

Beth hesitated but only for an instant. Then she was untying her robe. Wyatt's breath caught in a snag of anticipation. The front panels parted. Beneath it, she wore . . . flannel. Bright red, knee-length flannel with a frill of white lace at its conservative neckline. If she was at all aware of dashing his suspense to dejected smithereens, she didn't let on.

"That's new," he got out grimly.

"From my first experience with the northwoods. One can't be too warm."

Hell, he wanted to keep her warm. He'd hoped for some bit of nothing that would have her shivering. Then he could ease on up to rescue her from hypothermia. No chance of that with her in good ole flannel. No sir. At least it didn't have feet and a million little buttons. He was frowning as she slipped in between the sheets.

"What's wrong?"

"Nothing," he grumbled. "Can you reach the light?"

"Sure."

Darkness settled and with it, the anxious mood of uncertainty. The flannel had set Wyatt back and he was struggling to regroup his attack. Beth was still, trying to slow the race of her breathing. She didn't want him to think she felt anxious. Even if it was true.

"Comfortable?"

She jumped slightly. "Yes. And you?"

"Fine."

More silence.

Wyatt cleared his throat. "I seem to remember you were more comfortable over here." The covers rustled as he opened his arm, freeing the hollow at his side. She didn't wait for more of an invitation. She was there, filling the space with the round angle of her hip and shoulder, with the softness of bosom, belly and thigh. Carefully, he cinched up his arm, sealing her tightly against him. And he closed his eyes for a moment of sheer bliss.

Beth curled her arm about his middle and eased her cheek upon his shoulder. *I'm not going back*. There, he'd said it. But then, she'd known he was going to. She'd felt it right from the first.

189

This place had all the earmarks of a man making himself a home. Their apartment in Chicago was no better than a post office box. He was going to stay and she was . . . what? *What about me?* her heart cried out. *Where does that leave us?* her mind demanded. But she was silent. She couldn't speak through the fear clogging her throat. What if he told her there was no place for her in his plans? How could she stand it?

Did she want a place?

Beneath her palm, Beth felt the steady pulse of his heart. Her love for him was like that. Life-giving. Strong. Vital. But how could it continue once separated by physical distance? Especially when they were already emotionally miles apart? She had two weeks off. Then what? Back to Chicago, back to her meetings and her work while Wyatt stayed here developing his future without her? Would there be weekend commutes? Then she'd miss one because of a special event. Then another. Then several in a row. Until he didn't care if she came at all? Just like it was in Chicago. Was that what she wanted when she looked ahead? A long-distance relationship?

Would it be better to end things quickly or let them linger and die for lack of attention?

And what about the idea she'd been toying with? Staying here, living here with him. In the middle of nowhere? her sensibilities cried. There's nothing here, no city pulse, no challenging job, no . . . security. That was the fear that underlay it all. No security. She'd had nothing before. She

190

didn't want to go back to that. She was terrified of going back to that. She'd worked hard, made tremendous sacrifices in order to pad her future comfortably. Along with her love for Wyatt was always the safety of his name and his family. The relief of knowing she'd never go without. But if Wyatt cut his ties to his family, if he put all their money into this venture and he failed, where would that leave them? He wouldn't go to his father. She knew that. And in the back of her mind a horrible vision formulated: she and Wyatt in fifteen years, replaying the lives of her parents. Wyatt in a soiled T-shirt watching football on a snowy television screen, yelling for more beer while she was trying to budget the welfare check to meet their table needs. Kids underfoot, unkept and uncaring. A dead end. A nightmare.

And then the picture brightened. There was Denver. If the pain of separation got too great, if the emotional ties strained too thin to hold them together, if the risk of losing all was just too much to bear, there was always Denver. That was what she'd always wanted professionally. The perfect job. She had to consider it. She couldn't afford not to, given the situation.

Beth knew right then that if Wyatt didn't return to Chicago, neither could she. How could she work with the reminders ever at hand? His empty office. His glowering secretary. His parents. Their apartment. The staff's innuendo would be killing. She could persevere but did she want to? Not at such a cost. Without Wyatt, there was nothing in Chicago for her, either.

It was Denver or northern Michigan. In Denver, she'd have a job, security, success. Here, there were no guarantees.

Did she want a life on the isolated Keweenaw? Cut off from the challenge and excitement of the business world? Cut off from everything. With just Wyatt and his woods? Could a city girl survive so far removed from her element? No use asking those questions yet, not when the main one hung over her head. She hadn't been asked to stay in northern Michigan. If he wanted her here, wouldn't he ask? It was too much even for Wyatt Marston to assume she wouldn't need the invitation. A wife stayed with her husband. But there had to be a marriage, first. Did they have one anymore?

Asking her to share his covers for the night was not exactly the same as proposing she remain within them for the rest of their lives. But wasn't that what he meant when he took her for his wife? He hadn't asked that she give back that title.

The light stroke of his forefinger down the slope of her cheek distracted her from further thought. She lifted her head in inquiry and he met her with a kiss. A slow, sweet, will-crumbling kiss. Hers collapsed with the first feather-light touch of his tongue.

Wyatt hadn't expected it to last longer than a heartbeat. He'd been afraid if it did, she would push away. He'd meant to make the first move to

192

separate from the lush warmth of her mouth. He'd meant to, but then her lips parted and she sighed quietly. He didn't rush things. It was more important that the feelings evolve naturally, that they have time to experience all over again the simple pleasure of this mouth-to-mouth communion. It had been a long while since they'd shared such a satisfying conversation. He could think of eloquent things to say with the shifting slant of his lips, with his leisurely claim of her silken mouth. There was no fumbling for the right words, no worry that he'd phrase his feelings awkwardly or that he'd be rejected for expressing what resided in his heart. And as she returned his overtures, press for press, stroke for stroke, sigh for sigh, he no longer doubted that they were both saying the same thing.

"I love kissing you," he whispered against the welcoming softness of her. "I love the taste of you, the feel of you."

"Don't stop," she urged and he filled that yearning cavern with the deep thrust of his tongue.

She'd meant for him not to stop the words. She wanted him to continue them, to hear him say, *I love you*. As wonderful as his kisses were, they were no more explicit in meaning than his silences. They could have meant, *I love you*. They could have meant, *I need you*. They could have meant, *Don't ever leave me*. Or they could be saying, *It's been too long. I want us to make love*. And he didn't have to love her or need her

193

or want her with him forever and ever to say that. She twisted her head to one side, breaking from the luxury of his lips.

"Wyatt —"

But before she could ask him to be more specific, the mattress gave mightily and began a hard jouncing as Artemus leaped up onto the foot of it and walked, bold as brass, up between them. They had no choice but to separate to their own halves of the bed.

"Get down!" Wyatt ordered but the animal made a few spring-shaking turns and plopped, settling like a great furry barrier to any further intimacy. When Beth moved, he growled threateningly. "Artie, get down!" The dog began to lick Wyatt's face and Beth started to chuckle. "It's not funny!"

"Good night, Wyatt. Artemus." Beth put her back to the two of them and wiggled to get comfortable. She smiled at the sounds of her husband's savage curses. Artemus just moaned, oblivious to what he'd interrupted — or perhaps, very aware of it, and rested his muzzle on Wyatt's pillow.

"Your timing is lousy, pal," Wyatt grumbled, shoving the big head away. "Man's best friend. Hah!"

Artemus gave his thick tail several loud thumps in agreement.

The next morning, Wyatt tackled the stairs

194

with his crutches, wanting to eat a meal at a table instead of from a tray. With Jimmy on one side and Beth on the other, to lend support should it be needed, he made it down and Wyatt declared it worth the effort when he sat down to the breakfast feast Mani prepared. The boys had already left to meet the school bus.

It didn't take any great scrutiny for Wyatt to notice the difference in the room. It gleamed. The wood shone like satin, the window glass sparkled, dust balls had been shown the door. The heavy drapes were gone, leaving an unobstructed view of the cold Superior waters. The antique silver service was no longer black with neglect. It looked display-counter bright. If he hadn't known better, he'd have thought a whole cleaning crew had descended rather than one industrious wife. And he was proud as all get out of what she'd accomplished.

"Here are some more of those recipes."

Beth took the pile of brown papers from Mani, careful not to crumble the age-curled edges. She glanced through them and smiled in delight. "These are fabulous. What's a pasty?"

"It's like a regional meat pie," Jimmy explained. "The miners used to carry them down into the shafts hot out of the oven, keeping them warm by tucking them under their shirts. Then they'd heat them up on shovels at meal time."

"I'll make some for lunch," Mani offered.

"I won't have to carry it in my shirt, will I?"

They all laughed but Wyatt's attention was

drawn and held by the possibilities of being wedged between cotton and Beth's warm skin. And his thoughts could have kept a miner's meal hot for a week.

"I like the idea of a cookbook, don't you, Wyatt?"

Wyatt glanced at Jimmy and blinked. "What?"

"A cookbook?"

"Oh, yeah. Sure."

Beth smiled faintly and her cheeks grew rosy. Wyatt could almost suspect her of reading his mind. She studied the pages in her hand. "I'll have Frank, our chef, go through these and translate them into modern kitchenese. And when we have the books printed, we can include information on getting lodge reservations to experience the food firsthand. I think I could get copies into the hotel gift shops as well as into stores by Christmas. I'll check with my resources."

Jimmy was grinning, nodding at Wyatt with a certain degree of smugness.

"And we'll need brochures," Beth continued, her ideas gathering momentum. "I know a good printer. We'll need to supply photos. I'm sure we won't have any trouble getting some great four-color shots of sunsets and woods and of the lodge. And we'll need tourist information about what's to see and how much things cost. Have you got any kind of an agenda planned?"

Jimmy shook his head, still grinning. "No. Thought we'd leave that up to an expert."

It took Wyatt a while to get over her use of

"we" to voice the biggest roadblock to all her big schemes. "Wouldn't it be more prudent to wait until we're sure we have something to promote? We don't even know how we're going to finance this baby."

"Well, I can't help you there over the breakfast table, but I can get some basics going in the right direction."

Wyatt had to smile at the way she pushed aside their money problem as if it was a minor inconvenience. As if she had no doubts at all that he would, as promised, come up with something. As if she'd be on hand to see all the details through. He wanted to believe both things so badly, he brought up no further objections. It felt too good not to fight against the undertow of her enthusiasm.

Beth was slicing her ham steak into regimented sections. "So, what are you planning to offer the average tourist for his hard-won dollar?"

Jimmy leaned back in his chair, expression pensive. "The lodge accommodations, meals, sightseeing packages."

Beth pretended to yawn. "Very unique."

He scowled. "Naked native dancing?"

"That's better. Now, you're catching on."

"Well, there's Mani's cooking." He winked at his wife. "And the opportunity to stay in a fully restored historical site, I hope. Seaplane tours and shuttle to the Isle."

"Visits to remote ends of the earth only our STOL planes can reach." She was aware of

197

Wyatt's round-eyed stare and explained, "That's short take-off and landing."

"I know," he managed. What he was wondering was how she knew.

She smiled with a superior smugness and stirred creamer into her coffee. "It's sounding better and better. But we need a real hook."

"A place where the office can't find you—no phone, no fax, no frustrations," Wyatt interjected.

"Great." Beth had found a pen and was scribbling it down on her paper napkin. "I know some executives who'd pay an arm and a leg to have someone force them to relax. Leave your beepers at the door. They'd eat up the wilderness experience idea."

"If they're into the macho back-to-nature trip, we could offer a week in the woods like old-time loggers, with just a cross saw and axe," Jimmy suggested. "They'd get some honest blisters and the chance for some sweaty male bonding and we'd get our winter's supply of firewood."

"And we could offer overnight backpacking on the island with a guide. Once I'm mobile, that is." Wyatt grinned, falling right in with their snowballing excitement. "A cast wouldn't inspire great feelings of trust in the average tenderfoot."

Beth looked up from her notes. "If we put together a bunch of special packages like the logging and the backpacking and coordinate them with what's going on locally, I think we might have a winner here."

"A toast." Jimmy raised his coffee cup and the other three followed suit. "To the lodge and those foolish enough to invest their dreams, their time and their sweat to making it all come together."

Ceramic clinked. Over their cups, Wyatt met Beth's gaze and he offered up the faintest sketch of a smile. She returned it just as tentatively. It was a start.

Jimmy drained his cup and set it down. "Hey, Beth, I've got some rounds to make with the locals. You want to ride along and see what there is to see?"

"Sure. Let me grab my coat. I want to check with some of the area artisans. Mani, I need some names from you. I've got an idea about redoing the furniture. I think it would be perfect if we did it over the way you did the carriage house only on a grander scale, you know, all native influence mixed in with natural comfort. We could get some of that peeled pine furniture, some Indian basketry and woven seat covers and wall hangings. We'd be representing the area and keeping the money local. What do you think?"

"Sounds good. Wyatt?"

He nodded, unable to break from the study of his wife's face, so flushed with excitement and warmed by the thought of challenge. He knew Beth. She'd throw herself into a project wholeheartedly. But what would happen when all the arrangements were made, when all the details were set? What then? What could he offer to keep her busy and animated to rival the pull of city life? And how could he make sure she'd be happy with just him?

She had her challenge and now, he had his. And he could be just as determined as his tunnel-visioned wife.

After she'd driven off in Jimmy's Bronco, Wyatt decided the outdoors would do his chafing mood a world of good. Fitting the crutches under his arms, he practiced swinging through them, then, when he was confident enough, he maneuvered out onto the front porch. He breathed deeply, flushing the stagnant sickroom air from his lungs. He felt better, stronger, almost immediately. As he took in the sights and the sounds of nature, a sense of peace came over him and with it, an anxiousness for Beth's return. For the first time, he felt lonely in his favorite spot.

"Wyatt!"

He turned to see Mani waving from the back of the carriage house. He waved back.

"It's your father on the phone. Do you want me to take a message?"

Everything inside him seized up into a binding tightness. "No. I'll take it. Tell him I'm coming."

He picked his way along the pine needle path and was chagrined to find himself out of breath and sweating by the time he reached his friends' dwelling. Mani was waiting with the receiver in hand. The cord was long enough that he could stand on the back stoop.

"Hi, Dad."

"Wyatt. Is Beth there?"

His jaw clenched. "No, she's not."

"Do you know when she plans to come back home? Her clients are clamoring for her personal touch."

Were they? He was practically suffering lockjaw by then. "I thought she took two weeks."

"She did but I figured she might have cabin fever by now. You know how city girls are when you take them out of their element."

He was afraid he did know.

"I'll have her call you. You can discuss it with her."

"Do that. Oh, and how's the leg?" An afterthought. Like, "How's the weather?"

"Fine. And thanks for the plant."

"Plant?"

"Never mind."

And thanks for screwing up my life, you meddling SOB, he said to himself. Boyd wouldn't have the bad taste to bring up his coup, so Wyatt didn't either. No need to let the man know of his success in ruining all their plans. No sense in giving his father the chance to gloat.

"I'll have Beth call."

After he hung up, Wyatt worked his way laboriously back to the lodge. *Her personal touch.* The words rankled. So did the image that came to mind. Wyatt swore and took a misstep. A shaft of agony seared up his leg. For a moment, he hung on the padded support of the crutches, too blinded by pain and hurt to take another step. Then, through that haze of anguish came

201

one thought, crystal clear. Beth was here. With him. By her choice, whether it be motivated by guilt or greed or caring.

And he wasn't going to let her leave.

Chapter Twelve

Jimmy's idea of a little running around took the entire day. He drove them up and down Highway 41 and on a half dozen dirt tracks in between. By the time they returned to the lodge, Beth had a portfolio bulging with business cards and pamphlets on everything from living history museums and costumed interpreters to ghost towns and the turn of the century theater in Calumet where Sarah Bernhardt, Douglas Fairbanks, Jr., and Lillian Russell had played back in the Upper Peninsula boomtown days. She'd picked up itineraries for underground mine tours, Ojibway casinos and lighthouse museums. And she knew where to find cinnamon rolls the size of a catcher's mitt, thimbleberry fudge, dewberry jam and monk-made bread, and was carrying the samples to prove it.

The more she learned, the more she was impressed. It seemed the Keweenaw was an untapped paradise, a refuge from life's harsh realities where one could boat and fish the shorelines, creeks and many crystal clear lakes for trout, pike and walleye, where backpackers and campers could find any degree of physical challenge. It was ripe for rock hounds, bird watchers, morel seekers, driftwood collectors and photographers, a haven for hikers, history buffs and scuba divers eager to probe the old ship graveyards off the harsh coasts. It was beautiful, peaceful and still wild enough to hold a hint of danger. A lot like Wyatt Marston. And she was drawn to it in much the same way—knowing better but unable to help herself. The excitement and uncertainty were part of the appeal.

Then one fact held her stiff and silent for the ride back to the lodge. She was considering it. She was actually considering a life up in these rugged northlands.

It was craziness. She should be doing all she could to talk Wyatt into returning home, to their comfortable life, to their responsible and well-paying jobs, to the world they knew.

But even as her anxious mind fed her those arguments, her heart had the answer. To Wyatt, this was home. This was his world, where he felt comfortable. And the crazy part was, she could understand why. Maybe not completely but enough to know it would be wrong of her to insist he leave. This was the right place for him. But was it for her?

"You're quiet."

Beth glanced at Jimmy and offered a frail smile. "Just thinking."

"This is the spot to do it. Something about all

the clear air unclogs the pores in the brain. Something about our sunsets opens up the soul."

"Sounds good. Like something for the tour book." If only it was true.

"You're doing good things here, Beth," he ventured with a sidelong look. "The four of us could make one helluva team."

She said nothing and he respected her silence. But that didn't keep him from talking.

"Wyatt came up here to get in touch with those things in himself again. He lost them in Denver and in Chicago. He'd hoped to find them here, with you."

"What do you mean?"

"All I'm saying is Wyatt's the best friend I've ever had and I've always felt he deserved more than the Marston money could buy him."

She could picture Gretchen Marston cooing, *Give him my love*. "I'm not going to argue that."

"No?" Jimmy sounded surprised.

"No."

"Good." And he was grinning as he turned into the lodge's gravel drive.

At first, Beth thought the main building was dark. However, when Jimmy opened the front door for her, she could see the warm bronze of firelight radiating from the hearth in the great room. And when the two of them came closer, they could see Wyatt waiting there before it, stretched out on a thick quilt, sipping wine. Jimmy put on the brakes.

"I think I'll just say good night here."

"Oh, Jimmy come on in. Don't be silly." Did her voice betray the sudden quivering of nerves inside her?

"No. I think this is definitely a three's a crowd situation." He raised his voice to call, "Brought her home all safe and sound. 'Night, Wyatt."

"Thanks, Jimmy."

Noting the look of abandonment on the lovely Mrs. Marston's face, Jimmy pressed her arm with a bolstering fondness and gave a nod that she interpreted to mean, *Good luck*. She said his name suddenly but her request took him off guard.

"Jimmy, could you keep Artemus in with you tonight?"

"I—sure. I guess so. The boys would love to wrestle with him." Then he got the message loud and clear. Three's a crowd. He gave a low whistle and the big dog came trotting from the kitchen area. "Hey, you monster. You're coming home with me. Let's see what Mani has for dinner, shall we?"

The dog wagged his tail in full agreement.

Jimmy opened the door and Artemus bounded out. "Have a nice evening," he told her, his blue eyes crinkling with a wicked amusement.

"We will." That was a promise she'd do everything she could to keep.

She shut and locked the door behind him, then took a deep breath before advancing into the glow of the gathering room. She moved with a taut-muscled stride, senses both wary and expectant. The setting sizzled, like the big half-charred

206

logs in the fire, filling the room with sensual suggestion. Was that what Wyatt had in mind or were her own long-denied yearnings running away with her? Up to this point, the scene had been fairly safe. How much danger could a man with a broken leg present? She certainly wouldn't have any trouble outrunning him.

But she didn't want to run and therein lay the danger.

"Hi."

Wyatt looked up from his study of light playing upon crystal. Flickering shadows created an air of intense mystery over his lean features. His mouth moved in a brief suggestion of a smile. "Hi, yourself. Have a good time?"

"A great time. I didn't realize there was so much to see. I brought back souvenirs." She brandished her tote bag and continued to clutch it in front of her as if it would offer some protection against the hot blue simmer of his stare. "I've got lots of stuff we can go over."

"We can look at it tomorrow. Some wine? It's Pinot Noir. That's your favorite, isn't it?"

"Yes." He knew it was. She set down the collection of brochures she'd planned for a distraction, they were useless as a buffer now, and walked up to the edge of the quilt. He poured and extended the glass. She had to bend to take it.

"Sit down. You look tired. Jimmy wear you out with his sightseeing tour?"

"I enjoyed it. Really." She levered out of her

sensible boots and lowered herself to the make-shift pallet. It was soft, buffering the hardwood floor the way the logs did the evening chill. Cozy. Intimate. As intimate as the way his gaze moved over her. Her heart came to a standstill of antici-pation.

"Mani sent over some pasties for you to try. I've been keeping them warm for you."

She noticed for the first time, that a long-han-dled fireplace popcorn maker was angled in adja-cent to the flames. Wyatt pulled it out and opened the top half. He'd stuck the pastry cov-ered meat and potato pies inside to retain their heat. He lifted the two of them out gingerly. They were plump, the size of small footballs. And they smelled heavenly.

They dined on pasties and wine, not saying much but doing a lot of communicating through quick, darting glances. When Beth had eaten as much as her stomach would hold and the fruit of the vine had her as mellow as an aged vintage, she leaned back against the raised hearthstones and emitted a languid sigh.

"I'm stuffed."

"If you were a lumberjack, you could put away a half dozen of those."

"If I was a lumberjack, I'd be inappropriately dressed." She toyed with one of her dangling ear-rings. Wyatt smiled. His gaze moved from there to a leisurely study of her lower lip, then down to the curve of cotton over her very womanly con-tours.

"Can't argue that," he said somewhat hoarsely as he refilled her glass.

The fire snapped and crackled lazily, inviting a quiet mood to settle at its hearth. Beth stared into the flames, her expression becoming soft and wistful. Wyatt traced her profile with his gaze, wondering with a sudden shock of insight how the two of them could be married and yet be strangers to one another. He knew he was to blame for a lot of that. In all fairness, he couldn't fault Beth and her obsession for work with the isolation surrounding them. She was an open book as far as her past and her feelings, most of the time. He was the one who had trouble committing emotions into words. He'd begun to guard them close at an earlier age. It was a learned thing, sharing and trusting, and he'd never had the opportunity. He felt that lack within him now. Now when he wanted to reach out to the woman beside him.

She was near enough to touch with a caress. But touching wasn't the route of intimacy he desired. They'd had that kind of closeness before and it drew them together only up to a point. To a point where words were needed and he'd never been able to make himself say them. Here with her now, admiring the way firelight burnished her flawless skin, stirred by the way it played upon the moistness of her mouth, Wyatt knew they might never be this close again. He might not ever have the chance to speak to her of the things that mattered to him if he didn't speak them now. And cautions built by a lifetime of loneliness couldn't best the need to make contact with the one he loved.

"Thanks."

Beth turned to look at him. "For what?"

"For what you've been doing here. You've no idea what this place means to me. I'd do just about anything for the chance to make it work. I guess out of all the places I've been, this is the only one that's felt like home to me."

She nodded as if that was no surprise to her. Encouraged, he continued.

"My mom was from a little town near here. Her family goes all the way back to the early days of copper and logging, just like Jimmy's. She always carried a piece of this place around with her in her heart, in her soul. I must have inherited that from her. She never owned any of the ground up here. I know it must sound strange, but it was important to her and it got to be important to me. A piece of ground that had meaning, that stretched back generations. A place to belong. Dad never understood. He wanted to take what the land could offer, not give back to the land. He could see no value in these woods, in these waters. No monetary value, that is. And that's all he was ever looking for. They could never get together on that. Mom wanted permanence. Dad wanted position.

"He was working in the Michigan Avenue hotel as resident manager, so we were living there. I guess I kind of grew up in the business. Gretchen's father owned it and a chain of about six others—hotels and glitzy resorts. She liked my dad's ambitions and Dad like her business portfolio. I don't know how long they carried on before Mom died. She knew. Everyone knew."

Beth's fingertips eased over the back of his hand. He flinched at the unexpected overture and she began to draw away immediately. Instead of allowing her retreat, he twined his fingers around hers and hung on tight. There was a sense of security in that joined grasp and he clung to it.

"When Dad and Gretchen married—one of those merger arrangements, I'm sure, she got her manager and he got her money—we moved out to Denver. I lost more than my mom that year. I lost her affection and attention and I was cut off from her family and my friends up here. Dad couldn't see any reason to let me come back. He'd already decided that I'd get my college major in business and fall right in beside him making Marston money. Oh, he loved it. The Marston chain got the reputation of being the carnivore of hotels, chewing up anything weaker and swallowing it whole. What Dad couldn't incorporate, he destroyed. He thought of me the same way. Either I was with him or he wanted no part of me. So I conformed. Hell, I was sixteen, suddenly rich, in a new place, with all new people. Dad picked my friends and my school and the kind of car I drove. And I got used to telling myself it didn't matter, that he was doing it because he wanted the best for me, that it was his way of showing that he cared."

His smile took a twist of irony and Beth's heart ached for the aloneness she felt in him. How well she could relate to his sense of panic and isolation. She'd experienced it firsthand when they'd married. But she'd had Wyatt to get her through the difficult adjustments. He'd had no one. Not surprising that he'd adopted that shell of reserve to protect a frightened kid from an overwhelming situation. He didn't have her street toughness to fall back upon.

"I'm sure it was his way of telling you he loved you," she reassured him quietly.

Wyatt gave a disbelieving snort. "Yeah, well, I might have believed it once." He raked his fingers through his hair in frustration, still clutching at hers tightly with those of the other hand.

She wanted to believe it, because she genuinely liked and respected Wyatt's father. He'd been so good about giving his advice and support to her as he groomed her to follow his lead. But would he have been so generous, so charitable if she'd chosen a different path? For the first time, she wondered about the motive for Boyd Marston's benevolence as Wyatt continued talking.

"When I started college, Gretchen gave me an obscene amount of money, probably just to get me out of the way. I didn't have the kind of maturity to handle it. I thought of it as my ticket to independence. I was going to show my dad I could make it on my own. I invested in a couple of things, foolishly. Two of them went bust for lack of planning and the third turned out to be borderline illegal. I went from on top of the world to hip deep in debt, but Dad was there to bail me out. He paid off the right people to keep everything quiet and to keep me in my exclusive school and snotty clubs. Then he used it to step down hard on the back of my neck every time I tried to make a move on my own. I graduated from college and stepped right into my father's shadow. He had me thinking I'd lost the right to my own judgment. I didn't make waves, kept a nice conservative look about me and was vice-president of Marston Hotels by the time I was twenty-seven." Again he laughed caustically. "It was my destiny, he used to say. I believed him. I had no reason to think otherwise." He paused and looked up. "Until you."

Something warming and wonderful reached out to him through the tenderness in Beth's expression. It wasn't as blatant as a touch or a word, yet it penetrated to the heart of him where things lay broken and poorly pieced back together with a cement of defensiveness. He didn't feel that need to retreat and take cover now. Not with her. And for a moment, he experienced a terrible regret for not speaking these things to her long ago, for missing the strength she had to offer with her empathy and care.

"You gave me confidence, Beth. You made me feel like I was important, that I was capable of

213

great things, sound decisions. You believed in me."

"I still do."

"I haven't felt that from you for a long time." He said that quietly, without malice, without blame. Just a soft statement of fact. There were tears in her eyes when she replied.

"I'm sorry. What happened, Wyatt? What went wrong between us?"

"I don't know. If I did, I would have stopped it. All I know was one day you weren't there for me anymore and I didn't know how to get you back."

"Did you want me back?"

"I still want you back."

Wyatt leaned toward her and she moved to meet him. His shoulder bumped the glass she held and Beth gasped in dismay as wine spilled on the bodice of her blouse. She reared back instantly and began to swipe at the stain. She looked up at him in frustration.

"You'd better go rinse that out," he advised softly.

Beth hesitated. He'd just started opening up to her. She'd be dogged if she was going to let something like a wine stain come between a year of silence and the sudden flow of communication begun here on the hearth. "It's all right—"

"Don't be silly. Go change." Then, as if he understood her reservations, Wyatt smiled slightly. "Go ahead. I'm not going anywhere."

There was a patient look of commitment in his

face that convinced her she could risk the interruption. Still, she hurried, racing up the steps, flinging the shirt into the bathroom sink to soak. She wasn't about to let this moment pass by.

Wyatt was waiting, his expression pensive, his smile curving up on one side when he saw she wore her apricot robe. He refused to speculate on what she had on beneath it. It wasn't healthy. She'd bound her hair back in a loose braid, but trails of it strayed along her cheeks with a defining softness. A very feminine, very sexy look. Beth settled beside him, closer this time, ending the pretense of a companionable chat. And his instinct was to hold her at bay for reasons of self-preservation. He said the first thing he could think of.

"Dad wants you to call."

"Oh? Something urgent?"

"He didn't say."

It didn't take a psychoanalyst to recognize the edge creeping back into his voice. He was tensing, expecting to be put second on her list of priorities. And oh, how guilty she felt for conditioning him to think that way. Time to break those old patterns. She tossed back the tail of thick blond hair with a careless gesture. "If it was something vital, he would have said so. Since it's not, he can wait until morning."

Wyatt stared at her for a guarded moment.

"Where were we?" she prompted with a huskiness that ruffled all the right responses. She could feel him relax.

215

Wyatt looked at her lips, thinking of the kiss they'd been so close to sharing. Wanting it. Wanting her. But needing to set aside the physical long enough to reestablish the emotional.

"I was doing a lot of talking."

"Long overdue."

"I guess it is."

"Don't stop."

He sighed, forcing himself to overcome his inbred resistance to the type of soul baring she requested. "I want to make a go of this place, Beth," he began with a tenacious strength. "I want it more than I've ever wanted anything. I want to do something right, something good. This is it. I can feel it. Everything's here just waiting to come together. The past, the future, my friends. I know I can do this. I know it, Beth."

"I know you can, too."

She touched him then, briefly skimming her fingertips down one determinedly set cheek. Wyatt froze. When she did that, touched him like that, he never knew how to react. His first impulse was to jerk back to avoid—what? He wasn't sure. Her spontaneous gestures unnerved him, always had. Maybe because he couldn't reciprocate in the same easy manner. He was startled and wary of the unplanned. But this time, he held himself very still, going so far as to lean slightly into the pressure of her palm. Then he was rewarded by her lingering caress upon his face, his hair, the back of his neck. A little bit more of the barricade around his heart chipped away.

"I can't give up the things that are important to me, Beth," Wyatt spoke with firm conviction. "I won't be like my father. All he knows how to love is business. He doesn't give a damn about anything or anyone else. I'm tired of him using me in the name of family when he doesn't know the slightest thing about it. Family is what Jimmy and Mani have with their boys. It's all I've ever wanted. And I want it here, at the lodge. I want it here where he hasn't been able to spoil my memories or snatch away my hope."

"And you'll have it."

Beth leaned forward, her lips brushing over his like a whispered promise, then returning as a heated vow. He didn't so much as breathe, letting her mouth move on his, letting her tongue curl and stroke his hungrily. Then the reality of her desire hit and hit hard. And low. His hands came up to cup the curve of her rib cage as her forward momentum carried them down onto the thick quilt. Wisps of her hair spilled around his face, silken and scented. The remembered sweetness of loving her wiped all else from his mind. They were husband and wife and they belonged to one another. What else mattered?

He tasted of wine and urgency and Beth tasted deeply, frequently, endlessly. She inched up the bottom of his T-shirt until her palms had room to slide in next to his skin. He was warm and hard of frame. She rubbed her palms higher, luxuriating in his tensile strength and masculine furring. She dipped lower, finding and delighting in that same warmth, that same hardness, only here the proportions were on a much grander scale. He tensed. She shivered.

"Wyatt, I want us to make love," she breathed against his mouth. His eyes opened, staring up into hers, reading of a need to rival his own. And flat on his back with his leg in a cast, he smiled.

"As long as you don't expect any fancy athletics, we should do just fine."

She sat back on her heels and reached for the knot to her belt. "I'm all for old-fashioned simplicity." She parted the robe without the slightest hesitation. Beneath it, she wore—nothing.

His hands were there to push the warm fabric from the smooth slope of her shoulders. Then she melted down on top of him, a soft armful of feminine curves and evocative movements. She kissed his welcoming lips, at the same time gliding her knee over the fullness of him outlined boldly by the hug of cotton jersey. Wyatt's breathing shuddered and settled into a jerky tempo. His palms stroked over her lightly, charting bare back and silky upper arms, needing to hold her as much as he needed to hurry. The waiting was agony. The suspense was exquisite.

It wasn't as awkward as he feared it would be. The second he felt the fullness of her breasts straining against his palms, their peaks tight with arousal, Wyatt forgot all about the limitations of a leg cast. Beth made it easy for him to forget.

She was as creative as she was clever. She made it more game than struggle to get him out of his T-shirt and sweatpants. However, when she slid against him with the satiny warmth of skin on skin, the sense of play was swallowed up by some very hot and serious desire.

It couldn't last, though they both tried to prolong the moment with long, wet kisses and lingering caresses. Kissing, touching only added to the sensory urgency. The buildup of eager passions compelled them to seek a conclusion to the months of wearing tension, to seek release within one another.

Beth came down over him, surrounding him with the heat and strength of her body. She was liquid fire. And like a flame, she moved above him, consuming him, tormenting him to the edge of control with her soul-searing undulations. His hands were on her hips, encouraging the rhythm that would carry them to the pinnacle of shared relief. It engulfed them; they were consumed by fierce, shimmering waves of heat that burned down into a glowing warmth. Then, they lay content and tangled together, listening to the companionable pop and sizzle of logs in the hearth, to the satisfied rasp of one another's breathing.

"How's the leg?" Beth whispered.

"What leg?"

She smiled and drew her finger along the curve of his smile.

Wyatt glanced around. "I've been expecting Artie to barge in on everything."

Beth grinned wickedly. "Artie had other plans for this evening. He left you to your own resources."

"And how'd I do?"

She scooped the hair back from her face and smiled down at him. Then her expression sweetened with sincerity. "I'd wait a lifetime to share what we just did with you. Don't make me wait that long again. I've missed you, Wyatt."

He didn't say anything, but she couldn't overlook the sudden shadows clouding his gaze. It was as if he didn't quite believe her. But she would make him believe. If it took all night.

And she started with a convincing kiss.

Chapter Thirteen

The sleeping bags came in handy.

After dozing on the fireside quilt for an hour or so, it became quite apparent that the floorboards were not an innerspring mattress. Wrestling a one-legged and lethargic Wyatt up the stairs appealed to Beth about as much as taking the steps to the top of the Sears Tower would. So she put her creative mind to work and came up with the sleeping bags.

Wyatt watched drowsily as she spread the downy bag upon the quilt, then he obligingly angled onto it. After the first chilling contact, the fiber quickly warmed and became a cozy resting place. Beth zippered the other bag up over them to make a snug envelope that would have forced closeness — if they needed the encouragement to seek out each other's embrace.

Slowly, Wyatt accepted the fact that Beth was really in his arms, that she had been a full and willing party to their heated bouts of lovemaking. And with that realization came the unfurling of a fragile trust. He wanted desperately to believe in the goodness of what was happening between them, wanted to see it as a positive step toward a mutual healing. And he wanted to believe that was what Beth longed for, too.

He could have it all. Unfettered by the realities of misunderstanding and day-to-day stresses, he looked beyond to a future they could share, to one they could build together. Of course, he wasn't naive enough to think that all had been solved here before the lodge fire. There were some very somber facts that needed to be dealt with, but from the strength of what they were beginning would come the courage to confront those problems. And Wyatt was becoming more and more convinced that they would survive them intact. After all, the woman had been cleaning house for him.

"What are you thinking?" Beth asked. Her fingertip rubbed down the side of his face and he turned toward her. In the mellow glow of the fire's final embers, his features seemed cast in bronze and strong shadow. It was an intriguing contrast of rugged angles and softer highlights and Beth could have easily lost herself in fascinated study.

"I was thinking how much I'd like back what we had when we first met."

She fell silent for a second, searching his expression with an eager caution. Then she whispered, "I'd like that, too."

"Do you think we can get it back?"

222

"We can try. And if we can't go back, we can move on from here."

"Can we move in the same direction this time?" He sounded more careful, as if expecting her to object. "I want more from my wife than clothes in the closet and Post-Its stuck on the refrigerator saying, "Don't wait up." I want to be able to reach out and find you there beside me."

Beth slipped her hand over the back of his. He recoiled slightly but allowed her to guide him so that his palm fit over the curve of her hip.

"I'm here."

He was so intense, so serious, as if nothing was more important than for her to believe what he was about to say.

"I love you, Beth."

She went completely still. Then, with a soft cry, her arms were around him and the feel of her tears burned against his throat. "I'd almost given up on hearing you say that again. We're going to make it, Wyatt. I know we are."

And his embrace gathered her in tight, with a binding fervency. She closed her eyes, reveling in the feel of his lips upon her hair, against her temple. Responding to the spread of his hand with the offering arch of her body. And to the pressing evidence of his passion with an answering moan.

They made love again. It was slow and it was good. As Wyatt coaxed her up to unbelievable heights, Beth was sure in her heart that she had back the man she'd fallen in love with—the sensitive, slightly cynical and oh, so sexy Wyatt Marston. And as she drifted to sleep in his arms, she was smiling, certain she'd never let him go.

But morning came and with it, a certain degree of discomfort fell between them, the kind of tension that came when two strangers woke to find themselves lovers. They were intimately close yet uncertain of how to incorporate that closeness into their daily routine. Both wanted to believe everything had changed for the better yet neither had the confidence to put it to the test.

They started off with a rather awkward kiss, a bit of nervous laughter and some cautious touching. Finally, the spread of daylight across the floorboards was the excuse they needed to separate without either of them having to make that first move. Wyatt glanced at the brightening world around them and murmured, "Jimmy will be over soon," and Beth was levering out of the sleeping bags with a hurried, "I'll go get dressed."

Wyatt got a glimpse of sleek nakedness before she whipped her robe around her and headed for the stairs at a jog. Then he lay back and exhaled deeply, allowing the wonderful languor of the night before to overwhelm him. With the sharp edge of need finally whetted, he should have been able to look at things clearly and without distraction. But he didn't want to think. He wanted to feel, to enjoy the lazy sensations that only a prolonged bout of great sex could leave behind. He felt like he should have a cigarette and he didn't even smoke. With eyes closed and body lax, he brought back all the passion, all the tenderness he could remember, running them through his mind, over and over in hopes that the imprint would burn in deeply and remain forever. He wasn't thinking ahead to the rest of the nights they'd have together. He wanted to hang onto this one, the one that had more power over his heart and soul than even his honeymoon night. Because in the hours they'd spent before the hearth, they'd been reclaiming the treasures almost lost to them. And that made their value inestimable.

Finally, he made himself move. He could hear one of the spare room showers going upstairs and in the distance, the sound of Mani's boys as they noisily made their way to meet the bus. And as he dressed, he dared to wonder if children made by his wife and him would someday break that reverent silence of the morning woods with their precious laughter. Lord, he hoped so. It was the first time he'd ever given the thought much credence. Raising children between a Chicago high-rise apartment and some distant day-care center had never been his idea of having a family. Family was something you nurtured yourself, without the importance of a job intruding. God knows, he knew that better than anyone. Children didn't deserve second best. And for the first time, he wondered if he and Beth could put down family roots, here where little ones could have the room to grow unfettered by the confines of urban living and the distraction of career. Something to think about. Something he'd enjoy working on if Beth was in agreement. If she was going to stay.

That's what he thought he'd read as they made love. But he wasn't always real good at interpreting her actions. Staying would mean giving up her job . . . and more. It was a commitment he couldn't ask her to make, considering. She'd have to make that choice—between the hotel and lodge, between her extramarital freedoms and the total fidelity he'd insist upon if she were to remain here with him. It was all or nothing and he didn't quite have enough confidence in what they'd begun to demand she make her choice now. They had a week left. A week during which he had every intention of making it impossible for her to even consider leaving.

Later, as Wyatt sat on the porch to enjoy the cup of coffee she brought him, Beth rolled and packed away the reminders of their night before the fire. She knew they were treading on emotional eggshells, both wanting to believe things would be better now, both scarred and scared by the breakdown they were trying to put behind them. But they were trying. And she had to see that the forward momentum continued.

When she came out onto the sun porch, Beth went to stand at Wyatt's side. She placed a tentative hand upon his shoulder and was surprised, and pleased, when he reached up to engulf it with his own. He squeezed lightly as his gaze lifted to meet hers. And he gave her a frail, hopeful smile that shattered the awkwardness that had arrived with daylight. Her free hand curved around the strong line of his jaw, holding his face tilted up so she could bend to drink the taste of coffee and caring from his lips. His arm curled about her waist and with a tug, he brought her down upon his lap where they continued to feast on one another's affection.

Something sounding as subtle as a buffalo stampede raced beneath the windows. Beth glanced up to see Artie's plumed tail shoot past like a banner leading a cavalry charge.

"Damned dog," Wyatt muttered as he recaptured Beth's attention with the prompting nudge of his hand beneath her chin. It didn't take much for her to forget the dog. Just a return to the soul-shaking, mind-rattling kiss she'd longed for every time she looked at him. A stockpile of yearning had accumulated inside her over lonely months; the pile was too high to be depleted by one night, even one as glorious as the one they'd spent before the hearth. It would take many such nights, a lifetime of them. And that's what she was hoping for as his mouth moved slowly upon hers.

" 'Morning."

Groaning, Beth leaned away from her husband's luscious kiss to cant a glowering look at Jimmy Shingoos. "I thought it was supposed to be isolated up in these woods. We'd might as well be sitting in the middle of the Loop."

Wyatt's chuckle stirred a rumbling vibration. If he was annoyed by the intrusion, he covered it better. "Hey, Jimmy. Come on in for a cup of coffee."

"If I'm not butting into anything." But he was already opening the door. "I'm flying down to Baraga and wondered if you'd like to copilot."

He didn't have to answer. Beth could feel the jump of his affirmative reply. But he hesitated to ask sourly, "How are you planning to get me down the bluff? Block and tackle?"

"Not to worry. I idled her into a cove a couple of miles south of here. I can bus you down there in the Bronco. No problem, as long as you don't slip off the floats and sink like a rock. Thought you might like to get some wind beneath your wings."

"Would I ever. I feel like I'm beginning to sprout roots and grow moss." Then his fingertips traced the curve of Beth's thigh and he looked to her. "Want to come along?"

Beth shivered at the thought of being airborne. "Oh, no thank you. I've got some business to take care of here. You boys have fun."

Oh, yes, Wyatt remembered, stiffening. Business. She had to call his father. Hundreds of

228

miles away and the hotel still had the power to come between them. His voice was low and carefully neutral. "We won't be long. I'd better change."

"I'll bring some things down to you so you won't have to climb the stairs. What do you need?"

He told her and she was quick to hop off his lap and disappear into the body of the lodge. Jimmy lingered, not saying anything, yet saying plenty with his smirky grin. Wyatt wanted to drop his cast on the toes of his friend's sneakers. Nothing galled him like an I-told-you-so attitude. He should have been smiling, himself, but the taint of his father held his confidence in reserve. Boyd Marston could control things through the phone wires. He'd already sabotaged the loan deal. What did the man have in mind now? The only thing Wyatt had left of value was — his marriage.

With that thought tormenting him, Wyatt almost backed out of going. Things were still so fragile between him and his wife. But with Beth pushing and Jimmy pulling, they got him up and finally moving. And as the Bronco pulled out of the drive, the last thing he could see was Beth standing at the front door, waving goodbye.

Actually, Beth had forgotten all about Boyd Marston until Mani reminded her about him. Then, she subconsciously put off making the

229

connection with Chicago for as long as possible. She tidied their bedroom, did the dishes, even played fetch the stick with a mopey Artemus, who was missing Wyatt as much as she was. Finally, while a load of wash was running in the carriage house, she could make no more excuses.

"Bethany, how are you? Tell me what's going on up there. I was worried when you didn't call last night."

She responded to the genuine warmth of his tone by telling him what had happened since she arrived. He sounded regretful over Wyatt's loss of funding and happy to hear of their pending reconciliation. Then he moved on to talk about the hotel and her various accounts. As Beth discussed them with him, she was aware of a strange sense of detachment, as if the matters were no longer of much importance, these same things that had devoured her time and energy on a regular seven-days-a-week basis. And she found she was beginning to resent the fact that he was pushing business into her personal time. Time she deserved. Time she owed to her husband.

Boyd Marston hadn't gotten to his point of success without being able to read people. He caught on to the lack of usual enthusiasm in his PR director's voice and he could guess at the reason for it.

"Am I going to lose you to the northwoods, too, Bethany?" He made his tone light but there

230

was no mistaking the subtle confrontation of it.

"I don't know, Boyd."

His silence told of his surprise that she would even voice a hint of uncertainty. "When will you know? If I have to replace both my son and my daughter-in-law, I'd appreciate a little notice."

He sounded hurt and Beth responded with a pang of the guilt he intended her to feel. "It's not as though we're abandoning you."

"No. Of course not. We'll always be family. But where am I going to find someone to fill your shoes? Well, there's no need for us to worry until it actually happens. You have another week to decide. Who knows, Wyatt may come to his senses and return home."

Careful not to overstep her place between Wyatt and his father, she cautioned, "Don't count on that too much."

"But if he can't finance his white elephant up there—"

"There's always the stocks in Marston Hotels." Why hadn't she thought of that before? Of course. There was the answer to everything. Until Boyd planted another seed of doubt within her mind.

"Has he asked you to sign over your shares?"

Beth was taken aback by how sharp her father-in-law's tone had become. "No. We haven't really talked about it."

"Beth, be careful. I know you don't want to hear this but you've got to be prepared. What if it's not you he wants? What if it's just the stocks? What if that's what he had in mind when he asked you to bring them?"

I would do anything to make a go of this place. She heard Wyatt's passionate claim and it sent a shaft of pure terror through her. No, she wouldn't believe it. Not after last night. But then Boyd continued, playing on the worst of her fears, slipping that shadow of past pain into her subconscious mind.

"You could find yourself without anything. Of course, you'd still have your job with me to come back to, but you'd lose out on what you're entitled to. If Wyatt liquidates, you'd might as well flush that investment right down the pipes."

"I don't think that'll happen, Boyd."

But he could hear the wavering in her voice. And on his end, he smiled.

"Beth, protect your interests. Maybe I can help. Buy him out with my money. Then the stocks will stay in the family. I'll even reinvest them for you. That way, you'll have a financial buffer and Wyatt won't lose everything. You'll have the weight of the Marston chain behind you if you need it. And Wyatt doesn't have to know unless it becomes necessary. Then he'll be glad of it, too. I'll be a silent partner but Wyatt won't be out on a limb. If he's got to do this thing, he should be smart about it. You, too, Beth. I'm only thinking of the two of you. Wyatt hasn't been famous for his good judgment in the past."

"But he was on business training wheels then. How can you compare that with now?"

"So," Boyd drawled out. "He's told you."

"Yes. And I'm not going to let that color my opinion of his abilities." She wasn't. Was she?

"You're a bright girl, Beth, a survivor, just like me. I wish Wyatt had inherited some of those instincts. Buy him out, Beth. Don't take a risk you don't have to take. Will I see you Monday after next?"

"I'll let you know."

But when she hung up the phone, Beth wasn't as sure as she'd been before she dialed. She wasn't sure about anything.

Wyatt's first look at Beth's face flushed all the day's exhilaration out of him. When he was banking above the green pine forests and along the wave-tortured coast, his heart had soared with expectation. Now those hopes were firmly grounded by the reality he saw in her taut expression. Something was wrong. Something to do with her call to his father.

"Hi," he called out, skillfully maneuvering his crutches up the front porch steps.

"Back so soon?"

He paused, almost frowning. Was she happy to see him or not? He couldn't be sure. Instinct warned him to hang back until he could pick up on her signals. He could feel his own features pulling into a reflection of her impassive gaze.

233

They regarded each other for a long moment, the distance yawning wide between them. Then Wyatt realized what was happening and he knew he couldn't let it continue.

He hobbled up to his wife, ignoring the fact that she looked tense and wary. He put his hands to either side of her head, framing it gently. And he lowered his lips to hers. For a second, she was rigid and he feared he'd been wrong, that she'd resist. But then she went all soft and yielding and her mouth opened to his, inviting him sweetly inside.

"It seemed like I'd been gone forever to me," he murmured against that lush warmth.

His kiss and his words had the magic to wipe away her insecurities. Beth rested her head against the strong line of his shoulder and held to him, absorbing the feel of him, the shape of him, loving him so much for taking the first step that tears came to her eyes. If he would continue to come just halfway, they'd be all right. They would.

"Supper's ready," she told him as she rubbed her cheek against the scratchy wool of his shirt.

"What's Mani having?"

"I'm afraid you're going to have to trust your tastebuds to me tonight."

"Oh?"

"Mani showed me how to make several traditional northwoods dishes this afternoon. You're my guinea pig."

Beth was cleaning his house and now she was

234

cooking for him. He vowed to eat every last bite of what she prepared — even if it had the consistency of boot soles. "Lead me to the dining room. I'm starved."

"We'll be dining upstairs."

"Oh?"

"Sleeping bags were fine for one night, but I'm looking forward to a good mattress. And I'd just as soon not have to drag you up the stairs after a big meal."

"Sounds like you've got everything planned."

"I do."

"There's something to be said for an efficient wife."

She thought for a minute that he was being sarcastic. However, when she leaned back to look up at him, she saw the only thing that shone in his expression was a tender admiration. She smiled back, her caution evaporating beneath the warmth of his regard.

"Let's go," she urged. "Got your climbing gear on?"

"To be honest, I'd rather rappel a four-hundred-foot bluff on a shoestring than attempt those stairs. But my appetite will see me through the worst of it." And his blue eyes steeped with enough hungry meaning to set her shivering with anticipation.

The climb wasn't bad once they established a rhythm of push and pull. And Wyatt decided it was well worth the effort once he saw what she'd done with the room.

She'd brought a small cafe-sized table up from one of the parlors and draped it in lace and crystal and highlighted it with the flicker of candlelight. He could swear he heard wine chilling in the background. And romance budding. He liked those sounds just fine.

"Make yourself comfortable. I'll bring up dinner."

He glanced at the smooth beckoning surface of the bed and almost suggested they skip dinner and jump right to dessert, but Beth was already on her way downstairs. Wyatt sighed. He'd just have to take the courses to his meal in their proper order. Even if it killed him.

Beth's cooking may not have reached the sainted elevation of Mani's, but it was a far cut above average. Chased by an excellent vintage, the meal settled comfortably just as the mood settled comfortably. Artemus came creeping in to crouch at Wyatt's feet, snapping up leftovers he snuck off his plate and Beth didn't think to protest. She and the beast had come to a truce that afternoon. Besides, she was too aware that she would be testing the truce with her husband the minute she asked her question.

"Wyatt?"

"Ummm?"

"We need to talk about the lodge and how we're going to afford to keep it." She continued to throw out that all inclusive "we" and he had yet to correct her.

She'd expected defensiveness but certainly not

the easy way he leaned back in his chair, then reached out to cover the ridge of her knuckles with his hand. "If you've got any ideas, I'd love to hear them."

"You would?"

"Shoot."

"Okay." She took a big breath. "I've been thinking about our stocks in Marston Hotels."

"So have I. What have you been thinking?"

"That if I bought out your shares, for a good price naturally, you'd have enough to get things rolling. I know it wouldn't cover everything, but it would be a start. When you've got most of the remodeling completed, you can get the lodge on the Historical Registry and apply for federal funding. Then, no bank would turn down a request to finance the rest. You'd be going on faith for a while but I believe it's going to happen as much as you do."

A strange thing occurred as she spoke. Beth noticed how his expression set like potter's clay; by the time she was finished, it was as hard as rock. Though unreadable, his eyes took on a particular glitter when shielded behind half-slitted lids.

"Faith," he repeated softly. "It seems neither of us are ones for placing a great deal of store in it. Looks like you've got everything tied up neatly. I can almost hear my father talking."

Why did she feel things were not going well? She knew for certain when he drew his hand away from hers and returned to a straight-backed position. "Well?" she ventured. "What do you think?"

"I think I'm going to have to think about it."

"Wyatt—"

"I'll think about it." Crisp, curt, final.

And as she cleared the table of its dishes and good intentions, Beth wondered what had brought the wall of silence back down between them.

By the time she got everything cleaned up in the kitchen, it was dark and going on nine. They'd started dinner late. She switched off the downstairs lights as she went and finally climbed back to their shared room. The light was off there, too. Frowning slightly, she went to the bathroom and used the softer glow from the vanity cabinet to illuminate the interior of the bedroom. Wyatt was already under the covers, his back to her. And Artemus was stretched out in her spot. She assumed her husband was exhausted by the day's exertions. Beth had to remind herself that he was still on the mend and had to take things slowly. So what if the evening didn't come to the romantic end she'd hoped for. She'd have settled for a comfortable sense of closeness. But she feared she'd lost that at the dinner table.

Garbed in a chemise of apricot-colored silk — she didn't need flannel to keep her warm anymore — Beth approached the bed and the problem of moving Artemus. And was surprised that there was no problem at all. The big dog gave his tail several heavy thumps and hopped off the bed. She stared at him as he made a couple of quick doggy circles and dropped onto the rug. Absurdly pleased by the animal's concession, she slid under the warmed sheets.

From an impersonal distance, Beth listened to the sound of Wyatt's even breathing. She couldn't tell if he was asleep or just too worn out to move. Or avoiding her. She tried not to consider that last, but painful past experience asserted itself. Had they reverted back to the system of closed doors communication? Surely not after the strides they'd taken over the last twenty-four hours.

In the darkness, in her doubts, Boyd's cautions returned to torment the direction of her thoughts. It was the stocks. His mood had turned the minute she brought up using them for financing. Had he something else in mind? Was it a capital investment he wanted from her instead of a marital one? She shouldn't be surprised or hurt. Not when she considered the degree to which their relationship had deteriorated. Had he asked her to share in his wonderful plans? No. True, he hadn't discouraged her from including herself in the preliminaries, but that wasn't the same thing. It was the commitment from him that she needed.

She needed to be asked.

Sighing softly to herself, Beth began to shiver, feeling the chill of the night and the chill of her circumstance. To overcome both things, she edged up against the still figure beside her. Wyatt was wearing his sweat bottoms, but he was bare from the waist up. And the heat from him was immediate and irresistible. Carefully, she eased her arm around the slow-rising curve of his ribs and fit her palm over his heart, soothed by the steady tempo. He didn't move at first, then his hand covered hers and he hugged her arm to him tightly. It could have been a reflexive action, but she hoped it was more. Beth nuzzled her face into the hair at the nape of his neck.

"I love you, Wyatt," she whispered.

Did she imagine it, or did his whole body stiffen?

Chapter Fourteen

Wyatt lay wide awake, tortured by those soft words long after he felt Beth sag against him in sleep.

I love you, Wyatt.

How could she say that to him after boldly spouting his father's treachery? His eyes squeezed tight but not as tight as the pain squeezing about his heart. Faith, she'd said. Where was her faith? She spoke a good line about having confidence in him and in the future of the lodge, but where was the evidence of her faith in their future? She was one cautious lady. A business lady. That hadn't changed even when she put her brief case aside for a dustpan. She was making the best deals for Marston Hotels.

She was acting for Boyd Marston.

Why didn't she just come out and admit it? How stupid did they think he was? He knew she didn't have the money to make a buy-out offer. It was from his father, of course. But why? Just to make him look bad? To give him enough rope in hopes that he'd hang himself? So Boyd could keep his thumb on the direction of his future? He wasn't sure and at this precarious point, he needed to be sure. Of Beth. And she'd given him no reason for it. Dinner and some fabulous sex wasn't enough. He wanted something concrete, something he could hold up as proof positive. Was she just playing him along with all her sweet talk and enthusiasm? To coax him to accept the buy-out bid? After she helped engineer the collapse of his only other means of financing his dream? He should have suspected it, knowing how close she and his father were.

But he'd wanted to believe in her. Just like he'd believed when he'd married her. He'd seen the strength, the goodness in her then and had wanted those things in his life's partner. He saw her as the chance to relieve his loneliness, to share his expectations, as a recipient of all the love that had been massing inside him since his mother's death, just waiting to be heaped upon another. It should have been the perfect match. In a way, it was—his wife and Marston Hotels. And that left him on the outside, as always.

Dammit, why did she have to tease him with his father's offer? If she loved him, if she trusted him, if she believed in their future, why didn't she suggest they pool their stocks instead of choosing the halfway measure that solved nothing? The obvious tore through his earlier self-assurance. Because she didn't want to invest her fortune or her future in him. She was helping out, all right, but the way she was doing it left

242

her secure and the gate wide open should she want to get out fast. She wouldn't take a risk or make a commitment and how else was he supposed to feel about that? Like she was extending an olive branch only so far and was ready at the first sign of trouble to jerk it back? While he was standing on it. How was he supposed to believe in her when she'd betrayed him at every turn? With her obsessive dedication to her job. By her affair with Mark Casey. And now, in her refusal to take a stand beside him. How the hell was he supposed to trust her without leaving himself wide open?

He rolled onto his back and Beth cuddled in close, sighing gently as he adjusted the fit of his arm about her shoulders. He could just make out the exquisite contour of her face in the dimness. She looked so content. So happy to be with him. If only that was true.

I love you, Wyatt. How was he supposed to believe that when there were so many strings and conditions attached?

What it came down to after hours of fretful thought was whether or not it mattered. His father and stepmother's marriage was not a love match. It was business, pure and simple. Mutually benefiting, without emotional risk. He could accept Beth's terms; he could ask her to stay, could enjoy the fact of her in his bed at night and the brilliance of her managerial mind during the day. He could hold himself back from personal involvement, and the risk of being hurt would be minimal. He didn't want to let her go, but could he settle for such an arrangement just to keep her? It wasn't what he wanted, but he had to face the possibility that it was the best he was going to get. A companion and a business partner. A lovely face to stare at over dinner. A luscious lover to warm his sheets.

The more he thought about it, the more he rebelled against the cold and impersonal merger. It was what he had with his father. The man would see him well taken care of, would promote his future to the extent that it reflected well upon his own goals. He would give him money and a prestigious job but would never part with a grain of affection. He didn't want that in his marriage. Even if it meant giving up the woman he loved.

It was a point of pride. He'd had damned little of the latter when under his father's rule. This was his chance to control his own future, not just to wait like a contented parasite to get fat off the bankroll his father married into. He'd hated Denver. He'd hated the sprawling hotel chain. He'd hated being removed from people, from the process of accomplishment, from the chance to experience personal pride. He wouldn't let his father take that from him.

And if his wife stood on Boyd's side against him, he'd just as soon know of it now.

Both Wyatt and Artemus were gone when Beth awoke. It was mid-morning. She could tell by the

244

angle of the sun off the lake. Not one used to sleeping in, she was surprised by her lethargy. But she'd spent a restless night, filled with menacing dreams. Dreams of Chicago tenements and dark streets going nowhere. Dreams of emptiness, of loneliness. And the first thing she wanted to do when her eyes fluttered open was reach for Wyatt. He was the one she instinctively sought when she needed a sense of safety. But he wasn't there.

Her hand ran over the cool, vacant spot beside her and a painful feeling of abandonment twisted inside. She'd needed him to chase the shadows of her nightmare away. She'd needed him . . . It seemed sort of ironic, when she thought about it. She hadn't been there for him and now he wasn't there for her. She took an unsteady breath, bolstering herself with her own self-determination. She was a survivor, just like Boyd said. She was used to depending only upon her own wits, her own skills. Yet she'd woken this morning and it had been Wyatt she'd reached for instead of her own strength. And she'd been momentarily crushed by his absence. That was a pattern she wasn't going to see repeated. A husband and wife should be there to shore up each other in times of weakness. The ring on her finger meant more than just a new last name imprinted on her credit cards and a higher spending limit. It implied a union of two souls and that was something she and Wyatt had never established between themselves.

They'd always held zealously to their separate identities, their independent goals. And it had torn them apart. They'd committed themselves to a new beginning. If it was going to work out, they would have to begin as one, not as a distancing two. Not if she could help it. And she was anxious to tell Wyatt of her revelation. Maybe it was just the knowledge they needed to succeed.

She dressed quickly in her warm northern Michigan wardrobe and set about finding her husband. He should be easy to track if Artie was with him. The big dog had the grace of a moose and all the subtlety of a tank. They weren't in the lodge. It took only a pause to weigh the silence for her to discern that. That left Jimmy's. So she started there, uncertain of what mood she was going to find her husband in. They'd run a roller coaster in the last few days. She'd just gotten used to the exhilarating high when the downward plunge at last night's table caught her unaware. She didn't want to experience that ride again. There had to be a way to stop on the peak instead of in the valley bottom.

Beth was half way across the needle-covered trail when Artemus came bounding toward her. She bent to ruffle the big animal's ears and endured a number of enthusiastic slobbering kisses.

"Hey, guy. Where's Wyatt? Where's Wyatt?"

As if in answer, he turned and raced back toward Jimmy's. She followed and met up with the two of them at the Shingoos's back door.

"Good morning," she called cheerfully. Her greeting sounded as strained as her smile felt. "You seem to be getting around pretty good these days."

"I had some business to take care of this morning. Some calls to make." He left it at that and started the way she'd come, swinging with a confident strength between his crutches. It didn't seem to matter if she fell in step, so she took it upon herself to match his pace.

"Had breakfast yet?"

"Mani fixed me some."

"Oh. Coffee?"

"Enough to float a battleship."

"Oh." How quickly they exhausted the list of pleasantries on this beautiful spring day. So she cut right to the chase. "Have you given the stocks anymore thought?"

"Yes."

"And?"

"Thanks but no thanks."

"Wyatt —"

"I've found another buyer for my shares. You can do what you like with yours."

She stopped dead on the path, feeling as if he'd just kicked her away. He glanced back over his shoulder and lifted one questioning brow.

"I'm sorry, does that put you in a bad position?"

"No, it's just —"

"I thought you understood, Beth. I don't want

247

to do this under my father's shadow. I'm ready for this risk, even if you're not. I want to keep my personal and my professional life separate." And his confrontational look seemed to ask where she fell between the two. "I tried to blend them before and everything fell apart. Maybe things will work out better this way."

She didn't know how to reply. He'd just cut her off from one whole half of his future. Didn't he want her help? If not financially, then managerially? What was she to assume from his terse declaration? What would be left over? Washing his socks? Sweeping up the dog tracks on the floor? Surely he didn't mean to close her off from all means of being useful to him? The idea hurt.

She was somewhat surprised by how much she'd enjoyed involving herself in these planning stages. It was a challenge, like putting together a puzzle without the security of laying the outside edge pieces first. And she loved meeting the challenge with ideas, with suggestions, with ways to implement their dreams and meet their goals. Was Wyatt taking that away from her? To what purpose? Did he mean to relegate her to the position of dustpan management when she could help in other ways, too? Was this to be her punishment for becoming too engrossed in her last job? If so, it wasn't fair. It wasn't smart. And she wasn't going to allow it.

Wyatt started walking again, apparently not demanding she answer right away. She started to follow, more slowly, her thoughts tumbling wildly in an effort to make sense of what he was doing. Was it to spite his father or to spite her? Or both of them?

Wyatt didn't go into the lodge. Instead, he worked his way around the side and into the back where an irregular stone walk and about thirty feet of patchy grass separated the log wall from a sheer drop to the rocky beach below. He leaned on the pads of his crutches and looked pensively out over the water.

"Hot tubs, huh?"

"You liked that idea?"

He glanced at her and away. "Can't you picture it? Snow falling, water bubbling, the hair on the back of your head freezing to the edge, drinking something hot and more than a little potent."

"Goose bumps the size of baseballs, running back inside in subzero temps." She was smiling, but inside her emotions became all hot and turbulent at the thought of her and Wyatt immersed to the neck with breath pluming in the cold air.

"I thought we'd get some of those cedar lounge chairs for the less adventurous. They can lean back and watch the sunset and the leaves turn."

"Sounds nice," she agreed. His use of "we" had her wondering. "We," who? He and Jimmy? Or the two of them and Jimmy. She stared out through the dappled sunlight, blinking away a suspicious sheen that made everything sparkle like the water below. Her whole future was tied up in who was included in that elusive "we".

"I figure we can do half of the rooms for the

honeymooner crowd and make the others up for families and singles. We could turn some of the downstairs rooms, like the parlors and the den into small meeting spaces, all low key, of course. I'll be making over the library as my office."

"What are you going to do with the ballroom?"

"I don't know. What do you think?"

"You really want to know?"

"I've always valued your opinion, Beth. You've got good business instincts." That was a rather flatly delivered compliment, but she chose not to take offense.

"I'd leave it open. That way you can adjust it to fit the circumstances. You know, wedding reception, retirement parties, even small trade shows. You could rent it out if the guests in residence haven't booked it. No sense in letting the space go idle."

"That'd require some pretty tight organization."

"No big deal. Just some careful scheduling and some real mobile furnishings—tables, chairs, podium, portable risers, overhead screen, a few two-wheeled dollies, grunt labor and so on."

Wyatt was looking at her now, his features an intense study. "Maybe no problem for someone with your planning background."

"You offering me a job, Mr. Marston?" She made it light, so he could take it as a joke if he chose to. He smiled crookedly, not giving away the mood behind it.

"I doubt that the lodge could afford you."

"What if I offer my help for free?"

"Not a very good business move for a career woman like yourself."

"Oh, I don't know. Maybe I think it's just the right career move."

He didn't answer.

Oh, come on, Wyatt, Give me something, anything to go on! She was so exasperated, she was ready to kick one of the crutches out from under him. He looked so sure, so set, so independent braced there on the bluff, crutches firmly planted, expression set, as rugged as the landscape and just as resilient. *I don't need you,* he'd told her once before. That wasn't what she wanted to hear from him. What was she going to have to do to get some kind of reaction from him? Hit him over the head? Get down on her knees? What? It was rapidly becoming obvious that she would be a frustrated old lady if she waited for him to bring it up.

"I'm thinking of requesting an indefinite leave of absence from the hotel."

Lord, he was good at protecting his feelings. His only reaction was the slight widening of his eyes. "Why?"

"Whether you like it or not, you're going to need all the inexpensive help you can get to launch this project. I'm offering my services."

"As what?" Still, his expression was inscrutable.

"Anything you need me to be."

That brought a slight tic to the corners of his mouth. "Dad might not be willing to carry you that long. He really counts on you. One of us should have enough sense to maintain a healthy income."

"Your father can hire someone else. I'm not exactly unskilled labor anymore. I could get into another chain if I wanted to. Or I can get a job flipping moose burgers down on Forty-One."

He looked as though a smile was just dying to escape but he nailed it down. "Beth, have you thought this through?"

"Yes. And it's what I want to do. What do you want me to do, Wyatt?"

"It's not my decision."

"No? You don't think so?" She threw up her hands. "I give up. Getting through to you is like chipping through a brick wall with a toothpick. You think about it, Wyatt, and when you decide whether or not you want me to stay and in what capacity, you let me know."

She spun around and began to march away. She'd gotten about ten feet when his words stopped her.

"I want you to stay."

She took a deep, composing breath before she could risk turning to face him. It was too soon to let relief bring ruin to her mascara. When she came about, her expression was as sober as his. "As what?"

"My wife. My partner. Is that good enough?"

Time held the fragility of a heartbeat and the

promise of eternity as they looked at one another. Beth blinked. Dampness rimmed her lower lashes. Oh, damn, she hadn't wanted to cry. She swallowed hard and tried to adopt a cocky stance. "Good enough for starters."

He cracked a small smile and she filled his arms so fast, she almost bowled him over. Both of his crutches dropped, unnoticed, unneeded. She would hold him steady. Her face angled up and he was kissing her. Ravenously. With ounce for ounce of the same desperate yearning that made her go half crazy when she thought about a life without him.

"Don't go," he said against the part of her lips. "Don't go, Beth," he moaned into her ear. "Not for a minute. Not for an hour. Not ever."

"Just try to get rid of me."

He kissed her brow, her cheeks, the bridge of her nose and settled back deliciously upon her mouth. When she was almost senseless, he asked, "Are you sure?"

"About what? Whether it's day or night? No. About wanting to be with you? No question. Yes."

He was leaning into her, balancing on one leg. His hands were nudging impatiently up beneath the bottom of her sweater. "Oh, for that hot tub about now."

Beth moved against him suggestively. "It would make a mess out of your cast."

"I'm going to get one installed. I won't be wearing a cast forever. Then, we can celebrate the second this comes off. A little doctor-prescribed physical therapy."

"Ummm. Sounds good. But what are we going to do in the meantime?"

"There's always our bath tub." His fingers were fumbling with the rear clasp of her bra. It let go with a snap and his palms spread wide upon smooth bared skin. If they didn't get somewhere soon, she'd be dropping him right down on the pine needles.

"I'll settle for the bedroom," was her husky solution.

"Race you."

If there was an Olympic event for sensuous stair climbing, they would have been a shoo-in for the gold.

By the time they reached the room, Wyatt was breathing hard, partly from exertion, mostly from expectation. He dropped into the old rocking chair and awkwardly bent to wrestle off his left hiking boot. Then Beth was there, crouching over his cast, unhooking the rest of the leather boot laces, reaching up to peel down the pair of jeans she'd slit to the knee to accommodate the bulky wrapping. She took his elbows, meaning to lift him but ended up being pulled into his lap. At her questioning gaze, his smile grew all lazy and lecherous.

"I'm sick to death of being flat on my back in that bed."

"Something else on your mind?" she purred naughtily, enjoying the playfulness and the steamy anticipation. Wyatt was already reaching behind her knees, drawing them so they were wedged between his ribs and the rocker's bent wood arms. She wiggled her bottom and felt the hard outline of his intentions. "Oh, how ingenious. This just might work."

"Lock the door," he urged. "I don't want any two- or four-legged interruptions."

Beth squirmed down and went to turn the latch to assure their privacy. Then she crossed the room, boldly discarding clothing as she approached. By the time she reached the rocker, she was down to her socks. They were bright pink wool.

"You can leave those on," Wyatt suggested thickly. "They're sexy. "

"And so are you, for a one-legged man."

She proved it by climbing up onto his lap and fastening down on his mouth, all naked heat and wet velvet kisses. Wyatt's hands were at her trim waist, gripping hard, lifting her, settling her over and around him with a rough impatience. Beth gasped as a shudder of pleasure rippled through her. She tried to lift up but Wyatt held her still, imprisoning her with the strength of hands and body. Making her feel with devastating clarity how good it was to have him deep inside her. She looked at him through passion-glazed eyes, said his name in a desire-weakened voice. She arched rapturously as his mouth sought the sweet fruit of her breasts and cried out softly as he guided the rhythm of their union. And by the time they

255

reached the explosive end, it was a mystery of gravitational science that kept their wildly pitching chair from going over backwards.

Beth snuggled contentedly into the cove of her husband's shoulder. The sound she made was one of unashamed satisfaction as his hands made soothing forays up and down her spine. The rocker was now moving in a slow, sleepy arc that echoed the languorous beat of their hearts. Time moved quietly, unobserved by either one of them.

"We'd better make sure there's a rocking chair in each one of the guest rooms," Beth murmured and she thoroughly enjoyed the rumble of Wyatt's soft laughter.

"Maybe we should mention it as one of the lodge benefits in the brochure."

"Full-color pictures," she added.

Wyatt gathered her loose, heavy hair in one hand, sweeping it back from her face. "The only one who's going to enjoy this particular picture is me." He was smiling, but his voice was laced with what could have been promise or threat. Beth smiled back, not sure if she should be pleased by his possessiveness or alarmed by the subtle aggression.

Then, Wyatt was distracted by the drone of a plane swooping low along their beach. He craned his neck, able to make out the distinctive yellow and black of a Piper Cub on floats. He didn't know anyone who flew one.

"Company coming?" Beth asked, observing his interest.

He shrugged. "Could be."

"I guess this means you don't want to be caught with your pants down."

He looked away from the window and grinned. "At least not until later."

They dressed, then Wyatt coaxed her back upon his knees, seating her sideways so her long legs dangled over the arm and her head nestled beneath his chin. He was rocking them, stroking through her hair as he watched for the return of the plane. Sure enough, he heard the change in pitch of the Cub's engine and saw it glide down to touch on the glassy surface of their cove, taxiing in out of sight below the bluff.

"Company coming," he whispered into the silky blond hair.

"Tell them there's no room at the inn."

"I'll tell them there are no suitable bathrooms for rent at the inn."

They waited, both of them curiously watching the top of the path that led up from the beach. After several minutes went by, the figure of a man emerged: head, shoulders and tailored cashmere coat. Wyatt went dead still beneath her. He muttered four very distinctive words that blended into an oath and described only one man she could think of. She sat up straighter, surprised, straining to see for herself but there was no doubt.

Boyd Marston had come to call.

Chapter Fifteen

"So, this is it, what's gotten you to pull up stakes and abandon your obligations."

Boyd Marston stood in the central hall surveying the lodge interior with a jaundiced eye.

Beside her, Beth could feel the tension set in along her husband's tall frame. She glanced at Wyatt uneasily, very aware of how quickly he'd changed the instant they'd come downstairs and into the presence of his father. He was as remote and cold as the Alaskan tundra and she didn't like being included in his peripheral chill. It was as if he'd pushed aside all the tenderness of just moments ago as insignificant. If she'd learned anything about her husband during these last few days, it was that when he pushed the hardest, he needed her the most. She stepped in closer to him, reaching out to place a hand against the small of his back, pressing lightly to show her support. Though he allowed it, there was no lessening of the tension beneath her fingertips. Wyatt was strung taut as a guy wire.

"The only obligation I have is one of your making," Wyatt said with a quiet frostiness. "One you forced on me, not one I chose."

"Considering the choices you've made for yourself in the past, I'd say it's a damned good thing I did. I only wish you had learned something from it."

Before his son could reply, Boyd strode into the great room, studying the high beams with their lacy drape of cobwebs, regarding the fifties furniture with obvious, and well-founded distaste. And he made his pronouncement like it was carved irrevocably in stone.

"Throwing money down a well."

"It's my well."

The older man turned. His expression was between indulgent patronization and subtle contempt. "Not yet, I'm given to understand. And you'd be wise to back out now, before this place swallows you whole."

"I have obligations here, Dad." Wyatt's smile was a curve of cynicism. There was a glint of anger in his eyes, but he was holding it in. "And you know how we Marstons are when it comes to obligation."

"Don't be flip, Wyatt. Beth, I can count on you to talk some sense into him."

Both men looked at her and Beth felt suddenly jerked between two opposite poles. And the pull was fierce. Boyd was waiting, his expression mildly impatient, totally confident. Wyatt's was closed down so tight, she'd need a crowbar to pry

259

a speck of response from him. His eyes had gone flat, his features unyielding. He was waiting, too.

Beth looked at the elder Marston. "I'm sorry, Boyd, but I have to disagree. Wyatt's instincts are right on target here. This place has tremendous potential."

If emotional shock waves could be measured on the Richter scale, the readings from both men would have been up in the devastating seven to eight point range.

"Potential what? Investment drain? Beth, don't encourage him in this folly."

Was there a threat in that smoothly delivered line? A certain "Take my side or else" implication? Beth stiffened, resenting the manipulation from a man she respected. He'd never made such demands upon their working or personal relationship before. Or was that merely because she'd never had reason to disagree with his mandates? Well, she was disagreeing on this one. "That's not the way I see it," she told him softly. That softness was threaded with steel.

Wyatt's gaze never left her. He didn't give away much. Just a carefully shuttered glimpse was all she had to go on. But that sufficed. She saw the crippling effects of life beneath the heel of a man like Boyd Marston and she saw a relief so stark, it broke her heart.

Boyd snorted and tossed his hands up, as if they were both fools, deserving what they got. He stalked over to the windows, brushing some imagined dirt from his coat sleeve. He may have condemned the lodge interior, but he could find no fault with the breathtaking view.

"Beth, why don't you see if there's something you can put together for lunch," Wyatt suggested.

His stare was fastened on his father's straight back. It wasn't a friendly look. Beth wasn't sure she dared leave the two of them alone. She put an objecting hand on Wyatt's arm. He glanced at her, and seeing her concern, he smiled wryly.

"Go ahead," he urged. "I want to talk to my father."

If she could have, Beth would have grabbed onto him and surrounded him with her embrace, with her love, with her strength. She sensed he needed it. But perhaps it was enough that she hesitated to leave him, that she clung to his shirt sleeve, that she gazed up into his eyes in an effort to convey her support. It must have been, because he gave her a genuine smile and bent to brush his lips across her furrowed brow.

"Go ahead. I won't push him off the bluff." At her look of alarm, he relaxed into a grin. "How much damage can a man on crutches do?"

Beth pursed her lips, imagining he could do a great deal. And she warned in a low voice, "Don't let him kick them out from under you."

His smile tipped to one side, recognizing the merit of her suggestion. "I'll keep my feet — or rather, my foot — on the ground."

When the two men were alone, Wyatt neared the unapproachable figure of his father. His tone was level. "So, when are you leaving, Dad?"

Boyd laughed. "Now, that was subtle, Wyatt. Don't worry. I've no plans to wear out my welcome."

"I don't recall extending one."

He laughed again. "Afraid of a little honest advice?"

"Was that what you were planning to give me?"

"Condominiums."

"What?"

"Time-shares. You've got enough property here. Slap up a couple of units and use this for the social hub. Now that kind of development is savvy. And a golf course. Take down a few dozen acres of trees, plant a green and you'll—"

"No."

Boyd turned, brows raised at the challenging tone.

"No, Dad. That's not what I want to do here. You don't understand. But then you've never understood."

"It's that dreamy streak you inherited from your mother. God knows, I've tried to breed it out of you. What do you want, Wyatt? Some isolated little place in the pines where you can hide from your responsibilities?"

"Dad—"

"No, you listen. Stop this nonsense and get back to what you should be doing. You've got a business to run. A wife to take care of."

"I'm doing that," was Wyatt's frigid reply. "My business. My wife."

"And how long do you think either of them are going to last?"

Wyatt was silent as echoes and reechoes of past failure swamped over him. Damn the man, he always knew right where to stab and how hard to twist. He contained his temper but his voice was deadly. "Why let that worry you? It's not like you've ever given two minutes of your precious time to think about me one way or another. Unless it suited your purpose."

Boyd's lips narrowed and went white. His tone was curt. "Don't whine, Wyatt. It doesn't become you."

"Just like not being in control of everything doesn't become you. Like I said, how long are you staying?"

"My pilot's waiting. I didn't expect you to roll out the red carpet. I'm flying back to Chicago on the 4:15 out of Ontonagon. I've booked two seats: one for me and one for Bethany. It shouldn't take me that long to convince her to come with me."

An awful silence settled. Then, very softly, Wyatt told him, "She won't go."

Boyd chuckled. "Oh, I think she will. You never did understand her, not like I do. You don't know the lengths she'd go to bury her past and make something of herself. You don't know because you've always had everything handed to you on a silver platter and you don't appreciate any of it. You don't know what it's like to work up from what you're ashamed of. She'll come with me because I have what she wants." He saw his son stiffen and he smiled. "In Denver. With or without you?"

"You can take your position at headquarters and stuff it. Beth's staying here with me."

Boyd studied him, taking in the militant set of his jaw, the steely certainty in his stare. And his confidence faltered. So he turned to more aggressive, underhanded tactics.

"Why would you want her, Wyatt? You know what she is and what she's done."

"That's past," he ground out tersely.

"Is it? How far are you going to trust her if she decides to go shopping in Chicago or to visit friends and family? Without you. How often do you think she'll make those trips? Whenever Mark Casey's in town?"

"Leave Casey out of this."

"She came up here to divorce you, Wyatt."

That got the desired response. Wyatt jerked rigid, surprise blanking his expression.

"She's a smart girl, she was thinking out her options. She's got a good job waiting, one she's always wanted. How long do you think she's going to be charmed by the scent of pines and by the struggle to keep your fantasies afloat? Debt and distance have a way of getting under people's skin real fast. Especially when they know they've passed up something else. How are you going to look her in the eye knowing she gave it up for you? Knowing she regrets making the choice?"

Wyatt was breathing faster, trying to submerge

264

the fear that his father was right. He gripped his crutches, feeling vulnerable in body, vulnerable in heart.

"Wyatt, let her go. She'll only hurt you worse in the long run. I know about faithless women." A hard, bitter edge crept into his voice. "They take a terrible toll on your pride. If it wasn't for her controlling interest in the hotels, I'd have divorced your stepmother the first time she flaunted her infidelity in my face. Do you think Beth is any different?"

"You'd know, wouldn't you?" Wyatt said thickly. "How long did you cheat on my mother? I wish she'd had the courage to walk out."

The curtain of civility was torn away between them with those angry words. They glared at each other—two men held by blood but not bond.

"You're not going to get everything your way, Wyatt," Boyd said with a cruel sobriety. "It's time you grew up and started paying for the cost of being a Marston."

"Dad, I've been paying for that privilege every day of my life. And you know what? It's not worth a damned cent."

"You're going to regret this, Wyatt."

"No, I won't. And if you knew me at all, you'd realize that."

There was the sudden click of toenails on floorboards as Artemus trotted into the room. He drew up short the instant he scented a stranger and advanced, stiff-legged and bristled up

265

like a hedgehog, to stand guard at Wyatt's side, issuing a warning with the low drone of his growl.

"Artie, no," Wyatt snapped.

Confused by the sharp crack of his master's voice, the dog determined that the stranger was a threat. He leaped forward with a deep-chested snarl and Boyd was quick to put a chair between them.

"Call him off," the elder man demanded.

Just then, Beth came into the room. Assessing the situation and able to move faster than Wyatt on his crutches, she raced to the posturing animal and grabbed his collar. She jerked him hard enough to pull him off balance, then began to drag him toward the exterior doors.

"I'm sorry," she said over the scrape of toenails on wood. "That was my fault. I didn't think of what might happen when I let him in." She yanked open the door and shoved the dog out. He was instantly on his hind legs, fogging the glass with his angry barking.

"You've got about as much control over that animal as you have over everything else," Boyd grumbled fiercely as he struck the wrinkles from his coat with quick strokes of his hand. He didn't like being shaken from his usual composure and it wore on his ever shortening temper.

"Artie has pretty good instincts," Wyatt drawled. "I can trust them, most of the time." The he looked at his wife through narrowed eyes as if he was questioning her now.

266

Upon stepping back into the room, Beth had felt the tension strike her like a physical force. Artie reacted to it his way, by jumping immediately to protect Wyatt from the threat of danger, and she was startled because part of her responded the same way. As if Boyd was an enemy. That surprised her. She'd always thought herself fond of Wyatt's father, but had she been lulled by surface charm? Why else would her own protective instincts be so strongly set against him?

She looked between father and son, seeing them posed like combatants and she realized then that the ties of family were gone, cast off during whatever turbulent dialogue had occurred in her absence. Thinking to offer a safety valve to the impossible pressure, she called with a feigned congeniality, "Lunch is ready."

Wyatt's head snapped back around. He stared at her through glacial eyes. "I'm not hungry. Dad wants to talk business with you. I'll leave the two of you to it."

He maneuvered out on his crutches, brushing past her without a glance, without a hint of reassurance. Beth looked to Boyd for some sort of explanation, but for once the elder Marston looked as angry and rattled as his son.

"What kind of business?"

"I have a flight arranged for us to Chicago. This afternoon."

"What? Don't you think you should have consulted me first?" No wonder Wyatt was chewing nails, she thought in distress. Now how was she going to smooth this over? She couldn't. It was impossible. She would have to make a choice whether she was ready for it or not. Boyd had pushed her into an uncomfortable corner.

"Beth, I can see what's going on here. Things aren't better between the two of you. When are you going to stop hoping for a miracle? Wyatt is never going to trust you. He's never going to let you in. You'll never have a partnership with him, not like I'm offering you. Put this dead end behind you. Fly out of here now and go to Denver with me tomorrow. This is what you've wanted, the chance you've been waiting for. You are valuable to me and my organization. Wyatt is never going to appreciate you for who you are. If he did, wouldn't he have asked you to invest in this place with him? If he wanted you, if he trusted you, wouldn't he have included you? He's not going to change. Don't throw it all away on a risk you can't win."

Beth heard him speaking, heard the reasonableness of his words, the sincerity of his concern for her. And she didn't buy any of it. Because she was also hearing Wyatt say, *Stay with me, Beth. As my wife. As my partner. I love you, Beth.*

"I can't go with you, Boyd."

"Bethany, you're making a mistake. I'm offering you Denver, your dreams. What's Wyatt offering?"

"His dreams."

Beth found Wyatt out on the sun porch. He was staring out over the lake, his body locked

268

within the triangle of his crutches, his every muscle clenched and trembling with the strain of stress. She felt the change in him, the way he was deliberately closing himself off from her. It scared her. And it made her mad.

"What's going on, Wyatt?"

"Why didn't you tell me you decided to go to Denver?"

His voice was dead calm. A bad sign.

"I hadn't. Your father offered me the job there if . . . if we couldn't work things out between us." She kept her voice conversational, hoping he would let it pass, that he wouldn't sink his teeth into it as a bone of contention. But he did.

"So you came all prepared," he drawled out. "A no-lose situation. You covered every base. I applaud your foresight. I'm glad to know that if you decided I wasn't worth the effort, you had something to fall back on."

In a way, he was as good at manipulating guilt as his father was. Having one Marston jerk her around by the conscience was quite enough.

"Oh, no you don't. You're not going to put the blame on me, Wyatt Marston. You're the one who ran away from the way things were. You're the one who gave up on trying to work things out. What was I supposed to think? How long was I supposed to wait? You never even told me what was wrong! How dare you accuse me of anything!"

"I could accuse you of plenty."

Something in the atonal quality of his voice

269

cut her temper cold. Such a sensation of despair. She didn't know what to make of it even as she felt the rawness of his hurt. What had put such depthless desolation in him?

"What, Wyatt? Tell me. Get it out in the open. For once, don't leave me guessing."

He didn't answer. She could see tension working along his jaw in spasms. His hands were white-knuckled where they gripped his crutches. She didn't want to hurt him. He got that from every other quarter. He had to know he could trust her with the truth of what he was feeling. That she'd respond to it out of love for him. And he had to learn it now.

"What could you accuse me of?" she challenged gently. "Neglect? Yes, I neglected you and our marriage. But it was because I wanted to fit in with your family, because I wanted to make you proud of me. I didn't want anyone pointing a finger and saying, 'There's that gold digger from the tenements latching onto her free ride.' That's not what you were to me."

"You never had to prove anything to me, Beth. And you didn't need to prove yourself to anyone else, either."

"Maybe I had to prove it to me." She took a deep breath, understanding her own relentless drive to succeed as she made that admission. And it was true. She had been her own worst critic, so fearful of not living up to the Marston name. "You were the best thing that ever happened to me, Wyatt. Maybe I just had to prove to myself that I was worth it."

"You did," he said without inflection. "You proved it to everyone. You became the perfect Marston."

"For you. For me. For both of us. At least that was what I thought at the time. Maybe I was wrong. Maybe I did push too hard. But you could have slowed me down with a word. You could have stopped me if you'd told me what you were feeling. Why didn't you say anything?"

"You seemed to have everything you wanted. I didn't want to get in your way."

"In my way? Is that how you thought I viewed our marriage? As something in my way?"

"Why did you marry me, Beth? Because of who I was, what I could give you?"

"I didn't even know who you were when I fell in love with you. It didn't matter. It wouldn't have mattered."

"Finding out I was a millionaire didn't carry any weight at all?" His smile was a curl of cynicism. So she was brutally honest.

"Of course it did. I'm only human. I grew up with nothing. I had the chance to have the man I loved and everything his money could buy—all the things I'd dreamed of. A home, decent food on the table, nice friends who didn't hold up liquor stores or knock down old ladies on the street, a chance to step up out of the filth I grew up in. Why wouldn't I want that? But I wanted it from you, with you."

"Is that why you were willing to let my father buy you off?"

"That's not what he was trying to do. He was concerned about me, about both of us."

"*My* father? Please! Let's stick to reality here. My father only wants what's best for himself. He'd use you, me, his own mother to get what he wants."

"Maybe you believe that and I guess I don't blame you, but that doesn't explain why you couldn't trust me. Why did you come up here? Why did you try so hard to push me away? Wyatt, I love you. Why do you find that so hard to believe?"

He locked his jaw tightly and refused to speak.

Shaken to the soul, Beth watched him, knowing he would shut himself away again if she let him. Knowing how tenuous the situation was, she was afraid it wouldn't hold out against any added pressure. But she couldn't back down. Not now. Her pulse thick with trepidation, she said, "I want an answer now, Wyatt."

He gave a brittle laugh and shook his head. "You already know it, Beth." He looked at her then, without the slightest trace of emotion showing. "Can't you figure it out?"

That sear of sarcasm was the last straw. Fury and frustration collided, and like the Big Bang theory, gave birth to a host of fragmented feelings. She couldn't trust any of them to sustain her, so she held onto the anger, to her self-righteous belief that she deserved a reasonable response.

"I'm sick of trying to figure you out. You don't tell me anything, then dam up because I can't read your mind. Well, excuse me. You are not the easiest person in the world to read. I want to know what's going on and I want you to spell it out right now."

He looked purposefully away from her. She felt as if she'd smacked into a northern Michigan pine, the unyielding impact knocking all the breath and brass from her. She was horrified to find she was on the verge of tears. Hanging onto her poise by her fingernails, she stood straight and put every scrap of her tenacious spirit into an ultimatum.

"I want those answers, Wyatt. You are not going to avoid this. If you try, I'm going to get on that plane to Denver and I won't be back. Think about that and let me know."

Chapter Sixteen

The sound of the porch door slamming tore through Wyatt like a shot to the gut. He stood for a moment, weaving and wounded, unable to respond to her threat or to his own panic. He didn't know how to. The scars of his past ran deep, thickening about the walls of his heart. Trust her? How was he going to trust her?

How was he going to stand by and let her leave?

He stood there, watching her stalk to the edge of the bluff, watching her wrap her arms about herself in a defensive stance. He watched her, still loving her, and he cursed his father for bringing the taint back to that love.

But it wasn't his father's fault that Beth stood there while he stood here. He himself had put that distance between them. He'd allowed it to grow into an impossible cavern of misunderstanding and distrust. He'd encouraged it by doing nothing. He'd allowed her affair with Casey by doing nothing to stop it. When threatened, he backed into a corner. When confronted, he'd run.

He himself was to blame for the position he was in.

If he'd had faith in Beth's love, he would have confronted her with the facts of her infidelity. He would have done everything in his power to make things right. But he hadn't. Just like his mother, just like his father, because by not taking action, he wasn't risking anything. He'd been terrified that if he challenged her, he'd lose her. He'd been afraid to hear that she'd married him for all the shallow reasons that brought his father and stepmother together. And that she stayed with him for the same greedy purposes. He hadn't soothed his pride by ignoring the obvious, he'd torn it to shreds. Then he'd blamed everyone else for the tatters.

He observed his wife's courageous stance and he recalled the way she'd braved the elements over on Isle Royale. He remembered her wobbly tent and pathetic fire, the sad meal she'd made him. The way she'd splinted his leg, had stuck by him at the hospital and endured his temper once he was released into her care. He considered her suggestions about the lodge, her enthusiasm and confidence. And her passion. For the restoration. For him.

If she didn't want to make amends, why had she come? Why had she stayed? If she didn't want a future with him, why would she have bothered? If she didn't want him, why would she have put up so heroically with his foul moods and pushed so hard against his determined wall of silence? He'd forced her to be the one to admit she wanted to continue their life together, that she wanted a place in his life, a place in his dream. She'd come to him. She'd pushed her way through his arrogance to stand at his side. He'd made her make all the concessions, take all the risks. And she had, without complaint. All she'd ask was that he trust her, that he talk to her. Was that so much when she'd done all the rest? She'd given him every chance to take her back, to start again.

I love you, Wyatt. Just try to get rid of me.

Wasn't that what he was trying to do? With his sullenness? With his refusal to forgive?

Now it was his turn to trust. Or he was going to lose her.

It seemed to take him forever to cross to where she stood. She must have heard him. He was about as graceful as a crippled bulldozer. But she didn't turn.

His throat ached so badly he couldn't force words out. He tried to swallow to relieve the tightness, but the anxiousness wouldn't go up and it refused to go down. He angled in behind her and let one of his crutches drop so he could band her slender middle with the curl of his arm. He could feel her trembling. At that hint of her vulnerability, the tightness eased a bit. Still his voice was gravelly with it.

"Beth, I'm sorry I left you in limbo. I didn't do it to hurt you."

"Why didn't you talk to me first?" Her words

were frail, unlike her ultimatum of minutes ago. As if it had taken her all to mount that one glorious stand and now she had nothing more to give.

"I couldn't, Beth. I was afraid of what I might say. I wanted time to think, time to sort through what I was going to do."

"Why did you let me bring the portfolio here if you didn't want to see me?"

He wished just once the words would come easy, that he could just yank open his heart and spill out all the secrets and suspicions and the silent sufferings. So she could see how badly he hurt, how hard it was to come to this point of confession. It was such a struggle to drag emotion, kicking and screaming, up from the guarded shadows of his soul. Because never in all his life had speaking what resided there made one grain of difference. Usually, it made things harder. But Beth was demanding this purge, and whether he thought it would do any good or not, he couldn't deny her.

"I wanted to see you. I was dying to see you. I just didn't know how to handle it. Dammit, Beth, I didn't know what to think." He squeezed his eyes shut, still not knowing. She leaned back against him and the softness of her hair tickled his chin. He could smell its freshness. He breathed in deep until he was dizzy with it.

"Neither did I," she admitted. "But I had to come. Because I didn't want to lose you, Wyatt." She was clutching at his arm, her shivering more pronounced. He could hear the tears in her voice.

And that broke him down, finally making the words flow.

"I couldn't stay in Chicago, Beth. I couldn't face that situation the way things were. I was so hurt, I just wanted to crawl into a hole somewhere safe. This was the only place I could come up with. It was stupid, I know it. But somehow all the trust had broken down between us. I couldn't talk to you there. And once you got here, I saw the chance for us to pick up the pieces, to put things back together, but I didn't know if you'd still want to."

She inhaled raggedly. "I want to."

Relief gushed from him noisily. He pressed his face into the soft spill of her hair, his eyes closing tighter, his heart pounding so hard it crowded his throat. "I want to put the past behind us. I want to start over. We've got a lot of good things here, Beth, things we can share and work on together. Are you sure you can be happy?"

"I can be happy anywhere you are." A simple answer to a complex question. Almost too simple.

"It won't be easy. There's more wildlife than nightlife."

She chuckled huskily. "I've had the pleasure of meeting some of the fauna."

"It gets pretty lonesome, especially in the winter months. There'll be no benefits, no fund-raisers, no galas. Nothing like what you've been used to. I can keep you busy with all the details of the lodge, and I'm going to need you, but it's not going to be glamorous work. For a while it's going to be a lot of that elbow grease you were talking about."

"Then I won't have to wonder what to wear."

He didn't smile at her glib reply. He was working up to the main point that was stuck painfully between his ribs. "There won't be anyone but me."

"That's all I've ever wanted."

"Then why wasn't I enough for you before?"

He didn't mean to blurt it out. She stiffened against him and he feared he'd just shot his other foot off. Dammit, she was telling him everything he needed to hear. Why did he have to push it?

"What?"

"Never mind. It doesn't matter now."

"Wyatt, what are you talking about?"

"I know I'm as much to blame as you. I'd just as soon never bring him up again."

"Who?"

She didn't know? Were there more men than he'd suspected? So many she couldn't even take a guess? A jealous rage bunched in his belly. "Casey," he gritted out.

"Mark Casey?" His arm was still around her. She pushed against it, whirling to face him so fast, he almost lost his balance. "What about him?"

"For the love of God, Beth, don't do this. Did you think you could keep that sort of thing quiet? I'm not asking for an apology."

"You're not going to get one! I don't have any-

279

thing to apologize for. What are you saying, Wyatt? That you think I was having an affair with Mark Casey?"

He didn't have to answer. His expression said everything all too clearly.

Beth drew a shallow breath against the sudden hurt compressing about her heart. "How could you?"

He looked uncomfortable, a dull flush of color rising up his neck to betray his own struggle against pain. "Beth, please don't—"

"I didn't."

He stared at her. She spoke without hesitation, with appropriate indignation. Her eyes were bright with distress. But there wasn't a trace of guilt anywhere. For the first time, he thought to question the truth of what he'd heard. God, could he have been wrong about all of it?

"You weren't having an affair?"

"Not then. Not ever. What Mark and I had together were a few business lunches and a few social meetings in very public places. Wyatt, why on earth would you think it was anything more than that?"

His answer came out heavily. "Because I was told it was."

"By whom?"

"By my father. The day I left."

They were both silent, assimilating what they'd just learned.

At first, Beth was furious. How could Wyatt have believed the worst, without proof, without ever once asking her for her side of the story? But then, given his past experiences, how could he not believe his father? How could he believe in a fidelity he'd never seen in his own family? And how easy she'd made it for him to think the worst. With her frequent absences from home. With her long hours, with her socializing. With the remoteness that settled into all the aspects of their relationship. Wouldn't it be easy for him to hear the whisper of scandal and see all the symptoms of their unhappy marriage as the signs of her infidelity? Especially if those whispers were from someone he trusted.

It was then she understood what he'd been saying in his delirium when they'd lain together in their soggy sleeping bags on Isle Royale and he'd bared his soul. *Don't go, Beth. Don't go with him.* Wyatt had been pleading with her not to abandon their marriage, not to betray his love for her. She realized the hell he'd been through and all her anger melted away.

She put a hand to his face, half expecting him to rear back. He didn't. She moved it in a slow caress over the taut angles and lean hollows, absorbing his tension with the tenderness of her touch.

"Wyatt, I was never unfaithful to you. Not with Mark Casey, not with anyone. If I'm guilty of betraying our vows, it's because I wasn't there for you, not because I was with anyone else." She paused, searching his expression, needing to see the spark of belief that could carry them through

281

this terrible moment and on into the rest of their lives. It wasn't there. Nothing was there. Just a blank. "I love you, Wyatt. I can't make you believe that, but I hope you've been able to feel it over the last few days. It would kill me to think you didn't believe I cared."

Slowly, he put his hand over hers and he drew it to his lips, pressing them warmly into her palm. A shaky sob escaped her. Then her face was against his shoulder and he was holding her with enough force to crack her ribs. It was a wonderful compression. He let her cry it out, then murmured softly, again and again, how much he loved her. Then the magnitude of it all struck her and struck hard. Beth pulled away just far enough to look up at him.

"Why would he do it, Wyatt? Why would your father tell such a lie? He had to have known it wasn't true. Why would he do such a thing to us?"

"Maybe because he was afraid that having you was making me too strong. He was afraid of losing his control. That's why he sabotaged my loan application."

"He did that?"

"I thought you knew."

She shook her head in confusion. "Why would he do that, then send me to offer the means for you to continue on your own?"

"With the stocks?" She nodded and suddenly, it was no longer a mystery to Wyatt. It made a frightening sort of sense, especially after what his

282

father had said in the great room just minutes ago. "It was the stocks. What did he ask you to do, Beth?"

"He wanted me to buy you out, then he was going to purchase both our shares. I thought he was doing it that way because he was afraid you wouldn't accept help from him directly."

Wyatt's laugh was bitter. "Oh, no. That wasn't his reason at all. I did a little checking when I went looking for a buyer for my shares. Gretchen has always maintained controlling interest in Marston Hotels. That's why she's able to do pretty much whatever she wants without worrying what my father will say. But if he had our shares, he'd own the balance of stocks. He wanted control of the chain so he could divorce her without losing the hotels."

"And he was willing to destroy our marriage to get it?" Beth was stunned. All she respected about Boyd Marston was a lie. It was like waking up to find your best friend had used your car in a hit and run, then put the keys back in your hand to throw off blame. She was heartsick and, at the same time, angry and so very glad all had come to light before it was too late.

How clear it all seemed now. The job in Denver was Boyd's first clever wedge between them. He'd known Wyatt better than she did. He had to have known his son would balk at going, at surrendering her to the Marston hierarchy. But he hadn't counted on her saying no to the offer in favor of her marriage. So, he'd levered harder, playing upon Wyatt's insecurities with that dark little lie about Mark Casey. And it had almost worked. It had almost torn them apart. But again, he hadn't considered her determination to make her marriage work in spite of the fears he preyed upon so ruthlessly. Or in the strength of Wyatt's love that could overcome even his unforgivable lie. She shivered to think how close she'd come to getting on that plane to Denver. And so apparently did Wyatt for his face was a fierce study of contained rage. It would have taken the jaws of life to break his hold on her.

"Well, he's not going to come between us with his cheap tricks. Nothing is. We're going to work this out, Beth. So help me God. And with Jimmy and Mani, we'll make a go of this place. We're going to have a great future here."

All Beth could do was nod, believing it with all her heart.

Wyatt touched her hair, brushing it back so he could read the unspoken truth upon her face. And he was satisfied. "Let's go give the old man the good news."

They walked back inside, arm in arm, Beth taking the place of one of his crutches and Wyatt not ashamed to lean on her for support. Boyd was where they'd left him, looking impatient and then slightly threatened by the sight of them as a unified front.

"Well, I've got to be going. I guess from the looks of things, you'll be staying, Beth. I'll miss working with you. Wyatt, one last offer. You want to make this place work? I think it's madness, but if it's what you want, I'll see you have it. I'll buy both your shares in Marston Hotels at a price generous enough for you to fit this monstrosity out to the envy of Michigan Avenue. It's obvious you've never cared about the family business, so why hang on to sentimentality. Let's sever ties and part as friends."

Wyatt was smiling grimly. "Oh, I cared about family, it's just the business that didn't interest me. But they were always one and the same for you."

Boyd shrugged, not bothering to deny it.

"Thanks, Dad but I don't want your money. Beth can do what she chooses with her shares. I don't mind if she wants to hang on to them for security, but I've got an independent investor to buy mine." There was a savage satisfaction in seeing the man who'd nearly cost him his heart's desire suddenly go stiff and pale. "He may not offer as much as you, but I'll feel damn good about selling them to him. It won't be enough to finance the entire renovation, but I'm looking forward to the challenge. As long as Beth's willing to reinvest her faith into our marriage, that's all I need."

"You're a fool," Boyd spat, the veins on his neck distending with anger. "You'll flounder and fail up here. Then who's going to bail you out? Don't come crawling home to me for any favors."

"I won't be coming to you for anything," Wyatt stated evenly. And he smiled again. "I'm not planning to fail. I've got one hell of a management supervisor." His arm hugged Beth.

"That and a quarter will buy you—"

"Whatever he wants," Beth interjected softly. She squared up beside her husband, fueled by the trust in his words and free to see Boyd Marston for what he was at last. "We're not going to fail. Because I'm going to sell my shares to the same buyer Wyatt found for his if the man wants them. I'm going to reinvest the monies in a project I believe in with all my heart. I have a feeling it's the investment of a lifetime and I don't want to miss out on it."

"You're both fools."

But Wyatt paid no attention to him. He was staring down into the confident glow of his wife's eyes. "Dad, don't you have a plane to catch?"

Boyd snatched his coat and shrugged into it without further words. He stormed out of the lodge, forgetting one thing.

Artemus.

The big dog came barreling around the side of the house with frenzied barking. Boyd raced for the stairs leading down to the beach with the big dog snapping at his Italian leather heels.

"Wyatt, aren't you going to call him off?" Beth suggested halfheartedly as she leaned her head against her husband's shoulder.

"Naw. The exercise will do them both good. I'd rather find a bottle of Pinot Noir to toast our new partnership."

She sighed and snuggled closer, forgetting all

about Boyd Marston and Denver. "Sounds good."

"And then we can talk about what we should do first. We've got a business to get off the ground."

Beth didn't hesitate. She'd been planning for days what she'd say once she was sure that "we" included her. Now, she had no doubts. "Plumbing, then furniture. I already have some of it picked out. But first, we get the hot tub."

"There. We've reached our first corporate decision. Time to pop a cork."

"I'm going to like doing business with you, Mr. Marston."

"Then," he continued with a sultry smile, "I think we should see if we can both fit into the whirlpool in our bathroom."

"Sounds even better. I'll get the Saran Wrap."

He gave her a startled but not quite objecting look.

"To cover your cast," she explained with a chuckle. "Why? What did you think I was going to do with it?"

"Never mind." Then he grinned. "I'll tell you later."

And Beth was smiling in anticipation as she lifted her face for her husband's kiss.